LIES, SPIES, AND THE BAKER'S SURPRISE

BOOKS BY TERRY AMBROSE

Seaside Cove Bed & Breakfast Mysteries
A Treasure to Die For
Clues in the Sand
The Killer Christmas Sweater Club
Secrets of the Treasure King
Treasure Most Deadly

McKenna Mysteries
Photo Finish
Kauai Temptations
Big Island Blues
Mystery of the Lei Palaoa
Honolulu Hottie
North Shore Nanny
A Damsel for Santa
Maui Magic
The Scent of Waikiki
On the Take in Waikiki
Mystery of the Eight Islands

License to Lie Series
License to Lie
Con Game
Shadows from the Past

Anthologies with Stories
Paradise, Passion, Murder: 10 Tales of Mystery from Hawai'i
Happy Homicides 3: Summertime Crimes
Happy Homicides 4: Fall into Crime
Happy Homicides 5: The Purr-fect Crime

LIES, SPIES, AND THE BAKER'S SURPRISE

SEASIDE COVE BED & BREAKFAST MYSTERY
BOOK 6

Terry Ambrose

COPYRIGHT

ABOUT THE AUTHOR

Once upon a time, in a life he'd rather forget, Terry Ambrose tracked down deadbeats for a living. He also hired big guys with tow trucks to steal cars—but only when negotiations failed. Those years of chasing deadbeats taught him many valuable life lessons such as—always keep your car in the garage.

Terry has written more than twenty books, several of which have been award finalists. In 2014, his thriller, "Con Game," won the San Diego Book Awards for Best Action-Thriller. His series include the Trouble in Paradise McKenna Mysteries, the Seaside Cove Bed & Breakfast Mysteries, and the License to Lie thriller series.

You can learn more about Terry and his writing at terryambrose.com.

1

ALEX

Hey Journal,

Another day down! The big wedding's gonna be here soon. Daddy and Marquetta don't know it, but I'm working on Operation Honeymoon. They're kinda slow at this whole love thing, so I'm thinking if there's a way to get them off alone, they might figure things out sooner. What do you think, Journal? Will it work? It's worth a try. Operation Honeymoon is full speed ahead! And if that works, Operation Baby Brother can't be far behind!

My dad and Marquetta need to take a lesson from the new couple who checked in this afternoon. Well...maybe not. Their names are Tara and Henry Nicholas, but I think Henry has a secret. He's not really Tara's husband! Whoa! That's like so wrong. Do you think she knows? So there's no way they can be married. Right, Journal? I totally don't get why she's with him if he's already got another wife.

It's not like we don't get unmarried couples here. When my dad inherited the B&B a couple years ago, he was like, wait a minute, do we allow that? And Marquetta was like, why should we care? I guess 'cause she grew up around the B&B, she's seen it all her life. She didn't think it was a big deal. I think Marquetta's right. If a girl wants to go away with her

7

boyfriend, why shouldn't they be able to? Since I'm only eleven, my dad would totally freak if he heard me say that. But when I grow up, I'm gonna go places with my boyfriend. Guess I'd better wait a few years to tell Robbie about it. He's still kinda reluctant about the whole going steady thing.

The only reason I know about Henry's secret is 'cause he passed me on the stairs after I said goodnight to Daddy and Marquetta. I know I wasn't supposed to spy on him, but he looked like he was in a super big hurry, so I kinda hung out at the top while he talked on his cell at the bottom. It's not my fault his voice carried so far!

So what do you think? Does Tara know Henry's cheating on her? Oh wait, I guess maybe it's the other way around. She's like the other woman. Holy moley! Talk about complicated! So maybe she doesn't even know he's married? She seems awfully nice. Not like him. I don't trust him. Anybody who'd sneak downstairs to talk to their wife while their girlfriend waited upstairs can't be honest.

I'm pretty sure Henry's in the doghouse for not being home with his real wife. And you know what, Journal? He totally deserves it. He told her he was in San Francisco on business! Seaside Cove's only halfway there! So what's up with that? I'm convinced he's up to no good. I'm super confused about how to handle it, though.

Talk about a major problem. If I go to my dad, he's gonna tell me to stop butting into other people's business. But having somebody lie to both his wife and his girlfriend is super bad. Since it won't be long before Marquetta's my mom, I'll talk to her. She's smart about all this relationship stuff. At least when it comes to other people.

It's also bedtime, and if I don't at least make it look like I'm trying to go to sleep, my dad will get on my case when he comes to check on me. This being a kid sure can be tough.

Gotta go!

Xoxo

Alex

2

RICK

DESPITE THE FACT THAT HIS wedding to Marquetta Weiss was less than a week and a half away, Rick Atwood awoke feeling remarkably calm. There hadn't been any hint of trouble in Seaside Cove lately, which meant Alex hadn't been sticking her nose into police business. Best of all, the wedding planning was going smoothly. In nine days, he'd marry the woman of his dreams, who also had demonstrated herself to be Alex's soulmate. All in all, life was good.

After a quick shower, he went downstairs, once again looking forward to starting another day with Marquetta. He checked the upstairs coffee and tea station on the way and noted which supplies were low. With his first task of the day accomplished, he padded along the hall and down the stairs. There were no guests hanging around the living room, so he quickly nudged the two couches back into their normal spots. In the nearly two years that he'd owned the B&B, he'd never figured out why some felt a need to rearrange the furniture in the public areas. Then again, he was only the owner. What did he know?

The dining room was also empty. One table looked like someone had been there, so he returned the chairs to where they belonged, checked the place settings, then turned toward the kitchen. His spirits lifted as he pushed through the butler door.

"Hey, boss," Marquetta said when she saw him. She had her hair pulled back into a ponytail that she'd secured with a bright green scrunchie and wore her usual Seaside Cove Bed & Breakfast tee-shirt over a pair of jeans. She was in the process of chopping peppers for this morning's omelettes, but stopped when he approached.

"Hey to you, too, future wife." Rick went to her, put his hand at the small of her back, and kissed her.

Marquetta wrinkled her nose and returned her attention to the task at hand. "What have I told you about taking liberties with the staff while on duty?"

"You mean my staff of one?" Rick chuckled and kissed her on the cheek. "I'll try to control myself."

"You do that." The chef's knife returned to its swift, smooth, seesawing motion. "Did you check the upstairs coffee station?"

"Already done. I also checked the dining room. I'll get them both stocked up right now."

Rick took care of the upstairs station first and was about finished with the dining room when Tara Nicholas walked in. A trim black woman with an easy smile, she owned a bookstore and had met her husband at his bakery, which was just two doors down from her store. Yesterday, when they'd checked in, he'd discovered she was what Marquetta called a 'toucher', someone who communicated not only with their words and facial expressions but also by physically reaching out to the other person. This morning, her lighthearted air was gone, and she had her arms wrapped around her, almost as though she was cold.

"Good morning, Mrs. Nicholas." Rick gave her a friendly wave and backed away from the station. "Help yourself. I'm almost done here. Did you sleep well?"

"Not really." She grimaced and let out a deep sigh.

"Is there something wrong with your room?"

"No. It's wonderful. It's homey and comfortable." She paused, shrugged her shoulders, and added, "I just have a lot on my mind. That's all."

"If there's anything we can do to make it better, please let me know. Our goal is for your stay to be one you won't ever forget."

"Oh, I don't think I'll forget this trip," Tara said sharply. She winced and closed her eyes. "Sorry. This has nothing to do with you or the B&B."

Rick felt a pang of sorrow for the woman. Here she was on a trip that should be fun and exciting, and instead she was...what? Having regrets? Worried? "Is there anything we can do to help?"

Tara reached out, laid her palm on Rick's arm, and gave him a reassuring squeeze. She shook her head and said, "No. Really. This has nothing to do with you or the B&B."

Although he hated to see guests unhappy, Rick reminded himself this was the point where he'd tell Alex that asking more questions was interfering, so he gestured at a table beneath one of the garden windows. The sun was beginning to poke through the early morning fog, bathing the area in a soft light. Rick couldn't help but feel the view might soothe his guest. "Then I'll let you be. Feel free to grab one of those window tables. Personally, this is my favorite time of the day to enjoy the view."

Tara gazed at the table he'd indicated. The corners of her mouth curled up ever so slightly. "You're right. It is lovely. Maybe I will."

"Please, make yourself at home. The breakfast service starts at six-thirty, but until then we have plenty of fresh coffee and water for tea. Let me know if there's anything in particular you'd like. Marquetta's excellent at special requests." Rick rolled the supply cart back toward the kitchen, taking a last look over his shoulder before he pushed the cart through the butler door. Tara was still standing in the same place, staring out at the garden.

Alex came down to help with the breakfast service shortly before six-thirty. When she walked into the kitchen, her first words were, "Yay! Nine days!"

Marquetta gave Alex a hug and said, "And hopefully it will be another day without my mother trying to take over everything. I love her, but she's starting to act like this is her wedding."

"She just wants to help," Rick said.

Marquetta stared evenly at him, her expression giving away her skepticism. "I'll admit she's behaved very well, so far. I'm waiting for her to make her move. You watch, Rick. Mom will not be satisfied unless she's in control."

"You're strong. I'm confident you'll get what you want without offending her." Rick kissed her, then turned to Alex. "Six-thirty. Time for us to get to work, kiddo."

As they took their first orders, Rick noticed that Tara never had sat at the window table. Neither Tara nor her husband were even in the dining room.

Instead, the table was now occupied by Patricia Turner and her husband. This particular morning, they'd been joined by Adam Cunningham, Seaside Cove's Chief of Police.

"Morning, everyone," Rick said as he approached. "Pulled any cats out of trees lately, Adam?"

"You know, if you weren't my friend..." Adam's voice, which was accompanied by a deep scowl, trailed off.

"You have to pull cats out of trees?" Greg Turner asked.

Adam shot Rick another nasty look, then said, "You had to bring that up, didn't you?"

Rick ignored Adam's tweaked ego as he explained. "One of our oldest residents, Mrs. Cantwell, has a cat that likes to run away. Adam winds up saving the cat about three times a week."

"It's usually only one or two. The record was three." Adam chuckled, "I'll get you back, buddy."

"I'm sure you will. On a serious note, any further developments in the diving accident case?"

"We've got a name, Tiny Renet." Adam leaned forward and looked across the table. "The rest is up to the expert—Ms. County Coroner."

"That's Deputy Coroner, Chief," Patricia Turner shot back easily. But her brief exhibit of playfulness was quickly replaced by the same reserved demeanor Rick had seen since they'd first met. "There's not much. Other than we are putting some of the blame on Kiernan Walsh. He was Renet's dive buddy."

Rick couldn't believe a diver with any experience at all would misjudge his air supply so badly. "I don't get it. How does a diver run out of air?"

"Don't know yet, but I'm recommending the chief have another conversation with his quote-unquote dive buddy."

"What a tragic waste," Rick said.

"Yes. From what I've heard, they were both experienced enough to have known what they were doing was dangerous. Anyway, the full examination should be wrapping up today. In the end, the DA will probably decide it was nothing other than a case of a diver miscalculating a safe dive time."

Greg Turner gave a dismissive wave of his hand. "Stupidity running rampant is what I call it. Patty's too much of a professional to ever say anything like that, though."

"Greg…" Patricia gave her husband a mock don't-try-my-patience glare.

"Well, it's true. Isn't it? The law can't punish them, but life sure can." Greg cleared his throat, then regarded Rick. "Thanks again for putting her up on such short notice. After a long day, the road back to San Ladron can be pretty treacherous. I'm just glad my wife didn't have to drive. Besides, if she hadn't stayed here, I never would have come for a visit."

"I'm glad we had an opening, Mr. Turner. And I'm delighted you were both able to stay with us."

"We're leaving this afternoon," Patricia said. "I have cases stacking up."

"The work never stops, does it?" Rick said. "Adam, I have another question for you. Marquetta told me Joe Gray slipped and fell at the marina. How's he doing?"

"He'll be fine. He's got a broken arm and some aches and pains, but his ego probably took the biggest hit. Luckily, a couple of tourists saw him go down. One came over to assist."

Rick gave Adam a thumbs-up. "Witnesses are always good."

"Not in this case," Adam said with a shake of his head. "The guy wasn't much help. The other witness is Jennifer Martin. According to the report, she was at the Ugly Worm Bait & Tackle when she saw this Good Samaritan running over to help. Not exactly what you'd call great eyewitnesses."

"One of ours?" Rick's eyebrows went up. "If we've got a Good Samaritan staying here, I might want to do something nice for him."

"Not one of your guests, buddy. Some guy named Max Rado. He's staying at the Inn. Said he was taking a stroll down on the docks and ran into another guest from the Inn. While they were talking, Joe fell. He heard a noise and saw Joe was down. I'm going to get an earful later. Joe called me this morning and was carrying on about it not being an accident. I told him I'd stop by and talk to him. My guess is he's just trying to save face."

"I remember when Alex and I moved here. I was impressed because he was so sharp. Maybe that's not the case anymore. He is getting up there. Do you think he'll be well enough to give Marquetta away at the wedding?"

"If I know Joe, he wouldn't miss it. You know how he feels about Markie."

Rick bit his lip, and Adam gazed at him quizzically.

"What's wrong?"

"I hope having Joe walk her down the aisle isn't a mistake. That's all. I'd hate to have her memories about the death of her father come back to haunt her on her wedding day."

"I don't think it'll be a problem. According to Mary O'Donnell, the ghosts of the past no longer hold sway over Marquetta."

Rick snickered. "There's nothing like the opinion of an old Irishwoman to make sense out of life."

"Tell you what. If her prediction is as accurate as her cinnamon rolls are good, you've got nothing to worry about. Speaking of food, how about breakfast? I'm starved."

"You're always starved, Adam." Rick took their orders and moved on to the next table. He'd spent way too much time satisfying his curiosity, and he wouldn't blame Alex if she brought up the subject of him dawdling at any one table. After all, he probably talked to her at least once a week when she did exactly the same thing.

He took the last order and headed for the kitchen. Marquetta was plating two of Alex's orders when he entered. He held the butler door open for Alex and she waltzed by him wearing a smug grin.

"Who's talking too much now?" Alex giggled as she carried the plates back to her table.

"I'm never going to live this down," Rick said as he approached Marquetta.

"Nope. Boss, you've just given your daughter a license to talk. You are going to rue the day you took a few minutes to talk shop with Adam and the county coroner."

3

ALEX

I slip the butler door open and peek into the kitchen. My dad is standing with Marquetta and kinda whispering. "I didn't realize it was going to take half the morning to get a few questions answered."

Marquetta stands on her tiptoes and kisses him on the cheek. "I love you anyway, even if you are turning into a big gossip."

My dad? A gossip? That's like, not possible. He turns around and raises his eyebrows. "I thought I heard that door. How's it going out there, kiddo?"

"It's all good. So what did Chief Cunningham and Dr. Turner have to say?"

My dad's face gets all red. He totally looks flustered. He probably thought I was still busy in the dining room, but I hurried back because I'm super curious about the whole diving accident, too. I'll bet it wasn't an accident at all!

All of a sudden Marquetta whirls around and lifts her pan off the burner and slides the omelette onto a plate. "That was close. A couple more seconds and it would have burned." She gets a real stern look on her face, points at my dad, then at me. "Get to work, you two. We've got guests to deal with."

"Yes, ma'am!" Daddy says as he rushes past me. He looks so relieved.

I start to follow him, but stop. We're alone, and I have my chance to ask Marquetta about what I heard last night. "Sorry, Marquetta. I was gonna ask you a question."

"Alex, can we talk about it later?"

"I guess. It's about one of the guests. Mr. Nicholas."

Marquetta looks at the stack of orders she's got lined up on the counter and makes a face. "Oh, Sweetie, I've got a half dozen orders to prepare right now. Can it wait until this rush is over?"

"Yeah. Do you need help?"

"I'm fine, but I need you and your dad to keep the guests happy. And check the coffee station. Okay?"

"On it!" I push the supply cart out the door and see my dad coming back.

"I'll answer your question when we have breakfast," he says as we pass.

After the breakfast rush, I guess I'll get all my questions answered. The coffee's getting a little low, so I fill it up and then check on my tables. By the time I get back to the kitchen, Marquetta's plating my next two orders. One is for a family of four. They're like totally normal. One of the kids is super well behaved, but the other has ADD or something.

I pass my dad again as I'm going out and he's coming in. Marquetta is finishing up the order for the Turners, which is awesome because I'm delivering to a table near theirs and will be able to listen in. Daddy shows up at the Turners' table right when I'm putting the last plate in front of the kid that's behaving himself. I notice that Chief Cunningham is watching a man and a woman enter the dining room. He's got a funny look on his face.

"Who's he, Rick? Is that Victor Pallett?"

Whoa. Chief Cunningham doesn't know visitors by name unless there's trouble. What's up with that? I tell the parents I can get them some more coffee and water. They're happy neither of them has to leave the table, and I'm happy 'cause I'll get to eavesdrop. It's a total win-win.

Mr. Pallett totally has the male pattern baldness thing going on. I think he's kinda young to be losing so much hair, but my dad says people don't get a choice in their genes, unless it's the kind they wear. He always thinks that's funny, but it's so lame. Anyway, my dad still has all his hair, so he doesn't look old at all. Mr. Pallett's funny 'cause there's a little puff sticking up like a fuzzy island in the middle of a shiny lake. He's also kinda pudgy. To be honest, I don't get what his girlfriend sees in him. Her name is Kathryn Larkin. She's got a runner's figure—kind of on the thin side. She's totally not a good match for him. She could do way better.

My dad looks over at the door and nods. "It is Pallett. Why?"

"His name came up during Joe's rant about his fall not being an accident."

What? Marquetta was wrong about Mr. Gray? She's never wrong about that kind of stuff 'cause everybody tells her everything. Maybe I can get one-up on her. The dining room's not too noisy right now, so it's not hard to hear what they're saying while I refill coffee and water.

Mr. Turner shoots a look at Mr. Pallett as he pours syrup on his waffle. "Looks like he needs some exercise."

Wow. Even I don't use that much syrup. His poor waffle is like drowning on the plate. His wife is staring at the syrup lake. She gives him a light tap on the arm. "Says the man who's having fat and sugar for breakfast. You haven't been to the gym in a while yourself, Greg."

He winces like he's kind of embarrassed. "What can I say? I don't eat this way at home." He faces his wife and wrinkles his nose. "Just because you run five miles every morning. Rain or shine. But that guy looks like he's thirty going on forty-five. He's giving me inspiration to be more dedicated."

"Enjoy your sugar high, Mr. Dedicated." Dr. Turner grins at her husband, then takes a bite of her omelette and lets out a small moan. "I love sun-dried tomatoes. My compliments to the chef."

"I'll pass that on. She's my fiancée." My dad beams, then realizes I'm listening in. I can tell 'cause he winks at me.

Dr. Turner looks at me, raises her eyebrows, then looks back at my dad. "You're single? I thought you and your wife ran the B&B."

"I'm divorced, Dr. Turner. But In nine days, you will be correct. " My dad motions with his head like he wants me to join them.

I finish pouring the last of the coffee and water and step over to the Turners' table. "My mom was more interested in a stage career than a family. My dad raised me all by himself. Marquetta grew up here and knows the B&B better than anyone."

Daddy gives my shoulder a gentle squeeze. When I look up at him, he gives me the sideways look thing he likes to do. It's his way of telling me to not be so critical of my mom. I know he's right. He always wants me to be patient and kind. But my real mom was never around and I never knew her. It's hard to have feelings for someone you don't know.

"Marquetta and I met when I inherited the B&B from my grandfather. For me, it was love at first sight. And she and Alex get along as if they've known each other their entire lives."

"Marquetta's gonna be such an awesome mom," I add.

"Sounds like a perfect match. Nine days, huh?" Mr. Turner says.

"Yup," I say quickly. " I can't wait."

My dad chuckles. "I agree. I can't wait, either. Now, we need to attend to our other guests. Alex, would you seat Mr. Pallett and Ms. Larkin?"

"Okay." I hand him the carafes for the coffee and water. Just when I'm ready to seat Mr. Pallett and his girlfriend, the Nicholas couple shows up. There's only one table available, and it's a four-top, so I ask if they'd mind sharing.

Neither of the men looks happy, but when the women say they're okay with it, it becomes a done deal. I grab two more menus and guide them all to the table. As I seat them, I try to get some conversation going by asking Mr. Pallett what he does for a living.

"I'm starting a new business. As a matter of fact, we're here to scout out the territory. I'll be running tours."

Oh no, not another tour company. No way do we need another one of those. Ever since the discovery of the *San Mañuel*, the town's been totally flooded with all kinds of people looking for a big treasure score. My teacher at school says it's kinda like the California Gold Rush all over again.

"What's the matter?" Mr. Pallett sneers at me. "Why'd you make a face?"

"Victor!" Ms. Larkin snaps. "She's just a girl. Be nice."

He gives Ms. Larkin a nasty look, but doesn't say anything. My face gets kinda hot. I'm never supposed to make the guests angry, and if I start an argument between him and his girlfriend, my dad will ground me for sure. "It's okay, Ms. Larkin." Not really, but if I don't say the words, I'll get in so much trouble. "Mr. Pallett, we kinda have a lot of people who are doing the tour thing already. Most of them work out of San Ladron 'cause they get more customers there."

"Well, they're not doing what I'm doing."

Mr. Pallett still doesn't look happy. I feel like I've gotta smooth this over. "So what kind of tours are you gonna run?"

"The Joaquin Murrieta Haunted Treasure Tour," he says with a smug grin. "It's going to include lots of scary stories about old Joaquin himself, including how his head was kept in a jar and taken around the state so people could see he was really dead."

Mr. Pallett looks like Billy Thornton in school. He's a total bully and uses that smug look with the other kids when he thinks he's shown them up. One of these days I'm gonna punch him in the nose.

"Yeah. Pretty good. Right, kid?" Mr. Pallett leans back in his chair and crosses his arms over his chest.

Oh man, he's worse than Billy Thornton. On the other side of the table, Mr. Nicholas sits up straight. He looks like he's interested, but the two girlfriends don't look impressed at all. I'm with them. Marquetta told me once that people have been looking for buried treasure in the mountains behind Seaside Cove since like forever, and nobody's ever found it. This is a lame idea, but it's Mr. Pallett's money, and if he wants to throw it away, I'm not gonna stop him.

I hand out the menus and say, "He was like a big outlaw. Right? I totally have to check him out."

"He was a skilled horseman, a thief, and a cold-blooded killer. But my sources tell me he's got a stash of gold in these hills. Gold I intend to use to my advantage."

"Good luck with that, Mr. Pallett. I'll be back to take your orders in a few minutes. Help yourselves to the water, coffee, and juice."

Mr. Pallett ignores me and starts reading his menu. His girlfriend says thanks. She's nice. I like her. I don't know why she's with such a grump. As I walk away, I hear Mr. Nicholas asking about the tours. Omigod. He's not only a cheater, but he must be a total loser, too.

4

RICK

RICK WAS FILLING A COFFEE carafe when Alex burst through the door. She gritted her teeth, closed her eyes, and took a long, slow breath. He set down the carafe and knelt before her.

"What's wrong, kiddo?" He stroked her hair as he scrutinized her face. She didn't have to say a word for him to know something was bothering her. Her flushed complexion was a dead giveaway. His daughter was angry. In fact, he hadn't seen her this agitated in a very long time. "Does this have to do with one of the guests?"

"Mr. Pallett's a jerk. He's gonna run some bogus tours and take money from poor people who don't know any better and..."

Rick pulled her in close for a hug and rubbed her back. "Calm down. Breathe."

Marquetta watched from the stove. Rick saw the angst on her face and knew she wanted to help comfort Alex, but she was in the middle of preparing three orders and couldn't stop. When Alex pushed back, she sniffled and fixed her gaze on the floor.

Almost certain he knew what she was reluctant to ask, he said, "Do you want to swap a table with me? You can finish with the Browers." He gave Alex a slight nudge and added, "Mrs. Brower thinks you're adorable. And a hard worker. She's got a granddaughter who's about your age. You take them and I'll handle Mr. Pallett."

"I hate it when someone's so nasty."

"He was nasty to you? What did he do?"

"He's just like Billy Thornton at school." Alex shook her head and sniffled again.

"Sweetie?" Marquetta said from her spot at the stove. "Let your dad take Mr. Pallett. You've got one Billy Thornton already. You don't need another."

"Marquetta's right, kiddo. Besides, we've got a wedding coming up and we're going to need your help with a lot of details. That'll be plenty of stress for you." Rick kissed Alex on the forehead. "You okay with that?"

"I guess. I hate giving in to bullies," Alex huffed, then her mood lightened. "But I'm happy to help with the wedding."

Rick returned to the carafe he'd been filling when Alex walked in and topped it off. While Alex turned in her orders to Marquetta, he headed back to the dining room. Victor Pallett had assumed a boisterous tone with Henry Nicholas. Both of the women at the table looked exceedingly uncomfortable. Rick hoped he could intervene without making it look like he was reprimanding a guest, but if it came to it and Pallett started annoying the others trying to have breakfast, he wouldn't hesitate.

"Alex is on a break, so I'm going to be taking your orders. I'll start with the ladies. Do you have any questions about the menu?"

He got only shaking heads from the two women. Their quiet demeanors had him suspecting both were tired of being at the obnoxious table and would rather have a quiet breakfast together than put up with their significant others. They went through the ordering process. Everyone except Pallett was polite and respectful, but Rick was able to get through the order without losing his temper.

As he was walking away, he heard Kathryn Larkin hiss, "Victor! You need to stop this. First, you upset that little girl and now you're being rude to the owner."

"I'm the customer here, Kathryn. I don't have to do anything. His kid needs to suck it up and deal with it."

Rick spun on his heel and strode back to the table. "No, Mr. Pallett. My daughter does not need to learn to 'suck it up.' She's eleven. You, on the other hand, are an adult. And I'll expect you to act like one in the public areas of my B&B. And just so we're clear, the Chief of Police is sitting over there. In my opinion, he doesn't look one bit happy with you right now. I'd say it's because you're disrupting his breakfast, and he hates it when people do that."

Adam straightened up in his seat. He rotated his torso enough to put him facing Victor Pallett straight on and watched without blinking. Rick could tell the move wasn't lost on the man. Pallett crooked his neck from side-to-side, then gritted his teeth and grumbled an insincere apology. Rick accepted the empty words and excused himself. He saw Alex a few minutes later and told her what had happened.

"I want you to steer clear of that man, Alex. At least until he's had a chance to cool down. Okay?"

"No problem." Alex stepped closer and wrapped her arms around Rick. "Thanks for sticking up for me, Daddy."

Rick kissed her on the top of her head. "Anytime, kiddo. Anytime."

As they delivered orders to guests and bussed empty tables, Rick felt an unusual underlying tension in the dining room. He thought about how ridiculous Pallett's behavior was. It took a great deal for it to happen, but the B&B did have what they called the Naughty List. Much like Santa's Christmas list for bad little boys and girls, those on the Naughty List didn't get what they wanted. Instead, if they ever tried to book another reservation, they received a polite, "We're booked."

By the time the orders were ready for the table where Mr. Pallett sat, tensions at the table had settled down. Pallett was in the process of selling his Joaquin Murrieta tour business idea to Henry Nicholas.

"I don't know, Victor. I've got my hands full already."

"Your bakery?" Pallett scoffed.

"Along with something else. Something bigger."

Pallett leaned forward just as Rick was about to set down his plate. Rick pulled his hand and the plate back an instant before the food went flying.

"Victor, let Rick do his job," Ms. Larkin snapped.

"Sure. Whatever," Pallett grunted as he sat back in his chair, then ignored Rick and smirked. "What? That deal with the *San Mañuel*?"

Henry Nicholas looked as if he'd been slapped in the face. He sat back in his chair, a reddish glow filling his cheeks.

His wife, Tara, who had been picking up her knife and fork, stopped and stared at him. "What? You're here about a deal involving the *San Mañuel*? You didn't tell me about this, Henry."

"It's all still in the early stages. Negotiations going on. It's all very complicated. Don't worry about it."

Tara gaped at him, her gaze intense, her anger obviously percolating beneath the surface. Rick didn't blame her one bit. If he used such a condescending tone on Marquetta, she'd probably take him down with the nearest heavy object.

Pretending not to be listening, Rick went around the table to deliver Mr. Nicholas's order. As he put the plate in front of the man, he listened to him go on about the wonderful opportunity he was following for him and his wife. A chance to secure their future together. Blah, blah, blah. From the look on his wife's face, she and her husband were headed for a doozy of a confrontation. Worse, Pallett didn't look the least bit happy.

Hoping to keep the breakfast service from turning into a complete disaster, Rick said, "I hope you all enjoy your meal. Is there anything else I can get you?"

The two women still looked as though they might ask to be seated alone. There were no additional requests, but a cold silence engulfed the table as Rick left. He checked on his other tables and eventually got to the Turners.

"Sounds like you've got your hands full, buddy," Adam said.

Rick leaned over and lowered his voice. "Better that they're not talking than the alternative. And by the way, thank you for being here today. You saved my bacon."

Patricia held her coffee mug between her hands with her elbows resting on the table. "Neanderthals. If Greg acted like such a jerk, I'd divorce him in a heartbeat."

"It's true." Greg deadpanned. "She wrote it into our wedding vows—it shall be grounds for divorce if I ever treat women and children like chattel or act like a nineteenth-century male chauvinist."

Patricia cut her eyes toward Greg and raised her glass. "You're just lucky I didn't do that. If I had, I would have added several more conditions."

"Don't worry, Sweetheart. I'd have signed off on anything to marry you."

"I know." Patricia looked down quickly and smiled to herself. Rick wasn't sure, but she might have even been blushing. It was one of the few brief moments of anything other than professionalism Rick had seen from her.

A loud bleep cut through the hum of the guests. Rick turned to see whose cell phone was further disrupting the breakfast service. Of course, it was at the trouble table. Henry Nicholas fumbled with the phone, attempting to turn down the volume and see who was calling at the same time. To his right, Tara was staring down at the screen. She muttered something to herself as her husband stood and dashed out of the room.

"He's not much better, is he?" Adam said as he followed the spectacle.

"No. He's not," Rick muttered.

"How's the munchkin doing?" Adam asked as he watched Alex chat with the Browers while she filled their coffee mugs.

"She wasn't happy that I swapped tables with her, but I knew this guy would continue pushing her buttons. I get the feeling he likes doing things to upset people."

"Good observation," Patricia said. "That's one nice thing about my patients. They never give me any lip."

"That's right, Doc. And if they do start talking back, you'll know you've lost it." Adam paused to watch Tara Nicholas storm out of the room. "Uh oh. I think there's trouble brewing."

Loud voices drifted in from the lobby. Rick hung his head and sighed. "Great. Just what I need. Another problem. Excuse me while I go see what's going on."

"Family spectacle time," Adam quipped.

Rick rolled his eyes and went to see if he could quell the argument before it got any worse. In the fifteen seconds it took him to make it to the lobby, Tara's voice continued to escalate.

"Mrs. Nicholas," Rick said sternly. "Please. This is a public area. Let's keep our voices down."

"Tara, baby, it's not what you think," her husband stammered. "Last night was just a business call. You know, about that deal I was telling Victor about."

Tara stiffened. She pulled her head back and watched her husband's face. The muscles in her jaw relaxed slightly, but she looked as though she didn't know what to say.

Alex appeared next to Rick. She crossed her arms over her chest and looked straight at Henry Nicholas. "He's lying."

Oh, God no. So much for Alex not sticking her nose into other people's business. His heart sank. Somehow, he'd have to prevent this from turning into an all-out war in his lobby.

5

RICK

DEFIANCE PAINTED ALEX'S FACE. SHE maintained her determined stance, and it looked like she had no intention of backing down. One confrontation with a guest could be called a mistake, but two was practically a disaster. He also knew Alex would never deliberately cause a problem without a very good reason. Basically, he had no desire to reprimand his daughter. It didn't matter if she'd put him and the B&B in a terrible position. These guests were way out of line.

"Alex, what did I tell you about interfering in the guests' personal business?" Rick said softly.

"Yeah," Henry Nicholas added. "You definitely need to teach that kid some boundaries. Come on, Tara. Let's get out of here."

He reached out to grab his wife's hand, but she backed away. "No. I'm not going anywhere with you. I want to know what she means."

Rick's heart sank. This was heading downhill fast. He had two guests who were at odds, another in the dining room who was looking to cause trouble, and Alex was right in the middle of it. The only solution was to deal with this quickly. "Alex? Answer Mrs. Nicholas, please."

"This is preposterous. You're going to take the word of a child over mine? Tara, baby, let's go somewhere else."

"No, Henry. I saw the name when that call came through. I want to hear what this girl has to say. Alex?"

Alex looked up at Rick. He threw his hands up in the air. "Go ahead."

"He got a call last night. He was like down here at the bottom of the stairs talking to his wife. He told her he was in San Francisco on business. He kept telling her he loved her and said he'd be home soon."

"She's lying!" Nicholas blurted. "You need to reprimand..."

"Shut up, Henry!" Tara stood face-to-face with the man Rick had thought was her husband. She had her arms straight down at her sides, her voice held a bitter edge. "You lying scum. You lied to your wife, and you lied to me."

"Tara, baby. Come on. I didn't lie. We'll be separating soon and..."

"Just stop, would you? You told me you were divorced. Now you're saying you're not."

Tara's cheeks flamed an even brighter red as Nicholas sputtered a weak excuse about paperwork and formalities. The longer he went on, the more pathetic the man sounded.

"Why don't we take this up to my office?" Rick asked.

"Rick, I want him out. My real name is Tara Amengual. You already have my credit card, and I'm the one who paid for the accommodations. I'd like to finish out the reservation, but I demand you get this man out of my room."

Now what? Rick thought. He had two problems to deal with, Alex and this...couple, for lack of a better term. "Alex, would you go back and keep the breakfast service going? I'll finish here in a moment."

Alex nodded and left the room. Rick wasn't sure how he'd resolve the dispute between these two, other than to go back to basics. "Mr. Nicholas? Ms. Amengual has a point. I'd have to check, but if she's the one who paid for the room, it is hers. Will you leave peacefully?"

The man's jaw clenched as he took in a slow breath, but then he said, "What am I going to do?"

"I'll find you a place to stay. We're booked up, but there's the Happy Daze B&B and the town also has a motel, the Seaside Cove Inn. I'll get you into one of those."

"Whatever. You're going to regret this, Tara." He strode out of the room and up the stairs.

"Ms. Amengual, I need to go back and help Alex. I'd suggest you give Mr. Nicholas some time to vacate, but let me know if he doesn't."

"I should watch what he does, but I don't even want to lay eyes on that man right now. Do you know what I found in his bag last night? A little pink bakery box. All the way here he kept hinting about some big romantic gesture. I think Henry was going to propose...and now I find out he wasn't even divorced? Are you kidding me?"

"Um...Ms. Amengual..."

"Sorry. I know. It's not your problem, and you're not my therapist. I wish I could afford one. I'm going for a walk. That will help. I have a lot of thinking to do. Would you make sure he gets out of my room?"

Reluctantly, Rick said, "Of course." He felt sorry for the woman as he watched her leave. Marquetta had once told him she'd seen everything at the B&B. He wondered if she'd ever experienced this situation before.

It felt like all eyes were focused on Rick as he entered the dining room. Like some of the other guests, the Browers rose and walked toward the exit. "Mr. and Mrs. Brower..." Rick said.

The husband raised his hand. "It's no problem. We were finished with our breakfast and didn't want to interrupt out there."

Mrs. Brower nodded in agreement and added, "We think you handled the situation extremely well."

"Thanks. It's the first time I've come across that one."

By eight-fifteen, there were only three occupied tables. These were the late arrivals, the ones who showed up at the tail end of the breakfast service. Some wanted a leisurely meal, others simply loved to hang out. Anita Jones, a single woman who'd come in two days ago, was standing at one of the coffee carafes. She'd just poured herself a mug and taken a sip when she made a terrible face.

"Ms. Jones? Is there something wrong with the coffee?"

She set down the mug and pointed at it. "It tastes salty."

"Salty? Are you sure?" Rick waved his hand in front of his face. "Sorry. Stupid question. It's just that we've never had a complaint about our coffee."

"See for yourself." Anita picked up a mug, poured a small amount from the carafe, and handed it to Rick.

He took one sip and found himself making the same ugly face as Ms. Jones. "I'll get this replaced right away. I can't imagine what happened." Rick carried the carafe back to the kitchen. Alex was stacking dishes in the dishwasher and Marquetta was cleaning her twelve-inch skillet in the sink. He told them what had happened. At that point, Marquetta said she wanted to check for herself.

"Suit yourself. You'll be sorry." Rick handed her the mug.

She practically spit out the coffee. "That's terrible!"

Alex shook her head when Marquetta offered her a sip. "No way."

Rick filled a fresh carafe and carried it to the coffee station, where Anita stood guard over the other carafes.

"I think they're all the same," she said.

"What?" Rick blurted. He tested a sample from another carafe, had an intense urge to spit it out, but swallowed anyway. "Can you watch these while I get a cart to clear them out?"

"Sure. I'd say somebody doesn't like you, Mr. Atwood."

The comment stopped Rick in his tracks. No. There was no way. Or was there? Could Victor Pallett have done this? "I'll be right back." Rick set down the fresh carafe and returned to the kitchen.

He gave Marquetta and Alex another update. When he was done, he said, "I think we need to replace everything out there."

"I agree," Marquetta said. "Alex, would you fill some new carafes while your dad and I pull everything?"

"No problem," Alex chirped and got to work.

Rick and Marquetta headed back to the dining room, but Rick stopped her outside the butler door. Whispering, he said, "I think this was the work of Victor Pallett. He wasn't happy when I came down on him for being so hard on Alex."

"You'll never prove it, Rick. And while he's here, the only thing we can do is keep an eye on him."

"You're right, as usual."

"Of course I am." Marquetta winked playfully. "And don't you forget it, boss."

When they arrived at the coffee station, Anita had been joined by Patricia Turner. "Oh God, no. I hope we don't need the coroner," Rick quipped.

"We were just talking," Anita said.

"Yes. About the incident with the coffee," Dr. Turner added.

"Ladies, I can explain." Rick tried not to sound defensive, but his insides cringed at the thought of what a Deputy County Coroner might think of the entire morning's debacle.

The doc looked perplexed and frowned. "Explain? Why?"

"All the trouble we've had this morning. This is the first time we've ever had something like this happen with one of the meals."

"Oh. That's not what we were talking about."

"You weren't?"

"No. What? Did you think we were cancelling our stays because some clown was playing a stupid prank?"

Rather than go into how he saw the doctor as rigid, Rick decided it was best to let it go. "The thought crossed my mind," he said sheepishly.

She waved her hand in front of her face. "No way. This has been a very interesting morning. It's kind of like being a participant in one of those mystery games. Anita and I were just comparing notes about what we saw."

Rick's eyes widened. Wonderful. Maybe they had something he could use to find the culprit. "And?"

"And nothing," Anita said. "We came up with a big, fat zero."

"Right," Patricia added. "But the good news is Greg and I have decided to extend our stay if you have an opening."

"Extend...um, sure. Let me check the reservation list. I'm sure I can work something out."

"Good," Patricia said. "Let's add on three more days, if it's possible."

Finally, a bit of good news. Assuming they had a room available. Hopefully, Victor Pallet, or whoever had salted the coffee, wouldn't escalate things. And while he was finding a way to juggle reservations, Rick might as well work on finding a room for Henry Nicholas.

6

ALEX

IT'S ALMOST LUNCHTIME WHEN ME and Marquetta finish our chores. We had two check outs and we've got people coming in this afternoon, so we've changed the bedding and the linens, vacuumed, and cleaned the bathrooms. I'm starving by the time we finish. Marquetta says she wants to see how my dad is doing, so we're gonna meet in the kitchen in ten minutes. She says my dad's in his office pulling his hair out. I think that's funny 'cause I know what he's really doing is trying to find a way for the Turners to stay a few more days. The only way that's gonna happen is if we get a cancellation.

I'm thinking of sneaking a few potato chips when I get to the kitchen, but then I see Tara on the back patio. She's staring out at the ocean and looking kinda lonely. I wonder if she thinks she made a mistake by kicking out Mr. Nicholas.

I'm about to go talk to her when Marquetta comes through the butler door and says my dad's gonna join us. We start making sandwiches and salads for lunch. When my dad shows up, he tells us how he got Henry Nicholas a room at the Seaside Cove Inn and how the people who were coming in for one day cancelled. The Turners got lucky. They can keep their room like they wanted to.

Tara's still out on the back patio when my dad tells me I can go play with my friends for the afternoon. I text them and we all agree to meet at the park down the street. I get my stuff together, say goodbye, and go out the French doors at the end of the kitchen.

I find Tara standing on the deck of the gazebo. She's still watching the ocean and doesn't even hear me coming when I walk along the decomposed granite path by the flower beds. It looks like she's super deep in thought. When I get closer, I say her name. She kinda jumps the way people do when you startle them, but doesn't get mad.

She flashes me a smile that goes away as fast as it came. "Alex. What are you up to?"

"I saw you out here and thought you looked kinda lonely."

"How sweet." She sighs, then hugs her arms around her. "I just have a lot to think about. You probably wouldn't understand."

"I've got a boyfriend. I think I do."

She smiles again, and this time it lasts longer. "You do? What's his name?"

"Robbie Sachetti. He's got dreamy blue eyes, and he makes me laugh."

"Sounds serious. I felt much the same about Henry. Until this trip. I thought he was wonderful. Now I realize he's nothing but a rat. Sorry, I shouldn't be putting all this on you."

"It's okay. I know when I'm sad, my dad and Marquetta say it's better to talk about it."

"Your dad and Marquetta are getting married soon, aren't they?"

"Next week. Right here." I hold my hands out to my sides. "This is gonna be an awesome place for a wedding."

"You're right. It is." She laughs quietly to herself. "It's the perfect color, white. It's got a nice roof to protect the bride and groom from the sun. I'd say it's an excellent place for a wedding." She runs her hand along the handrail. Her fingers catch on a flake of paint, and a little white speck falls to the floor. She winces and apologizes.

"It's okay, Ms. Amengual. That part gets the afternoon sun and the most wind. We need to have our handyman do some touchup on the paint."

"Other than needing a little touching up, it's in perfect condition."

I point to the side facing the shed where I keep my bike. "One of our guests did some damage to the lattice work underneath when he was hiding something he stole."

Tara's eyebrows go up and she walks over to look down. She looks kinda skeptical, like maybe I'm making this up.

"We call it treasure fever. People do crazy things when they think there's a lot of money involved."

She takes in a long breath and then she hugs herself. She looks lost, like she's alone in the world. Her forehead gets puckery, and she stares at the ocean again. "How did they get together?"

"Who?"

"Your dad and Marquetta. How did they know they were right for each other?"

I get a picture in my head from the first time I saw them kissing and laugh. "It took like forever to get them to figure it out. I spent almost a whole entire year playing matchmaker. It wasn't until last Christmas that I caught them kissing in the attic."

The puckering goes away and Tara gets a lopsided grin on her face. "In the attic?"

"They were searching for decorations, but they finally realized they were perfect for each other."

"How romantic. What happened to your biological mother?"

"She..." I stop and take a deep breath. It still hurts to think about how we got here. "She didn't want us."

"I'm sorry. I was raised by a single mother, so I get it. "

"What happened to your dad?"

"He left one day when I was five. My mother had to work two jobs to put food on the table. At least your dad's got this place."

"If it hadn't been for Captain Jack, we never would have come here. And we never would have met Marquetta."

"Who's Captain Jack?"

"My great-grandfather, but everyone just calls him Captain Jack. He kinda helped raise Marquetta 'cause her dad died when she was ten."

Tara gets another lost look in her eyes. There are little creases in her forehead that weren't there a second ago. "Wow. So here we all are, in the house of broken families."

"It's okay. I totally love Marquetta with all my heart. I'm sorry Mr. Nicholas treated you the way he did. Is he really still married to his wife?"

"Apparently. I guess I just wanted to believe him so much when he told me he was divorced. It was the only reason I agreed to come here with him. Did your dad find him a room?"

"At the Inn. It's only a motel, and it's not as nice as here, but it's a place to stay."

"There's some consolation in that he's getting a downgrade." Tara laughs, then covers her mouth with her hand. "Sorry, that's not nice. Is it?"

"It's totally okay. He kinda deserves it."

She looks off toward the ocean and takes a deep breath. "Yeah. He does. You look like you're headed somewhere."

"My bike's in the shed over there. I'm going to meet some friends."

"Good for you. Are you meeting your boyfriend, too?"

"Him and my best friend Sasha."

She looks sad as she says, "Good for you, Alex. Stay in touch with your friends. They'll help you through the tough times."

"Do you have someone you can talk to, Ms. Amengual?"

"I've spent too much time focused on work." She lets out a heavy sigh. "And Henry. I'm going to move on and reconnect with some of my friends when I get back."

"Good idea."

"You're a pretty lucky young lady. Do you know that?"

"For sure. Is there anything I can get you before I go?"

"I'm fine. But thank you."

I say goodbye and start to leave when she calls after me.

"Hey Alex, thanks for talking with me."

"No problem."

"And one more thing. Call me Tara."

It's funny how I kind of feel both good and bad for her. I wanted to make her feel better, and I think maybe I did. But I totally get how someone lying to her would have hurt so much. If Robbie or Sasha did that to me, I'd be devastated.

I roll my bike out of the shed and onto the decomposed granite path. As I go toward the street, I wave goodbye. Tara waves back, and I realize she's got a problem. How's she gonna get home since she's not the one who drove here?

7

RICK

THE FOLLOWING DAY'S BREAKFAST SERVICE was back to normal. With Henry Nicholas absent, so many things ran much smoother. Tara Amengual sat by herself, but was more at ease. Victor Pallett acted like a normal, polite guest. With no tirades or obnoxious behavior, the entire service felt almost, well, boring. Climbing the stairs to his office, Rick held a strong appreciation for simple group dynamics. He wouldn't have picked Henry Nicholas as a magnet for trouble, but magnetism was one of those mysterious forces the eye could not see.

When Rick reviewed his messages, he discovered two had come in overnight. Both wanted reservations later in the season. It was easy to deal with those quickly, and he was preparing a bank deposit when his cell phone rang. He checked the screen, saw it was Adam Cunningham calling, and answered.

"How's my favorite chief of police today?"

"I need your assistance." Adam's voice was somber amidst a backdrop of activity around him.

No, thought Rick. It can't be. Not again. "Why?"

"Henry Nicholas is dead. It looks suspicious to me. I'm calling in Dr. Turner. I'm pretty sure we've got a murder investigation on our hands."

"Adam, I'm getting married in eight days."

"I know. I'm sorry. But the mayor was quite explicit when I called her with the news. She wants you to help."

"There are times I really regret making that deal with her."

"Everybody thought it was a onetime thing, but this keeps happening. Sign of changes in town, I suppose."

"Can't have it both ways, right? Where are you at?"

"The Inn. Lydia discovered the body when she came in to do the out clean."

"What do you mean? Henry Nicholas was leaving? I booked that room for three nights. When did he check out?"

"He changed the reservation after lunch yesterday. He told Ray he was driving back to LA first thing this morning."

A thousand and one questions ran through Rick's head as he tried to reconcile Henry's initial plans with the sudden change. The only thing he could come up with was that the breakup had affected Henry more than anyone suspected. "I'll be there in fifteen minutes."

"You might as well walk over with the doc. She's on her way, too."

"It looks like Dr. Turner's vacation is over. See you soon."

After disconnecting the call, Rick looked around his desk. The good thing was he could turn all of this paperwork over to Marquetta. He'd have to talk to her next. And Alex. It wouldn't take long for her to hear about what had happened.

Rick found Marquetta in the laundry room. Her hair was pulled back and tied with a red scrunchie, and she again had on a Seaside Cove B&B tee shirt over jeans. She had one load of linens in the washer and another in the dryer. "Hey, are you done with the rooms already?"

"It appears we have a lot of guests who understand the concept of protecting the environment. I only had to replace linens in two rooms." Marquetta's brow furrowed. Her gray eyes searched Rick's as though she were trying to read his mind. "Something's happened, hasn't it?"

"Henry Nicholas is dead." He relayed the details Adam had given him and, before he'd even finished, could tell Marquetta understood what was coming next.

"This means I need to keep Alex busy again. Doesn't it?"

"I doubt that we'll have this wrapped up before she hears about it, so yes. I'd like to keep her from launching her own investigation."

"She's up in her room right now. I'll let her know you had to leave, but won't tell her why. I'll make up something if I have to."

After finalizing their plan to keep Alex occupied, Rick kissed Marquetta goodbye and went to the lobby. There, he found Patricia Turner already waiting.

"Let's go, Doc. I'll explain on the way."

"We're walking?"

"Yes. It's just down on Front Street on the other side of the roundabout."

"Most convenient murder scene I've ever been to."

Unlike the B&B with its intricate Victorian architecture and bright colors, the Inn was bland to the nth degree. Painted in earth tones, it stood in stark contrast to many of the other brightly colored buildings in town. Two Seaside Cove Police four-by-fours were parked out front.

Patricia Turner practically gasped. "Seeing this place reminds me of how thankful I am that I was able to stay at your B&B and not this..."

"Product of the sixties?"

"Amongst other things. Clean, affordable lodging? Really? That's all this place has going for it?"

"Ray's not big on frills. He's more of a just-the-basics kind of guy."

"You might also call it a clone of a million other cheap motels. And believe me, I've ended up in a bunch of them. Your place is so much nicer."

"Thanks." Rick felt a flush of pride, the same one he always felt when guests complimented the B&B.

They entered through the lobby door, which had been propped open. Ray Villari greeted them with a scowl. "About time you got here. Upstairs, Room 210. You can't miss it. It's the one crawling with cops."

Rick thanked Ray and led the way. As they were crossing through the pool area, Dr. Turner said, "Not a happy man, is he?"

"Cheery to the end," Rick quipped as he pointed out the room. "There's no elevator. Sorry, we'll have to take the stairs."

The doc's gaze followed the stairway to the second floor. "At least it's not a mountain. No problem."

Adam was waiting outside the room as they approached. "Body's inside, Doc."

"Thanks, Chief. That guy downstairs said the place was crawling with cops. Is it just you and Deputy Kama?"

"Yup. The entire available Seaside Cove Police Department is here. Both of us. My other deputy's reading water meters today."

Patricia Turner shook her head and looked back toward the main office. "Strange man."

"Ray's an acquired taste," Adam said with a smirk.

"I'll pass." Dr. Turner responded, then entered the room.

"What have we got so far?" Rick asked.

"Lydia discovered the body about forty-five minutes ago. She knocked, didn't get an answer, so she announced herself and entered. The victim was lying on the floor near the bathroom. It looks like the carpet soaked up a lot of the blood."

"Ray's going to have a fit."

"I know. He hates spending money. What he'll really hate is having to hire a new maid. Lydia freaked out, went down to the office, and quit. Ray's furious because she walked out right then and there."

Rick considered the shock of walking into a room and finding a dead body. It was stressful enough seeing one when you were expecting it. "I can't imagine what Lydia must have felt when she walked in. If I found a dead body at our place...man, I'd freak out, too."

"Exactly. Shall we go see your ex-guest?"

"Why not? Every minute we stand around out here is another minute we're not working the case."

Inside the room, Patricia Turner had fully slipped into her role as coroner. She was kneeling next to the body, inspecting it closely. Deputy Amy Kama stood nearby. She waved to Rick, then said to Adam, "Doc's already got some thoughts, Chief."

Each time Rick walked into one of the Inn's rooms, he said a silent thanks that he'd inherited the B&B and not a place like this. Ray's sense of interior design straddled the line somewhere between boring and depressing. He'd carried the earth-tone color scheme on the outside of the Inn into the rooms. From the brown quilted polyester bedspread to the knockoff prints on the walls, everything screamed one word—cheap.

"Tell me, Doc, what have you got?"

Dr. Turner straightened up and stretched her back. "Well, Chief, from the positioning of the body and the type of wound, I'd say your victim fell backwards and hit his head. Probably on the corner of the dresser. From the smudges on that corner, it also appears someone tried to clean it up. The crime scene techs will solve that puzzle. I won't be able to give a final opinion on the wound until I do a full exam. Preliminarily, I'd estimate that Mr. Nicholas died more than twelve hours ago." She frowned and paused. "I've never examined someone I'd actually known before. I mean, yesterday, you and I were sitting a couple of tables over while this guy was egging that jerk on. And today..."

"I know, Doc. Strange feeling, huh?" Adam took a look around the room. He pointed at the bedspread. "He never even slept here. So you think he died sometime last night, huh?"

"That's just a preliminary estimate. I'll get you something more accurate as soon as I can."

"Thanks, Doc." Adam looked at Rick. "Any questions before we start searching the room?"

"Not really. But since Dr. Turner's here, let me walk through a theory. There's no sign of a struggle. Therefore, the killer either surprised our victim, or they knew each other. Right?"

Rick got nods from both Adam and Dr. Turner.

Deputy Kama joined them and stood next to Adam as Rick continued. "And the body fell here on the opposite side of the room from the door. There should have been some sort of struggle. Something should be disturbed."

"I think we can assume the killer and Henry Nicholas were friendly," Adam said.

"Exactly," Rick added. "So our killer was invited in, then they got into an argument. The victim gets pushed backward, hits his head, and the killer realizes what's happened. What's strange is that rather than calling 9-1-1, he tried to clean up and left."

"Makes sense," Dr. Turner said. "I hope I can get you some more details."

Rick was hoping one of the three professionals would disagree with him. But the evidence all pointed to a single conclusion. And, quite possibly, one suspect. "Henry Nicholas only knew one person in town, and until yesterday, they were very friendly."

Adam grimaced as he surveyed the scene. "It gives me no pleasure to say I think you could be right."

Deputy Kama raised her eyebrows. "Care to share? Do you two have someone in mind?"

"Tara Amengual," Rick said. "She and Henry posed as husband and wife when they checked into the B&B. Things fell apart when Henry's real wife called him and Tara found out about it."

"She was furious with him yesterday," Dr. Turner added. "You talked to her. Do you think she was angry enough to come over here and kill him?"

Rick studied the body for a few seconds. "I don't know. Henry Nicholas was a stranger in town. Other than the guests he and Tara had breakfast with yesterday, he knew only one person —Tara. I'm sure he would have let her in if she showed up at his door. But I'm really hoping she kept her distance."

"For someone who wants to be wrong, you made a pretty convincing argument," Adam said.

"I know. And that's what worries me. I think Tara is the easy solution. What if there's someone else?"

8

ALEX

Hey Journal,

I don't know if I'm gonna get a chance to see Robbie or Sasha today. Marquetta says we're having a planning meeting about the wedding with her mom and Traci Peterson down in the kitchen. It's kinda weird that she'd do something like this so early in the day 'cause we have a lot of work to do. I guess maybe it's the only time Grandma Madeline and Traci can get away from their jobs. We're all meeting in the kitchen in a couple minutes.

I've been thinking about Tara, too. The talk with her made me appreciate the time I had with Sasha and Robbie. When I met them yesterday, they both said I was acting kinda weird, so I told them what happened between Tara and Mr. Nicholas. They didn't get why I feel so sorry for Tara, but that's okay. It's kinda different for me 'cause I was part of the reason she's going through this. It's nice she wants to stay for a few days. I'm gonna talk to Marquetta and see if maybe she can suggest some things Tara might want to do.

Gotta go now!

Xoxo

Alex

* * *

Grandma Madeline and Traci are on one side of the island, and Marquetta is on the other. They get quiet when I walk in, and it feels like they just stopped because of me. Marquetta pats the barstool next to hers, so I give Grandma Madeline a hug, say hi to Traci, and then sit on the stool.

"How are you doing, dear?" Grandma Madeline asks.

"Good. Did I miss anything?"

Grandma Madeline and Traci both look at Marquetta. Uh oh, they really were talking about me. "Did I mess up by being late?"

"No, Sweetie. You didn't mess up at all. Traci was telling us she found a special candle set for the wedding."

I can almost feel Grandma Madeline and Traci let out the breaths they've been holding.

"Yes, and it's my contribution to the wedding," Traci says. "There'll be enough candles to cover the perimeter of the gazebo. I've been having trouble getting supplies lately, so I contacted a friend of mine. She's a professional chandler in Maine and would be happy to make them. She's promised me the candles can arrive a few days before the wedding."

"They sound wonderful," Marquetta says. "Thank you, Traci. That's so sweet."

But Grandma Madeline doesn't look happy. She's got on a grumpy face as she looks at Marquetta. "I don't know, dear. It's a daytime wedding. Do you really need candles? They probably won't even be noticeable."

"Mom, I think it's a wonderful idea. Candles will provide a lovely ambience."

"I thought you wanted to keep the ceremony simple," Grandma Madeline huffs. "I also think this relying-on-shipping business is cutting things rather close. Are you sure you wouldn't rather do something more traditional? More reliable. Wouldn't you agree, dear?"

I bite my lower lip to keep from smiling. Marquetta says her mom knows how to push her buttons. I can totally see that 'cause I know Marquetta would love those candles. I'm like a hundred percent sure my dad would think it's cool, too.

Traci's been kinda quiet, but it looks like she's getting mad about this turning into a big deal. "Madeline, my friend is very reliable. If she says she'll have everything here before the wedding, it will be here. And I have to disagree. Candles add a nice touch of elegance to any setting. Day or night."

"Me, too. I think candles are awesome."

Grandma Madeline's jaw gets tight, but then she gives everyone a forced smile. It's the one she uses a lot. "Well, then. I guess it's settled."

Marquetta reaches across the table. "Mom, I do want to keep things simple. But I also want to have some nice touches."

"Very well, dear. I'm glad you feel that way."

Grandma Madeline gives us all a firm nod, like maybe she's made up her mind on something. What's she up to?

"I have a contribution of my own I'd like to make."

Uh oh. This is gonna get super complicated.

9

RICK

RICK HAD WATCHED THE REACTIONS of Dr. Turner, Deputy Kama, and Adam as he'd laid out his theory. He'd hoped for resistance, but they all agreed Tara was the most likely suspect. She'd certainly had reason to argue with Henry. She could have easily pushed him. The only question was, had she been here? The problem was, since Tara was his guest, he didn't feel right about his role in this investigation.

"Adam, I told you before I was reluctant to help with this case because of the wedding, but I also think you and Deputy Kama can handle this. You don't really need me."

"Nonsense, Rick. You bring a different perspective to these cases. The reason I called you is not just because of the deal with the mayor, but also because I'd like to have you involved."

That wasn't the answer Rick wanted. A heaviness filled his body. He felt so conflicted. "I don't...feel right about being involved in this."

"Why?"

Rick rubbed the back of his neck. He knew the moment he said the words, they'd feel more real than they did as no more than a wayward thought. "I just don't."

"That's not like you, buddy. What's up?"

"I feel responsible for his death," Rick blurted. "I'm the one who caused all the trouble between him and Tara, and I'm the one who got him this room. If I'd have done things differently, Henry Nicholas might not be dead."

"First off, this isn't your fault. The munchkin started all this by sticking her nose into their, um, affairs. But even at that, you're not responsible for our victim's actions. And neither is Alex. Henry Nicholas got himself into his situation. All you'd be doing is trying to find out who did this to him."

Adam's support didn't erase how Rick felt. In fact, it sounded like nothing more than a friend practicing sympathy over reason. "That doesn't make me any less reluctant."

"Let's step outside for a minute." Adam looked at Deputy Kama and Dr. Turner, then pointed at the open door. "We'll be right back."

Once they were outside the room, Adam turned left. "Let's walk for a minute."

"Pep talk?" Rick asked.

"More like a free therapy session."

They'd gone only a few feet when Rick stopped and put his hands on the railing. He surveyed the pool area. It was the best feature about the Inn. A lovely courtyard overflowed with ferns and different types of palms. Small, flowering broadleaved plants occupied the few gaps. It all worked together to create a delightful, tropical atmosphere.

"Too bad Ray didn't use this as his inspiration for the rest of the place," Adam said.

"This could have been a real gem if someone had put the money into it." Rick turned to Adam and sighed. "So, are you going to make me do this?"

"You're not an employee of the town, Rick. I can't force you to do anything. You're a consultant, which means you have every right to walk away. But I don't believe it's in your DNA to do that. Do you really consider this to be a conflict of interest, or is it the wedding you're worried about?"

"I don't know, Adam. Things went so wrong when I married Giselle. I was working a lot of hours at the paper and she was chasing her Broadway-stardom dreams. Work sent us in opposite directions. I know this isn't an actual job, but I don't want it pulling me away from Alex and Marquetta."

"Believe me, Marquetta understands. She knows how important it is to solve a crime like this."

Adam's green eyes held Rick's gaze. The first time they'd met, there had been an innocence in those eyes. Today, they looked more seasoned.

"But what if we can't solve this one right away? I don't want to be conducting a murder investigation on my wedding day."

"I wouldn't let you do that."

"That's what you say today."

"Don't worry. I won't change my opinion later."

"I might get distracted by the wedding."

"Rick, does this even have anything to do with the wedding? Maybe this is really about Alex."

And there it was. The real reason Rick's throat felt thick with guilt. Alex. Eleven years old and fascinated by murder. Precocious enough to get herself into trouble, but not out. "Once she hears about this, she'll want to investigate. You know that, right?"

"I do. But ask yourself this—what happens if you don't help with the investigation and Alex discovers you backed away? Do you honestly believe she won't get involved if you're not? Or will she double down on her efforts because she sees a bigger need?"

Rick closed his eyes. He knew the answer to the question. Pretending this murder hadn't happened was only going to work until Alex heard about it through the grapevine. And even if she wasn't a junior reporter for the Cove Talkers Newsletter, she'd hear the news in a matter of hours. By dinner, she'd know every little detail.

"You're right, Adam. This isn't going away on its own, and I'm really setting a bad example for Alex if I don't help you out."

Adam nudged Rick in the ribs. "I wasn't going to play the set-a-good-example-for-your-daughter card, but since you brought it up..."

"No need. I'll help. Let's get going."

Dr. Turner was on her way out when Rick and Adam walked back into the room. "You're leaving?" Rick asked.

"Not much I can do at this point. Any poking around I do here will only complicate my job later."

"Will you be doing the autopsy, Doc?" Adam asked.

She shook her head. "Maybe not. Technically, I'm on vacation for a few more days. My boss could decide to assign this to one of my colleagues, but I've been here and at the crime scene. So it's also possible he'll want me to see it through. I'll ask and let you know."

It was only a few minutes after they said their goodbyes that the team from the Coroner's office showed up to transport the body. Rick snapped a few photos to provide himself with a reference later in the case, then went back outside while the team set up. Adam joined him a few seconds later.

"Getting a little crowded in there," Rick said.

"I know. I had Kama stay so she could witness the transportation, but there's no need for both of us to be in there."

As they waited, a scruffy man with a thick gray beard walked toward them. He had a room key in his hand and studied them with wary eyes. The man's jeans and jacket were caked with dirt and Rick suspected he'd been crawling around in the hills and caves in search of something like Joaquin Murrieta's treasure.

When the man was a few feet away, he stopped and gestured beyond Rick and Adam. "Excuse me. I'm in the next room."

Adam held his ground as he displayed his badge. "I'm Chief Cunningham of the Seaside Cove Police. I'd like to ask you a few questions. Were you here yesterday afternoon?"

"Checked in about a week ago. Questions about what?"

"The guest who was staying in this room died sometime yesterday. We're looking into his death. Were you in your room yesterday afternoon, Mr...?" Adam craned his neck forward and regarded the man.

"I don't like getting involved with cops." The man averted his gaze and his brow furrowed. "I haven't done anything."

Adam planted his feet shoulder width apart and leaned forward slightly, forcing the man to take a small step back. He pulled a notepad from his pocket and his voice took on an official edge. "Just answer the question, sir. What's your name?"

The man grimaced, then reluctantly said, "Oscar Johnson."

Adam wrote down the name, then regarded the man closely. "Mr. Johnson, where did you have dinner last night?"

From what Rick had seen of the treasure hunters who came to town, most weren't interested in spending money on fancy dinners. And with only two restaurants in Seaside Cove, both of which were relatively upscale, he felt certain this man chose a different option.

"What's that got to do with anything?" Johnson demanded.

"Mr. Johnson, so far I'm considering you a witness, but if you continue to obstruct my investigation, I'm going to start wondering what you have to hide."

"Alright. No need to get all heavy-handed. I grabbed some takeout from the deli at the Seaside Cove market. I was in the market about five, then came back here and was in my room for the rest of the night. I watched TV for a while, then fell asleep around nine."

Rick gestured at the open door. "Did you hear anything coming from this room last night?"

"No. I'm...a little hard of hearing, so I keep the TV up. In fact, the front desk called me about eight and told me to turn it down. You can call them and ask if you want."

Yes, indeed, they could. And they would, just to close the loop. "Did you see anyone go into or come out of this room last night?"

"Not really. But there was a woman leaving about the time I came back. I don't know if she was in that room or not, but I passed her on the way up the stairs."

"Can you describe this woman?" Rick asked.

"Black lady. Wore a denim jacket and those tight jeans all the young ones like."

Adam shot a glance at Rick, who felt his neck muscles tighten. Tara Amengual had been dressed like that yesterday. Had she come over to talk with Henry? Yell at him again? Though he resisted the urge to spin the scenario, Rick had seen Tara's temper. If she'd been angry, he truly believed she might have come here, fully intending to give her fake ex a tongue-lashing. Instead, it turned into a literal head bashing.

"How old was this woman?" Rick asked.

"Hard to say. Young. Maybe late twenties? Early thirties?"

The tightness in Rick's neck was being replaced by a giant knot in his stomach. The more detailed Johnson's description became, the more it sounded like Tara. "Anything else you remember about her?"

"No. We just passed on the stairs."

After getting Oscar Johnson's contact information, they let him go and went back into the room. It still bothered Rick that the victim hadn't even slept in the bed.

"I don't want to believe Tara committed murder," Rick said. "But Johnson's description fits her almost exactly."

"We'll check to see if there are any guests here who Mr. Johnson could have seen, but we'll also need to talk to Ms. Amengual."

"Do you think we might be able to narrow down the time of death without an autopsy?" Rick asked hopefully.

"Deputy Kama took the victim's phone into evidence. If we could get access to it, we might be able to determine his last activity."

"That's what I was hoping, too. I might have a way to get access. It's possible Tara knows his password. If not her, maybe his wife."

If one of those women had the password, they could access the call log. He hoped the phone activity would exonerate Tara just in case she'd been the last one to visit Henry Nicholas before he died.

10

ALEX

GRANDMA MADELINE NEVER LIKES TO be outdone. She's super-competitive, even though she'd never admit it. Marquetta's actually the one who told me what she was like when we were first discussing her mom being involved in planning the wedding. Marquetta's been real quiet since her mom said she wanted to make a contribution of her own. I don't know what it's gonna be, but I can see Marquetta's not happy.

"Grandma, what is it you wanna add?" I kinda hope that it's not a big deal, but the only way to find out is to ask. Right?

"Well, dear, I was thinking about a string quartet."

Whoa. That's a lot more than a few candles.

Marquetta's phone pings with a message. She reads the screen and nods to herself. As she's pocketing her phone, she shoots a look at Traci, who seems to know exactly what she's thinking. Traci fingers her lower lip and says, "Madeline, don't you think a string quartet would be overkill for a small wedding?"

"No more so than filling the space with fancy candles we don't need."

Traci's not the kind to get flustered, but her face gets red, and she takes a deep breath. "Marquetta has always loved candles, Madeline. You know that. Why shouldn't she have something truly unique for one of the most special days of her life? And then afterwards, she'll be able to place them around the house wherever she likes."

"I think the music helps to make the day special, too." Grandma Madeline turns to Marquetta. "Wouldn't you agree, dear?"

"Mom..." Marquetta looks at her mother and talks kinda slow, like she's choosing her words carefully. "Traci is giving us the candles as a gift. They're something we can use afterwards. But a string quartet? Really? We can't afford to be hiring live musicians."

Now Grandma Madeline's cheeks get pink and she gets kinda flustered herself. "Well...I've been saving my money and can certainly afford a small extravagance."

"Hiring four musicians is hardly a small extravagance, Mom. I don't want you to have to pay for something so expensive."

Oh boy. This could like go around in circles for a while. I can see why Marquetta didn't really want her mom involved in the planning.

The two of them eventually agree that we're not gonna do the string quartet, but Grandma Madeline can provide the bridal bouquet.

After we finish with the meeting, Traci and Grandma Madeline leave. Me and Marquetta are sitting at the table, and I wonder if she needs to talk. I get up to give her a hug. "You were right about Grandma. She totally wants to take over."

"I know, Sweetie. We'll work through it. I'll try to be more understanding when it's your turn."

"No way. If this is what it's like to get married, I never wanna do it!"

Marquetta laughs and hugs me tight. "You'll change your mind someday. Right now, we have baking to do."

"But I thought we finished with the breads for tomorrow morning."

"We need cookies for the lobby." She wrinkles her nose. "And maybe a few for us."

"Is this, like, therapy?"

"It's baking, Alex, not psychoanalysis."

"What's psycho..."

Marquetta gives me a fake laugh. "A very expensive option for people who don't like to bake. Let's go."

She gets up and I follow her into the kitchen. This is all kinda weird 'cause Marquetta's not acting like herself. I wonder if the whole wedding planning thing is getting to her. It only takes us about a half hour to get the first batch out of the oven.

"Let's put these out for the guests. Okay, Sweetie? I'll bring this batch and you clear a spot on the buffet."

Miss Larkin is standing right next to where the cookies are gonna go when I walk into the dining room. I'm surprised that she's alone, but she looks like she wants some quiet time.

"Hi, Miss Larkin. Would you like a Chocolate Chip Macaroon? We just made a batch and Marquetta's bringing them out."

She darts a look toward the door. "A little something sweet would be very nice. Thank you."

Marquetta shows up with the plate of cookies. "Miss Larkin, would you like one?"

"Alex was telling me you just baked these." She picks one up, and her mouth opens a little. "They're still warm. I can't remember the last time I had a cookie straight out of the oven."

I clear off a spot on the buffet and Marquetta puts down the plate. "It doesn't usually happen that way. You got lucky."

Miss Larkin lets out a slow moan when she takes a bite. "If only I could get as lucky with men."

"Relationships can be difficult," Marquetta says."Meeting Rick was, well, maybe it was fate. But to be truthful, we almost never got together. We were both carrying around a lot of pain."

"I can tell you one thing. I wish I'd never met Victor. The man is impossible."

Marquetta cocks her head to the side and frowns. "How long have you been together?"

"Three years. When we first met, I thought he was so funny. He was always joking around and telling ridiculous stories. He also liked to play little practical jokes on people. Most of the time, it really made everyone laugh."

"So, when did things change?"

Nice, I thought. It's amazing how good Marquetta is at this asking people questions stuff. She gets them to talking and they tell her everything. It's how she learns all the good news first.

"It wasn't any one thing. But his little jokes became less funny. It was like they became more mean-spirited...or maybe they were just more desperate. I really don't know what happened, but the whole situation got completely out of hand last Halloween. We were on our way to a Halloween party." Miss Larkin makes a face and shivers. Not the kind of shiver when you're cold, but more like she's trying to shake off a lot of anger.

"What happened?" I ask.

She huffs again and I think maybe she doesn't want to talk about it. Marquetta raises her little finger. It's her signal for when she wants me to be patient, so I just wait. After a few seconds, Miss Larkin starts rambling.

"We were going to a fundraiser being held downtown in an old hotel. We were walking along the street when we passed a homeless man. He was hunched over and hobbling along. Victor was wearing this awful vampire costume. He jumped out and yelled 'boo' as we were passing the poor man. It caused him to stumble. His foot slipped off the curb, and he fell into the street and was nearly hit by a car. I told Victor I thought we should help, but he threatened to leave me alone if I didn't keep up. I wasn't comfortable being alone on that street, so I..."

"Left without lending a hand?" Marquetta asked.

Miss Larkin nods. Her eyes look super sad and she doesn't say anything.

"What happened to the homeless guy?" I ask.

"Another person who was walking by called 9-1-1. When we heard the sirens, Victor grabbed my hand and practically dragged me away. I suppose he didn't want to get involved. And, to be honest, I didn't want to cause him trouble. I'm ashamed to say I never tried to find out if the man was seriously injured."

My feelings about Mr. Pallett deserving the name Mr. McNasty are getting stronger each time I hear something about him. Especially now 'cause Miss Larkin feels terrible about herself. And he's to blame. Marquetta steps closer to Miss Larkin and takes her hands. "Unfortunately, we learn the most about ourselves from our mistakes. I'm sure the next time you face a difficult decision, you won't let yourself be pulled away from the right path."

"How true that is," Miss Larkin says. "I've regretted letting Victor bully me since the day it happened. It's also helped me to see Victor in a new light. I'm actually thinking of leaving him."

Talk about a bummer. Staying at the B&B usually brings couples together 'cause it's so romantic. And now we have two breaking up? I hope that's not gonna become our new thing.

Marquetta looks at me and takes a deep breath. "Follow your heart. It took the longest time for me to realize it was what I needed to do. Alex was the one who brought me to my senses."

I gape at Marquetta, feeling kinda stupid 'cause she never told me that before. "I did?"

"Yes, Sweetie, you did."

Miss Larkin looks off to the side, and her eyes get misty. "I know what my heart wants. What I don't know is if I feel safe doing it."

11

RICK

RICK AND ADAM STOOD ON the second-floor walkway as the team from the Coroner's office carried the stretcher down the stairs and out the back exit. It was now just the two of them, an all-too-familiar situation as far as Rick was concerned.

"Adam, why don't you let me talk to Tara about the code for Henry's phone? She may not even know yet that he's dead."

"Good point. I certainly don't see a need to upset one of your guests without proper cause."

Rick nodded. "She's already upset. I don't want to make things worse by having her feel like she's a suspect."

"Not yet, anyway."

"Right. Not yet." Ever since his first case with Adam, the thought of accusing one of his guests of murder had become Rick's worst nightmare. And because of what Tara had already been through, he felt even worse about the possibility.

Adam gripped Rick's shoulder with his right hand. The pressure he applied was firm and reassuring. "Look, Rick, I'm happy to keep this low key for now. We don't have proof Ms. Amengual did anything, and until we do, we can hold off."

"Do you want me to ask if she came here to see Mr. Nicholas?"

"Let's wait for that question. We can always turn up the heat later. I'd like to have a firm time of death before we start."

"Sounds good to me. If she still looks guilty when we have something firmer, as much as I hate the idea, I'll go along with it. The main thing is, we need to catch the killer."

"Great. We have a plan. Do you want to track Ms. Amengual down while I compile some background on our victim?"

"Will do. But what about Ray? And Lydia?"

"I'm not worried at all about Lydia, but you know how Ray is. He doesn't reveal anything he doesn't have to. I'd like to talk to her first, then deal with him."

Rick's gaze instinctively drifted to the lobby door off the pool area that led to the Inn's office. Marquetta had once told him about Ray's background and how he'd just shown up one day after he purchased the Inn. "Any idea why he's so secretive?"

"Ray doesn't confide in anybody. So nobody in this town knows his background. However, my predecessor once told me he's married."

"Where's his wife?"

"Chief Jackson got his information from the mayor, who claimed Ray told her she lives in Boston. According to the story he heard, the chief thought Ray suffered some emotional trauma that caused them to separate. I don't know how true it is, but if Ray's learned to be distrusting of people, it would explain a lot."

Rick wondered if his own history with his ex might not be similar to Ray's situation. The difference might be that in Rick's case, so many things had led him to this moment where he was again open, trusting, and ready to marry. It had all begun with inheriting a B&B he hadn't even thought he wanted, and now he couldn't imagine living anywhere else.

"Yes, I can see how Ray might have gotten to be the way he is," Rick said. "I'll go find Tara and ask her about the phone access code while you look into our victim. Let's meet in your office in about an hour."

Glancing toward the lobby on his way down the stairs, Rick decided he didn't have time to deal with Ray Villari and his moods. Rather than risk running into him, Rick slipped out the rear exit. After a quick left in the alley behind the Inn, it was only a short walk to Front Street.

Rick turned right, then followed the roundabout. On the other side, he gazed down the street to the B&B. The house, large as it was, stood like a sentry standing guard over the ocean. With its white paint and dark shutters, the old Victorian maintained a sense of elegance Ray's cheap motel could never attain.

Climbing the stairs to the front door, Rick's thoughts were still dominated by his feelings of guilt about Henry Nicholas's death. He was reaching for the doorknob when the door opened. Patricia and Greg Turner both started when they saw him.

"Rick? Are you okay?" Dr. Turner asked.

"Yes. I'm fine." He stood to one side and gestured for them to come out.

When all three were on the front porch, Greg said, "I hear you and my wife have been hanging out."

"Actually, I wanted to talk to you about that, Dr. Turner."

The young woman's thin eyebrows arched as she gazed at Rick. "I'm happy to talk about it, but there's not much more I can tell you until we finish the autopsy."

"Actually, I wanted to talk to you about a different aspect of the murder. My daughter has a tendency to insert herself into police investigations...especially when there's a murder involved. She's of the opinion we need her help."

The couple exchanged a look involving raised eyebrows, then Dr. Turner shifted uncomfortably. "So I've heard. The chief told me she's very...persistent."

"Did Adam also tell you I keep trying to prevent her from getting involved and she keeps finding ways to investigate on her own?"

"Yes, he did." She pulled on a strand of her long, dark curls, then took her husband's arm. "We've been trying. I'm hoping we have a daughter who's as well-behaved and smart as Alex. And, don't worry, I already think I know what you're going to ask. I haven't revealed anything about the murder to her, and I won't."

It felt as though a huge weight had been removed from Rick's shoulders. He knew it wouldn't last long, but at least he had a temporary reprieve. "Thank you. I'm at my wit's end because I know a police investigation isn't a place for a child, and yet, my daughter feels exactly the opposite. I appreciate your help. She'll hear about the entire incident soon enough."

"I'll do my best to avoid giving her the opportunity to ask those types of questions."

"Thank you. And if she asks about the case, feel free to tell her it's none of her business."

Dr. Turner held Rick's gaze, her skepticism clearly showing. "From what I've heard, she won't accept that answer."

"Unfortunately, that's all too true." Rick felt suddenly embarrassed. Lately, he'd been breaking all of his rules about getting too personal with the guests. He stuffed his hands in his pockets and tried to sound upbeat. "Well, enough of my family drama. I'll let you get on with your day."

"We thought we'd take in a little more of the town. Patty's boss called—he wants her to come in and do the exam on your murder victim."

"So you're leaving?"

"We're negotiating. I have a lot of vacation time built up. Sorry, but we're not sure yet."

From a purely selfish standpoint, Rick really didn't want them leaving. He'd just gotten them squared away in their room, and if they left, he'd have an unplanned vacancy on his hands. "Well, Dr. Turner, I've got my fingers crossed for you. Enjoy your trip to town."

As Rick went through the front door, he checked the lobby, saw it was empty, then continued on to the kitchen.

"Rick just walked in. Let me call you back," Marquetta said. She disconnected the call, placed her cell phone on the kitchen island, and approached.

"What's up?" Rick asked.

"That was Traci. Thanks to my mom, I had to do a little damage control after our wedding planning meeting."

"What happened?"

"Just Mom being herself. How'd it go with Adam?"

"I'm definitely involved."

Marquetta put her arms around his neck and kissed him. "Was there ever any doubt?"

"Only in my deluded little world where my daughter actually does what I ask her to."

"Ah, the same world where Mom doesn't think she knows best."

"That's the one." Rick took in a deep breath. "So, what happened with your mom?"

"After the meeting with her and Traci, Mom called me back. She was quite upset because I didn't like her idea for the wedding. She wants to hire a string quartet."

"A string quartet? Isn't that kind of..."

"Overkill? Ostentatious?"

"I was going to say expensive, but those, too."

"She says I only have one wedding, and she'd like her gift to be an elegant addition. Something 'befitting of the atmosphere' at the B&B." Marquetta threw her hands up in the air. "How could I say no after that? I finally agreed. Anyway, I asked Alex to do some research for me. She's in her room. I'm hoping that's what she's actually working on."

"You've given me about the best news I could possibly hope for. And while Alex is occupied, I need to find Tara Amengual." He went on to explain his and Adam's theory about the phone and being able to narrow down a time of death. "Anyway, we're hoping she has the password."

"I haven't seen her, but she was out on the back patio. Since then, I've mostly been in here."

"I'll check her room. If she's not there, I'll walk into town. I still have the grocery list you gave me earlier. There are only a couple of things, so it won't be a problem to combine my trips. She's probably gone in for lunch. Speaking of which, what are we having?"

"Alex and I are having a salad. You, on the other hand, had better go before Alex sees you and starts asking questions about where you disappeared to this morning."

Rick hurried upstairs to the Port Room, which was located in the same wing as their personal quarters and included Alex's bedroom. He mentally kept his fingers crossed that Alex wouldn't hear him as he knocked lightly on Tara's door. After a few seconds with no response, he tried again. Rather than make more noise, he padded back down the stairs and left through the front door.

As Rick walked up Main Street, he still recalled the shock on Alex's face when they'd driven through town the first time. He also recalled how little the town had changed since his one and only visit when he was a child.

The only major change the town had ever experienced was its metamorphosis from a fishing village to a vacation destination. After that conversion, the brightly painted old homes on both sides of the street had been turned into quaint shops and become the heart of the downtown. A combination of space constraints and a fierce resistance to outside development had kept the town looking, and feeling, much the same for nearly a century.

Having come from a city where there were more restaurants on any given block than there were in the entire town, both he and Alex had gone through a bit of culture shock. But the Crooked Mast and the Rusty Nail weren't the only options. As Oscar Johnson had mentioned, the Seaside Cove Market had a small deli. And then there was Crusty Buns—a jewel for anyone interested in baked goods. They did a booming business even though they only sold coffee, tea, and muffins. It wasn't going to take long to see if Tara Amengual was in any of those places.

Rick chuckled at the memory of Alex's incredulous response when she'd realized how small Seaside Cove really was. In classic tween drama, it was the point when she declared her life was over.

The truth was, that's when it had really begun.

12

ALEX

—*HEY SASHA, SOMETHING'S UP. MARQUETTA asked me to check out some musicians Grandma Madeline wants to hire for the wedding. I don't get why she wants me to do that. Do you think she's just trying to keep me busy?*

Sasha doesn't answer my text right away. She's probably in yoga or dance class 'cause her mom keeps her super busy with activities. I'm gonna try Robbie next.

—*Hey, you around?*

—*Hey, Alex. Mom's driving me to my piano lesson. What's up?*

—*Marquetta's got me doing busy work.*

—*Oh. Boring.*

—*Yeah. Anything big going on in town?*

—*Don't know.*

I scrunch up my face and take a deep breath. That's Robbie. Marquetta says he's a man of few words. I think it's super frustrating.

—*We're there. Gotta go.*

—*Miss you*

—*Yeah*

I slam down the phone on my bedspread and grit my teeth. Boys! A second later, I pick up my phone. I could send him a few heart emojis...but Robbie's kinda like my dad. Clueless.

I bring up the browser and look up the name of the group Grandma Madeline was talking about. There is one in San Ladron, but there's like nothing on them. At least, nothing helpful. They have a gig coming up in a couple days at a small neighborhood craft fair.

My phone pings with a message. It's Sasha.

—*Hey Alex, I heard my mom talking on the phone with someone about a guy who died last night. He was like a guest at the B&B and then he moved to the Inn. Kinda weird, huh?*

—*That must be Mr. Nicholas. He's dead? He was a guest here, but he was lying to his girlfriend and she kicked him out.*

—*Yeah, my mom said it's all over town. So you knew the dead guy?*

—*For sure. Did she say anything else?*

—*Nah. Hey, gotta go. Yoga's about to start.*

—*Let's keep this on the down low. I don't want Marquetta or my dad to find out I know.*

—*K*

Cool. Sasha's gonna keep quiet. At least I figured out why Marquetta sent me up here. I'll bet my dad put her up to giving me busy stuff to do. He's totally paranoid about me getting involved. Well, two can play the secret game.

I'm gonna call Mr. Gray and ask him how he's doing. I'll tell him I just found out that he fell and ask him if he thinks it was an accident. He's like a super big gossip. I'll bet he'll tell me everything there is to know without me even asking. I dial the number. Mr. Gray answers on the second ring, and I tell him why I'm calling.

"Fell and broke my arm, Alex. Now I'm in a cast and my wife won't leave me alone. She thinks I'm an invalid."

"But you're like super active. You can't just not do anything. Right?"

"I wish Angela felt that way, but after thirty-seven years of marriage, I guess she's decided she knows what I need better than I do."

"Was your fall an accident like Chief Cunningham said?"

Mr. Gray grunts, and I can almost see the lines on his face getting all tight and pinched. "No, it was not. In fact, it was one of your guests who caused this. Victor Pallett tripped me because I called his business plan a sham."

"Mr. Gray, what's a sham?"

"A fake. A scam. The man's entire scheme is based on lies, Alex."

Holy cow. Maybe that's why he got so mad at me yesterday. If Mr. Gray told him it was a scam, and then I kinda did the same thing...so he, like, had a temper tantrum and salted our coffee and...Mr. Gray's still going on, and I realize I haven't been listening.

"I'm sorry, Mr. Gray. My phone cut out for a second."

"Happens to me all the time. I said Pallett claims he knows where there's a stash of Joaquin Murrieta's treasure. My first thought was, if he's so smart and has the location of this treasure, why doesn't he just go and get it? So I asked him. You know what he said?"

Duh, of course not. I wasn't there. "Uh-uh. What'd he say?"

"That he doesn't have the exact coordinates, but he's planning to lead expeditions to find it. He wants to charge people to traipse around the mountains looking for nonexistent treasure. And if by chance they do come across something, he'll get the bulk of it."

"So he gets people to pay to work for him and then he only splits part of the treasure with them? That doesn't sound very fair to me."

"Exactly. But that's what he thinks he's going to do. I'd bet money he doesn't know the first thing about Joaquin Murrieta."

Mr. Gray's kind of an expert on local history, so if anyone's gonna know where there's buried treasure, it's him. "I haven't heard that much about Joaquin Murrieta, Mr. Gray. Our teacher said we'll be studying him later in the semester."

"I'm glad to hear you'll be reading about him. The man was fascinating. Nobody really knows whether he was a cutthroat or a hero."

This is totally going the wrong direction. I shouldn't have said anything about buried treasure. I need to get Mr. Gray back on the subject of why he thinks he was tripped. "Maybe you could come talk to my class when we study him."

Mr. Gray clears his throat. He's quiet for a long time, which is totally not like him. "Well, thank you, Alex. I'd be honored to do that if your teacher wants me to, of course."

"I'll ask her. So did you tell Mr. Pallett you thought his business plan was a scam? I mean, like, to his face?"

"I sure did. He acted like he took it well enough, but as I was walking along the dock, he ran to catch up with me. He bumped into me hard enough to send me down." Mr. Gray pauses for a second, then says, "I'm surprised you haven't asked me about the murder."

Thank you, Sasha! Thank you! I'm not gonna sound stupid. "Was it Mr. Nicholas?"

"Yes. I heard someone bashed him over the head last night."

"Like with a club or something?"

"Well, I don't know exactly. But I would think so."

Mr. Gray doesn't sound too sure of his facts. Kind of like he's filling in the gaps. That's one reason I think writing for the Cove Talkers Newsletter is so important. I'm like my dad. I want to get to the truth and then print it. And if I'm gonna write about this, I need the facts. "Does Chief Cunningham have any clues?"

"Not that I've heard about. How come you're asking me? I thought you'd be right in the middle of things...oh, wait. I get it. Your dad hasn't told you what's going on. Has he?"

I could grumble about it being totally unfair, but there might be a better way. "I'm gonna write a story for the Cove Talkers Newsletter."

"Good idea. Get all the facts and not just spread gossip like all these people do."

I'm super glad there's no video on this call. I wouldn't want Mr. Gray seeing my face right now. My dad always says Mr. Gray talking about other people gossiping is like the pot calling the kettle black. "Who told you about it?"

"Jennifer Martin, who heard about it from Mary Ellen Herbert, who heard about it from Lydia Smith. She's the one who discovered the body."

I'll bet Marquetta knows Lydia Smith. I've never met her, but Marquetta knows everybody in town. The problem is she won't want me investigating, either. Unless, maybe, I get her to help me. "Are there any suspects yet?"

"Not yet. Wait a minute, Alex." The sound on the other end gets muffled. I can kinda hear Mr. Gray talking, but I can't make out the words. "Sorry about that. Angela just gave me the high sign. She says I'm gossiping. I guess if you want the facts, you'd be best off talking to Adam. According to my wife, I've said more than I should."

Rats. There goes my source. "Okay. Thanks, Mr. Gray."

June 6

Hey Journal, me again.

I just had a super interesting talk with Mr. Gray. He told me there's been another murder in town! Now I know where my dad's been all day. He's gotta be helping Chief Cunningham with the investigation. With the wedding so close, I'll bet my dad's super-stressed.

Do you think I should help them solve this case? Chief Cunningham says my hunches are pretty good. Daddy doesn't like to admit it, but he agrees. The thing is, I know where the cops will go with this. They'll look at Tara as a suspect because she had a big fight with Mr. Nicholas the day before the murder. But Tara's not the kind of person to kill somebody. No way it could have been her.

Well, guess what, Journal? I already have a suspect. Mr. McNasty! He's like the only one that makes sense. I'll bet he's the only other person in the whole town who knew Mr. Nicholas. And Mr. Nicholas was just a visitor, and he didn't do anything mean to anybody like Mr. Pallett did. The way Mr. Pallett acts, it's like if you disagree with him, he hates you. I'll bet he salted our coffee, then tripped Mr. Gray on purpose, and then he went on to kill Mr. Nicholas. Probably because Mr. Nicholas changed his mind about that stupid business idea.

That's it, Journal! I'm in. I'm gonna prove Mr. McNasty is the killer and did all the other bad stuff. The problem is, how am I supposed to do any investigating and not get caught? My dad will ground me for sure if he finds out I'm doing this again.

Maybe Marquetta has an idea. I'll find out.

Bye for now,

Alex

13

RICK

THE FIRST STOP IN RICK'S search for Tara Amengual was the Crooked Mast. It was closest to the B&B, and it was the town's most upscale—and expensive—place to dine. A perky girl with reddish hair, gleaming braces, and familiar eyes greeted him when he walked through the door.

Rick held out his hand and introduced himself. "I don't believe we've ever met."

"I'm Cecelia. Jennifer Martin is my mom."

Rick lightly smacked himself on the forehead. "Of course. I've seen you down at your mom's bait shop. I thought there was something familiar about you. It's nice to meet you, Cecelia. I'm looking for one of my guests. Her name is Tara Amengual. She's a black woman. Mid thirties. Hair comes to about here." He gestured to a spot on his neck just above the shoulder.

"Sorry, but I haven't seen her," Cecelia said.

Strike one, thought Rick as he left and moved on to the Rusty Nail. His route took him along Front Street and past Ray Villari's Seaside Cove Inn. As he passed the tired-looking motel with its drab, basically brown paint colors, he again wondered how Ray had become so distrustful.

At the Rusty Nail, which was still upscale but not as expensive as the Crooked Mast, Rick got the same answers. It wasn't that much of a surprise, given Tara's situation. He hoped to have better luck at Crusty Buns.

Rick went back down Front Street and turned right at the roundabout. His path took him by the Crooked Mast again and then by Scoops & Scones, the ice cream shop owned by Mayor Francine Carter. There were a few customers inside, but there was no sign of Tara. Rick kept looking up and down the street as he walked. This was a small town, and a search like this shouldn't be very difficult, but rather than waste time searching for her, why not just go home and wait for his guest to return?

He'd almost convinced himself giving up was the right decision when Tara Amengual walked out the door of Traci Peterson's candle shop with a Bee's Knees bag in her hands. She kept her gaze on the stairs and bit her lower lip as though she were lost in thought.

"Ms. Amengual!" Rick hurried forward to meet her. "I've been looking for you."

The young woman looked up, shifted the bag from one hand to the other, and cleared her throat. "Henry's dead?"

It appeared the grapevine had been working overtime. Within the next hour or so, everyone would know what had happened. And that included Alex. "Yes, he is."

"The woman inside told me." Tara threw a glance over her shoulder toward the front door of the Bee's Knees, then hoisted the bag in her hands. "I guess I should be more upset than I am, but after he lied to me, I can't summon any sympathy for the man. This is retail therapy. It's helping a lot."

Rick stepped aside for a family of four. Mom and dad were doing their best to keep their two small boys under control and entertained, but they were still taking up a good portion of the sidewalk. When the family had passed, Rick said, "I can see how you'd be upset with him. What I don't understand, though, is why you participated in the ruse in the first place. Why not simply tell us you were an unmarried couple? We wouldn't have cared."

"I know. It was stupid. I let Henry talk me into it. The same way I let him talk me into this trip." She paused, shifted the bag again, then began to ramble. "I feel so pathetic. My first marriage didn't last long. My husband cheated on me almost from the beginning. So when I met Henry, and he started telling me how much his wife hurt him and how his marriage was on the rocks, I thought I'd found someone who really understood." She paused, then added, "I hate being lied to."

Actually, after what he'd endured with Giselle, Rick understood Tara's anger completely. "Do you think he was lying all along?"

"I think they were having problems, but it never occurred to me that Henry might exaggerate what things were like. Maybe I was just a way to bolster his ego."

"Your registration card said you own a bookstore. Was Mr. Nicholas's bakery near your store?"

"Two doors down. Everything got started when I told him about the *San Mañuel*."

A twinge of suspicion inched its way into Rick's thoughts. Why had she not mentioned being interested in the *San Mañuel* before? "I didn't know you had such an interest in sunken treasure."

Tara shook her head. "Henry, more than me. I'm a bit of a history buff and enjoy reading about it, but Henry wasn't like that. He was actually sort of a penny-pincher. Then, one day, he said he wanted to get away for a few days. I didn't want to do it at first, but then he accused me of not being adventurous enough. That hurt because my ex said the same thing. So eventually, I agreed we should have a little adventure all our own."

"And the man-and-wife ruse?"

"Henry said it was our chance to live a secret life. We'd have a secret nobody else knew. I thought it was stupid at first. But, I have to admit that the way Henry made a game of it whenever we were together, it added some spice. So by the time we arrived, I was into it, too."

"And then he started getting phone calls from his real wife."

"Like I said, pathetic, right?"

"I don't see you as pathetic, Ms. Amengual. Perhaps you were just a little too willing to accept what you thought was love."

There was a long pause, and at the end, she winced. "Before I started laying all my troubles at your feet, you said you were looking for me?"

"Yes. Chief Cunningham asked me to find out if you have the password to Mr. Nicholas's phone."

"I wish I did," the woman snorted. "Maybe I wouldn't have wound up becoming the classic other woman in Henry's little love triangle."

"I'm sorry you had to go through that."

"I'll go back to my books and eventually I'll get over it."

Rick gestured at the bag she'd been shifting back and forth between her hands. "What did you buy?"

"Chocolate and candles," she said with a laugh. "Two of my favorites. When I get home, I'm going to break out a bottle of Zinfandel, light the candles, and binge on these chocolates until Henry's nothing but a memory."

"Sounds like a good plan. I'll let you continue your shopping."

"Yes. I've heard Scoops & Scones has some chocolate ice cream, that is, if you'll pardon the expression, to die for."

After finishing the conversation with Tara, Rick walked up the street to the one building along Main Street that bore an architectural kinship with Ray's motel—the police station. With its split pea soup exterior and purely functional windows, it looked more like it belonged in a bedraggled big city than here. The only semblance of style was the striped awning over the front door, which was color coordinated with the paint colors. Rick sighed as he looked at it. The stripes of pea green and white simply didn't measure up to the brightly painted homes in Seaside Cove.

Adam was seated at his desk. Without even looking up, he raised a hand and pointed at the chair in front of him. "Hey, buddy, any luck in finding Ms. Amengual?"

"She was coming out of the Bee's Knees. She had one of Traci's big bags, and it looked kind of heavy. Apparently, she's a huge candle fan."

"Traci had to love that. Did you learn anything?"

"She didn't seem very upset over her ex-boyfriend's death. Her ex-husband, the real one, not Henry Nicholas, cheated on her right out of the gate. She's never really gotten over it. I guess this latest incident has dredged up a lot of those old memories."

Adam turned away from his screen, his brow furrowed. "Do you think her anger might have given her motive enough to kill?"

"It's too early to say, and it's entirely possible she's in shock over Henry's death. At this point, I'm not really sure."

Adam locked his computer, stood, and donned his hat. "I think we should keep an eye on Ms. Amengual, but in the meantime, are you ready to pay Ray a visit?"

"I thought you wanted to talk to Lydia first."

"I called the house and Matteo told me she was resting. He asked if we could come by in about half an hour. Much as I hate to do it, we'll go see Ray first."

"Lead the way, Chief. But I'm letting you handle most of this."

"I know. At least I can arrest him if he's too big of a pain."

When they arrived at the Inn, Ray was standing behind the front desk. He wore his customary scowl—a look that made him look perpetually angry.

"Afternoon, Ray. We have a few questions for you about Henry Nicholas," Adam said.

Ray ran his fingers through his reddish hair and his scowl deepened. "I don't want to hear that name, Adam. That man's brought me nothing but grief. My maid quit after she found the body and now I've got nobody to clean rooms. I'm going to have to shell out a bunch of money to replace the carpet. This is going to be the talk of the town for at least a month. Do you know how much I hate that?"

"I know, Ray. Unfortunately, I can't stop the gossips. And I don't know of anyone who's looking for a job right now."

Ray huffed and swatted the air as if he were trying to kill a fly. "You mean you don't know anybody who wants to work for me." It looked to Rick like the man was trying to freeze the houseplant on the counter with his cold stare.

It was tempting to shoot back a retort about working conditions and pay, but Rick let the comment pass.

"How you run your business is not my concern, Ray. What I'm interested in is the law. And I need you to tell me what you know about Henry Nicholas."

"Don't know anything about him. He paid for his room. I don't get involved in their personal lives."

"We've been down this path before, Ray. Don't make me arrest you. Or maybe I'll have the mayor get on your case. You rented the man a room, and someone committed murder in that room. Bottom line, let's cut through the crap. What do you know about him?"

Ray grumbled for a minute, then scrawled a hasty signature on a piece of paper. "Sure. Whatever. He was quiet enough. Didn't make any noise. I have no idea why he was heading back to LA this morning. That's it. We done?"

"No. We're not done. Did the man have any visitors?"

After a long sigh, Ray said, "Some woman came in here about five yesterday afternoon. Tara something-or-other. I rang the room for her. She told him she was here, then she went up to see him. That's all I know."

Adam made a quick note, then peered closely at Ray. "Are you sure it was five?"

"Of course, I'm sure. Clock's right there on the wall. She walked in here, brazen as could be, and said she wanted to see him."

Rick suppressed a groan as he thought about what this could mean for Tara. While Adam made another note, Rick said, "What about Oscar Johnson? Did you get a complaint about him last night?"

Ray rolled his eyes and shook his head. "Guy's deaf as a post. Had to call and tell him to turn down the TV."

Adam looked up at Ray and gave him a curt nod. "Thanks for your time, Ray. We'll probably have more questions later. Let's go, Rick."

By no means did Rick think this conversation was over, but Adam obviously had something in mind, so Rick followed him out the front door and down the steps to the street. He caught up a few seconds later.

"Adam, I'd never classify Tara Amengual as brazen. I've seen her be pleasant, friendly, and even angry, but she's not the kind of woman who's overly bold or forward."

"I agree. But, I realized something while we were talking to Ray. We really do need to leave him for later. He's not going to talk without some pressure. The best way I can think of to create that, short of threatening him again, is to get information from Lydia, then come back here and put him on the spot."

"I just don't understand why Ray is so reluctant to cooperate with us. Instead of wanting to help, I feel like he's trying to make the investigation as difficult as possible. Back there, I was tempted to ask him what his problem was, but I knew that was a can of worms neither of us wanted opened."

Adam pulled on the driver's door handle of his Seaside Cove 4x4 and watched Rick over the hood. "Don't worry about Ray. With the right kind of pressure, he'll talk."

14

RICK

MARQUETTA SAT NEXT TO RICK, her knees tucked under her. He had his arm draped over her shoulders and was enjoying the perfectly romantic moment when she giggled.

"What's so funny?" Rick asked.

"God bless Tommy Cat."

Rick couldn't help from laughing along with her. "How'd you know that was Adam's emergency call?"

"Nine times out of ten, the only emergency that happens in this town is when Tommy Cat runs away. And since Mrs. Cantwell is so..."

"Crotchety? Cantankerous?"

"I was going to say...assertive, she gets what she wants—a handsome, young man to bring him back. Anyway, I'm just happy to have a little free time with you in the middle of the day."

With his eyes closed, Rick took a long, slow breath. In this quiet moment, he could feel his heart beating in his chest. He ran the back of his fingers over Marquetta's cheek. "Yes," he sighed. "This is just perfect. We get to shut out the world for a few minutes. Here's to many more quiet moments alone in the future."

Arching her eyebrows, Marquetta pulled back slightly. "I don't know, Mr. Atwood. You've been talking about wanting more children. How are we going to have time alone if I'm chasing around this big old house after a half dozen little Alexes?"

The double take he did to look at Marquetta nearly wrenched Rick's neck. His chest tightened as he croaked, "Who said anything about a half dozen?"

"Oh, did you want more?" Marquetta gave him another impish smile. "Maybe you want an entire baseball team."

"You're trying to kill me, woman." He pulled Marquetta close and kissed her. "But, if you're that into sports...I suppose I could muster the energy to make the necessary contributions."

Marquetta smacked Rick's shoulder, then leaned into him. "Party pooper. Ruining all my fun." She let out a contented sigh. "I can't believe we'll be married next Wednesday."

"I know. I just wish I had more time to spend here helping you prepare for it. This murder..."

"Rick, it's okay. Adam needs your help right now."

"I'm not so sure. He's turned into a very good investigator all on his own."

"He wasn't when you got here. You're part of the reason he's doing so well."

Was he the one responsible? Really? True, Adam had been forced to go from part-time deputy/part-time meter reader to Chief of Police in a very short period of time. And it would have been so easy for him to fail—just as Rick's grandfather, the infamously hard Captain Jack, had almost failed. The big difference was that Adam had succeeded where Captain Jack's vanity had nearly sunk the ship.

Rick studied his office. Brazilian mahogany throughout. Coffered ceiling. Bookshelves lined the wall to his right. Recessed lighting. A massive desk. It would cost a fortune these days to reconstruct this room. Actually, it had cost a fortune when Captain Jack remodeled the entire B&B, and nearly drove it into bankruptcy.

"If it hadn't been for you, I never would have made it when I inherited this place. You're the one who kept it going when it should have failed. If it wasn't for you, we never could have brought it back from the brink."

Marquetta studied his face, then shook her head. "I think we helped each other. Between you and Alex, you both helped me finally get past my dad's death."

And there it was, the only real issue he'd worried about with the wedding. Even though Adam had assured him Marquetta would be fine, Rick felt a need to ask. "Are you sure you're okay with having Joe Gray walk you down the aisle?"

"I'm more than fine with it. Joe and Captain Jack were my dad's best friends. If it hadn't been for Captain Jack helping me and my mother, I don't know how we would have survived. And Joe was the one who was there the most for me when Captain Jack died."

Rick closed his eyes again and let relief wash over him. He released a breath—the one he felt he'd been holding for weeks, ever since Marquetta had told him about Joe.

"What?" Marquetta asked.

"I was worried—no, I think I was terrified—about having Joe give you away. I kept thinking it was going to bring back the memories that haunted you for so long."

"Only in a good way. Somehow, it feels like all the tragedy is finally behind me. I understand now that if you don't let bad things eat you up, they can turn into something good." Marquetta nudged Rick with her elbow. "Kind of like your deal with the mayor to consult with the police. Your willingness to step in and help Adam has earned you a tremendous amount of goodwill."

"I know. It's almost as if the entire town is a marketing machine for us."

"That's right. And it's part of the reason we've become so successful."

Rick let out a heavy sigh. "That's why I feel so guilty right now. In the back of my mind, I'm still playing what-if scenarios about Henry Nicholas even being at the Inn."

"It's not your fault. He needed a place to stay after he lied to Tara, and you helped him. That's all there is to it."

"Logically, I know what happened," Rick said. "But emotionally, this one's taking a toll. At least you've been able to keep Alex out of it. That makes me feel better."

"I don't know how much longer it will be before she gets the news. I wouldn't be surprised if that's why she was so eager to go to her room."

"I'll check on her in a few minutes."

"If you don't mind, let me do it. There are a couple of things I want to talk to her about."

"Oh, preparing something special for the rehearsal dinner?"

"No. Nothing like that. I told you about how Mom wants to hire a string quartet for the wedding. Well, she came back later and started asking me if I'd go to San Ladron with her to check them out. I explained that I can't get away right now, not with all the other last-minute preparations and you having to be gone. But I think it would be a great job for Alex. "

Rick leaned over and kissed Marquetta. "Brilliant. Alex will hate the music, your mother will get discouraged, and we'll keep the junior detective off the case."

"I thought it was a good solution."

"It's much better than good. It's great. You said you had a couple of things to talk with Alex about. What else?"

"Oh no, the others are a secret."

Rick kissed Marquetta again. When she sighed, he whispered, "I guess I have to bring out my secret weapon."

Marquetta pushed him away and shook her head. "Oh no, Mr. Atwood. I am impervious to your charms. You have no power over me."

"Are you sure?" He reached out to pull her close, but Marquetta stood abruptly.

"I have too many things to do to let you distract me. Besides, there is something else I wanted to tell you."

"I know," Rick snickered. "You're madly in love with me and can't wait for our wedding night."

Marquetta waved dismissively and quirked her cheek. "Meh. I suppose." When Rick stuck out his lower lip in an exaggerated pout, she covered her mouth and giggled. "Oh, stop it, you big baby. What I really wanted was to talk to you about Tara. She was in her room when I went in to change the linens today and we started talking. Well, she did most of it."

"Yes, I know how you are. You listen, other people bare their souls." He'd always been amazed at Marquetta's ability to listen more than she talked. It was a balancing trick any private detective would be proud of. "What did Tara tell you?"

"I asked her if she'd gone to straighten things out with Mr. Nicholas. She said she had. When I asked what time she was there, she told me it was about five o'clock."

Rick's breath caught. "So it's true. We have two witnesses who put her there at the time. I was hoping they were mistaken, but now I wish I'd asked her when I saw her on the street." He told her about Adam's reasoning, then said, "Anything else?"

"I hate to tell you this, but Tara immediately changed her story when I made a comment about the time. She told me she hadn't actually gone to see Henry. She said she was partway to the Inn when she decided he wasn't worth the effort and went to the lighthouse for a little solitude instead."

"That's a big problem for her. It's going to look like she's lying if she denies being in the Inn's courtyard."

"In the courtyard's not the same as in the room."

"I know, and so far we don't have anyone who actually saw her go in. On the other hand, I'll bet there was nobody at the lighthouse. At least, nobody who would be able to identify her. What it comes down to is she has no alibi."

"I almost felt like she was using me as a way to establish one."

"When we first met Tara, my impression was that she's a very honest person. But it's beginning to feel like I'm playing whack-a-mole with her and her versions of the truth."

"You said you have two witnesses who saw her?"

"Yes. Ray talked to her on her way in, then she was seen by a guest on her way down the stairs. We've got her before and after, just not actually going in or coming out of the room."

"Mr. Nicholas was in a second floor room?"

"Exactly. I don't know what game Tara's playing, but right now it's looking like my initial impressions of her might have been wrong. I don't want to believe it, but maybe this was a premeditated murder."

"Or a case of bad timing," Marquetta countered.

Rick sighed and rested his elbows on his knees. "Could be. It's also possible we're chasing the wrong leads altogether."

"You and Adam will figure it out."

"One thing's for sure. I'll be able to focus a lot better if I know Alex is out of town with your mother. She's the last one I would expect to tolerate any sleuthing activities."

Marquetta's face puckered. "You're not happy with me for helping her in the past. Are you?"

"Actually, I'd rather have you keeping one of Alex's investigations under control than letting her operate on her own. At least I know you'll keep her from getting into too much trouble. Besides, we've both seen what happens when I ground her. She gets more creative. I think that's what scares me the most."

Rick's phone pinged, and he checked for a message.

"Adam's here. He's waiting out front. We're on our way to interview Lydia. Since she found the body, we want to see what she remembers. After that, Adam wants to talk to Ray again. Hey, before I go. Did you know Ray Villari is married?"

"Of course. Can you keep a secret?"

"Sure."

"You can't tell anyone this. Not Adam, and certainly not Alex. Ray and his wife are separated, but she's been talking about wanting to reconcile. He thinks she just wants half the Inn, so he's doing what he can to keep her away."

Rick stared at Marquetta for a long moment.

"You'll catch a fly if you don't close your mouth, Mr. Atwood."

"How do you do that?"

"Do what?"

"Get information nobody else knows. Adam knows Ray was separated, but he doesn't know about a possible reconciliation."

Marquetta nodded to herself, then started toward the door. Before she opened it, she said, "Oh no, a girl has to keep some secrets. And besides, you have a ride waiting for you."

She blew him a kiss over her shoulder and left.

15

ALEX

Hey Journal,

I'm supposed to be trying to find information about the band Grandma Madeline wants to hire for the wedding, but I'm too stressed to think about it. The wedding's becoming a super big deal around the B&B. I was talking to Miss Jones, and she told me she's been a bridesmaid four times—twice for the same friend and once when she was a spy! She wasn't like actually in the field or anything, but she was responsible for finding a secret message that was part of a photo. That's pretty awesome. I've never known a spy before.

When I told Miss Jones I'm a junior bridesmaid, Mrs. Brower overheard us. She thinks it's awesome I'm gonna be involved. She sure is excited about the wedding, too. She says Marquetta's going to make a beautiful bride.

I think the only guest who's not happy about the wedding might be that grumpy Mr. Pallett. He's totally a guest I hope never comes back. But maybe that's why my dad and Marquetta are in his office right now.

Do you suppose they're talking about the wedding? Or me? Do you think I'm in trouble, Journal? They don't talk like this in the middle of the day very often, but when it happens, it usually means I'm gonna get grounded. But I haven't done anything yet. Unless Mr. McNasty is trying to get me in trouble. I wish I had a way to put a spy cam in my dad's office, but that wouldn't be cool, either. He'd be super mad if he ever found it. I'm just gonna have to wait to see if I get grounded for something I don't even know I did.

Uh oh. Maybe I'm in trouble because I was talking so much to the guests about the wedding. I totally don't understand that 'cause Daddy and Marquetta have been open about it with them. Do you suppose they think I said too much? Daddy always says we're supposed to maintain some distance, but I think that's boring. The guests are just people, and we're kinda like their home away from home. Right?

Somebody just knocked on my door. I think it might be Marquetta.

Gotta go,

Alex

I unlock the door and peek out the crack. Marquetta is standing there, smiling at me. I guess I'm not getting grounded. So far.

"Got a minute, Sweetie?"

I like have a million of them right now. "Sure." I step back and open the door to let her in. "What's up?"

"Let's sit over on the bed." Marquetta puts her hand on my back and we go to sit. I cross my legs when I plop down, and she tucks hers under her when she sits on the bedspread. She looks around and I can see how happy this room makes her, too. "I love the colors in here, Sweetie."

This is my favorite room ever. Teal walls. Purple accents. Marquetta painted it before me and my dad ever arrived in Seaside Cove. The white furniture was hers when she was my age and it feels like it ties us together. "I love it, too. Thanks for calling my dad when you found out we were moving here."

"I wanted to make sure I got your favorite colors. By the way, your dad and I were just going over some things about the wedding. And yes, that includes Mom wanting to hire a string quartet."

Oh yay! They weren't talking about me. It was about Grandma Madeline! Uh oh. I haven't done the research Marquetta asked me to do. "I'm sorry, Marquetta. I haven't checked out that band yet."

"It's okay. There's been a new development. Mom came back to me later and said she wanted some help evaluating this group. She made a strong case, and I told her I'd ask you about it." Marquetta scrunches up her nose for a second, then reaches out and takes my hand.

Talk about making Marquetta's life harder. Now I'm really bummed 'cause I didn't do what she asked me to do. "I'll get right on it."

"I don't think checking them out online is going to be very helpful. I was thinking of an in-person visit."

"But there's less than eight days left before the wedding. How are you gonna do that?"

"That's what I wanted to run by your dad. You remember when I asked you to be a junior bridesmaid, and you wanted to know what you'd be responsible for?"

"For sure. You said something would come up." And it has. Operation Honeymoon.

"Well, I'm swamped and can't get away. So would you do me a favor and go with my mom to check out this quartet? They're probably not even available, but she's being very insistent."

I can feel my mouth drop open a little. "You want me to make the decision for you? What if I don't like them?"

"It's no problem. I trust your judgement. You and Traci both know what I like."

"Is she going, too?" That might be fun. Me and Traci really get along well.

"No. Traci can't leave right now. Between the Bee's Knees and the wedding preparations, she's swamped, too." Marquetta lifts my chin with her finger. She winks at me. "And besides, I don't know if I trust Traci's taste in music. She's becoming a little too ethereal."

"What's that?"

Marquetta laughs. She rests one hand on the bedspread and leans to the side. "I wish I could describe it. Let's say it doesn't sound like it's from this world...lots of echoing sounds, synthesizers...that sort of thing."

"Oh. I get it. The same stuff she plays in the store."

"Exactly. So, my one and only junior bridesmaid, will you do this for me?"

"For sure."

"Great!" Marquetta leans over and kisses my forehead. "Thank you, thank you."

"No problem." I totally want to help Marquetta, but I feel kinda like this is one of those jobs she's having me do just because she wants to keep me busy.

Marquetta gets up and starts toward the door. But then she stops and sits down again. She looks at me and lifts my chin again. "What's wrong, Sweetie? I thought you'd be happy to get out of the house with my mom."

I know I should be. My shoulders slump a little and I sigh. "I am. Kinda."

"But..."

I scoot over so we're sitting next to each other. She puts her arm around me and pulls me closer. I lean my head against her shoulder and it reminds me of what I missed when I was little. "Nothing," I mutter. I think I should just be happy I'm gonna have Marquetta as my mom.

"It's not nothing, Sweetie. I know you. This is about Mr. Nicholas. Isn't it?"

It's an awesome feeling knowing Marquetta gets me so well. And it's scary. I don't think I could ever keep a secret from her for long. "I wanna help."

"I know you do." She kinda hugs my shoulder a couple times. "And I'm sure you're aware that I've been keeping you busy. Right?"

I nod, but just watch the floor.

"Alex, you remember what your dad told you about being patient and kind with people like Mr. Pallett?"

"Yeah. Even when they're not nice."

"Your dad and I are both worried about him. We're thinking he's the one who salted our coffee."

"Mr. Gray says his fall wasn't an accident. He thinks Mr. Pallett tripped him."

"All the more reason to keep someone like him at a distance. And if you start to investigate, it could bring you much closer to him. In fact, he might see you as a big problem. He's not the kind of man who is patient or kind. Do you understand?"

"You think he's dangerous."

"We don't know for sure. But until we do, the best way for us to make sure you're safe is to keep you away from him. And that means..."

"No investigating," I grumble. "Got it."

Marquetta watches my face for the longest time. Her eyes are sad. I wonder if it's 'cause of me. Probably. I feel awful. This is happening right before the wedding. "I don't wanna make you sad, Marquetta."

"I'm not sad, Sweetie. I'm concerned about your welfare. I tell you what. You'll be going with my mom this afternoon. Tomorrow morning, we'll talk again. I think your dad will agree to let you do some investigating if I'm working with you."

"But you don't have time to babysit me."

"Sweetie, I always have time for you. And I doubt if this could be called babysitting by any stretch of the imagination. This is more like finding a way to keep a lion cub from getting herself in over her head."

16

RICK

THE TWENTY MINUTES WITH MARQUETTA had gone by in what felt like a single heartbeat. The problem was Rick knew if he flaked out on Adam, he'd hear about it. Adam would never complain, but the mayor? Oh yeah. And Alex? Definitely.

He felt sure Marquetta would be back in his office this afternoon, so he jotted a note telling her that Devon was supposed to finish painting today and left it on his desk. He also asked that she contact Devon if he didn't show up. He drew a big heart at the bottom of the note, then went to his closet and grabbed a jacket. On his way downstairs, he considered what to do with Alex. The bottom line was, once again, he and Marquetta needed to channel Alex's energy, not try to suppress it. When he climbed into Adam's 4x4, he and Adam exchanged greetings.

"How's Mrs. Cantwell's cat?" Rick asked.

"I'm pleased to announce that Tommy Cat is safe and sound."

Rick chuckled as he buckled his seatbelt. "Another case of the Seaside Cove Police coming to the rescue."

"To protect and serve, that's our motto." Adam chuckled as he pulled away from the curb.

"Marquetta thinks you need to hire a handsome, strapping young man as your next deputy."

Adam rolled his eyes and deadpanned, "I'll add it to the job posting. If the mayor ever lets me hire another deputy."

"Be sure to ask about a cat allergy," Rick smirked.

Adam cast an evil grin at him. "Or maybe I should just have my consultant deal with Mrs. Cantwell."

Rick cleared his throat, suddenly eager to end this conversation. "So, how are we doing with Lydia? Is she ready to talk to us?"

"Let's find out."

The drive to Lydia Smith's home took only a few minutes. She, her husband, and their three children lived in a well-kept Craftsman house out near the end of Whale Avenue. As they drove, Rick realized just how tiny his world had become. His time was consumed by the B&B, walks to and from the Seaside Cove Market, and an occasional shopping trip to one of the downtown stores.

He noticed that the further they got from the center of town, the smaller the homes became. The bright colors of the downtown faded. A few of the larger houses were well-maintained, but many were in need of paint, repairs, or landscaping.

"I've never been out to this part of town, Adam. It's a very different feeling."

"These were the homes for the workers back when this was a fishing village. Some of the owners have finished off the attics, but these were originally just a standard box layout with a living room, kitchen, and two bedrooms."

"I'm sure they've still got more square footage than a lot of apartments in New York."

Adam laughed as he checked his mirrors. "The places in this neighborhood might not be in the best shape, but I'd be surprised if anyone around here wanted to leave for a small apartment in the big city. Lydia's place is at the end of the block."

Rick watched out the side window, inspecting the homes carefully. Even though some of them were borderline dilapidated, he thought Adam was probably right. And now that he'd become a property owner here in Seaside Cove, he had no urge whatsoever to move back.

Lydia's home stuck out for several reasons. First, it was in better repair than most of the surrounding homes. Hers had a fresh coat of white paint from top to bottom. The landscaping, though very basic with just a few agapanthuses, rhododendrons, and an old oak tree in the front yard, was also well-maintained. But the defining feature that made it so different from others on the block was the porch. It had been extended to wrap around the entire house.

"It's not much," Adam said.

"Maybe not, but you can see the pride of ownership. And the covered, wraparound porch—wow. Someone did a nice job."

"Matteo. He was a general contractor at one point. He did a lot of work in San Ladron. But once the kids started coming, he had to be around more. He still does some remodeling, but mostly it's just handyman-type stuff. Of course, with Lydia quitting her job, I'm not sure how much longer they'll be able to stay. Her parents owned this home when her father was a fisherman. Now that she's unemployed, things are going to get tough for them."

Rick's remorse over Henry Nicholas's death came rushing back. He practically felt like he'd been body slammed by a large wave. If only he hadn't booked the room at the Inn. "I feel so responsible, Adam."

"Why? Because you helped the guy out by getting him a place to stay?"

"By kicking him out of the B&B. He was safe there."

"You didn't have a lot of choice. And you can't be sure that he was safe. If someone was after him, this could have happened at your place."

Rick grimaced. "You might be right, but we won't know for sure until we find the killer. Let's get on with this, okay?"

Adam agreed. They exited the police 4x4 and walked to the screen door. The screen material itself was new, and the wooden frame, though old, had a fresh coat of paint. Even the porch columns had been sanded and painted and were in excellent condition.

"If I didn't have a handyman already, I'd consider hiring this guy," Rick said.

"Matteo's pretty good, but Devon's been taking care of your place for decades. He knows that old house better than anyone."

"Don't worry. I have no intention of making a switch. But when Devon does retire, I'll definitely keep this guy in mind."

"Good plan." Adam knocked lightly on the wooden frame of the screen door.

A middle-aged Hispanic woman wearing a UCLA sweatshirt and jeans greeted them. Her eyes were rimmed in red and her pain, obvious. "Thanks for calling ahead, Chief."

"Lydia, how are you holding up?"

The woman dabbed at her cheeks with a tissue and shook her head. "I'm not the squeamish type, but the blood on the carpet was too much for me. I've been fighting a wicked headache ever since I walked into that room. When I tried to tell Ray about it, he went off on me like I was the one who killed the man."

"Lydia and Matteo both served in Iraq during the War on Terror," Adam said. "That's where you met, right?"

"Yes. We were talking one day and found out he lived in San Ladron. Here we were, halfway around the world, and we were almost neighbors at home. We saw some difficult conditions. We stayed in touch and got together after we both got out." Lydia paused and looked at Rick. "Mr. Atwood, are you helping the chief on the case?"

"I am. And, please, call me Rick. It must have been quite the shock when you found the body."

Lydia rested a plump shoulder against the doorframe and crossed one leg over the other. "I knocked on the door to Room 210, got no answer, so I announced myself and unlocked the door. Ray had told me the guest had checked out and left, but I never trust him." Her face screwed up into a disgusted grimace. "He expects people to get out at the crack of dawn. He gets irritated because a lot of them wait until the last minute."

"I take it you've had your share of surprises working at the Inn?" Rick said.

"Oh yeah. You just got to be flexible, you know? But Ray, the word's not even in his vocabulary."

"How right you are," Adam said. "Lydia, what happened after you unlocked the door to the room?"

"I cracked the door open and called out again. There was no response, so I went in. I put the doorstop in place and moved my cart. I was surprised that the bed looked like it had been made. I was still doing a mental inventory of what needed to be done when I almost tripped over the body."

"Did you scream?" Rick asked.

Lydia's olive cheeks flushed. She raised her hand with her thumb and index finger held an inch apart. "A little, yes. It was such a shock."

"Your reaction is perfectly understandable," Rick said. "If I stumbled over a dead body in one of my rooms, I'd probably scream, too."

Lydia cocked her head to the side and gazed skeptically at Rick. "They say you covered the crime beat in New York."

"For a number of years. In looking back, I realize it took a toll on me." Rick felt a pang of sympathy for Lydia because her peaceful life in Seaside Cove had been shattered by a part of life she thought she'd left behind. Hoping to not dwell on his own past, Rick asked, "How long have you worked for Ray?"

"Going on ten years."

"And I'll bet you've never come across anything like this before."

"Nothing this bad, no."

Rick shot a sideways glance at Adam, who was jotting down notes on his pad. When he finished, he gave Rick a thumbs up, then returned his attention to the notepad and jotted down something else. Apparently, Adam was happy to let Rick take the lead. "We're trying to reconstruct what happened leading up to the murder," Rick said.

"We're looking for witnesses who were around at the time of death," Adam added.

The crows feet around Lydia's dark eyes creased. She massaged her temples with her fingertips, then said, "You two work pretty good together. Sorry, but my headache's coming back. Anyway, I did see someone. It was at the end of my shift on Monday. A woman went into the room."

"So you actually saw her enter?" Rick asked.

"Yes."

"Can you describe her?"

"How about a name, instead? When your victim greeted her at the door, he called her Tara. She went off on him almost immediately. I thought they were going to get into it right there on the walkway, but then he grabbed her arm and pulled her into the room."

17

RICK

THE LITTLE HAIRS ON THE back of Rick's neck stiffened. Could he have been so wrong about Tara? Yes? No? He cursed his indecision. "You said he pulled her into the room. Did she resist?"

"Hard to say. If she did, it wasn't very much. She saw me and could have yelled for help, but she didn't."

"Do you have any idea how long she was inside?"

Lydia shook her head. "No. I was leaving for the day. And you know how Ray is, don't see and don't tell. I'm just supposed to do my job and keep my mouth shut."

Adam put down his pad and frowned at Lydia. He craned his neck forward slightly. "Lydia, what exactly are you saying?"

Crossing her arms over her chest, she gazed back at Adam. She chewed on her lower lip, then sniffled. "I feel terrible about not doing something at the time. What the heck? Ray won't want to give me my job back. He was in the office. He knew the woman's name. I said I thought we should check to see if she needed help, and he told me she was his wife. Then he ordered me to go home."

"So you think the murder could have been prevented if you or Ray had done something right then and there?" Rick asked.

"I'm sure of it. It did not look like things were going to go well between those two. I guess I was right."

Rick wanted to return to the B&B, to the sanctity of his office, and do nothing more than sort through the events of the past two days. But he had to push his own desires off to the side. There were plenty more questions to be asked and answered. Chief among those was if Lydia had seen anyone else besides Tara.

"No, I didn't see anybody else go into that room. The Inn isn't like the B&B, Rick. Your place is smaller and more intimate. The Inn is just, well, a motel. Ray had me put out those cheap pastries and coffee each morning, but most people only try those once. They learn their lesson and start going to Crusty Buns." Lydia stopped and snickered. "Unless, of course, they're exceptionally cheap."

"Did you see Mr. Nicholas earlier in the day?" Rick asked.

"When I was restocking my cleaning cart. It was kind of hard to miss him. He was in the lobby yucking it up with a couple of the other guests. Two men. I don't know their names since I never saw them enter or leave their rooms. Besides, they were being obnoxious, and I was trying to ignore them."

"Can you describe these two men, Lydia?" Adam asked.

"One was a hipster—you know, the plaid shirt, scruffy beard. He had dark, short hair. The other guy was bald and wore black-framed glasses. I remember because they kept slipping down, and he had to push them back up."

Rick snuck a look at Adam. "Ray should know who these guys are. Right?"

"If he saw them together, he should. Was Ray there at the time, Lydia?"

"He was in and out of his office because there were a couple of checkouts. I can't imagine he didn't notice."

Adam jotted a note, then said, "We'll talk to him. Lydia, I might have to put pressure on Ray to get him to open up. I'm hoping your name won't come up, but you realize that's a possibility. Are you okay with that?"

"Don't worry, Chief. Not only would Ray not want to hire me back, but I don't intend to work for him ever again. I've had enough of Ray Villari and his royal cheapness."

"Then I think we're good. Unless you have more questions, Rick."

There was one question in the back of Rick's mind, but it had nothing to do with the case. Mentally, he ran down the checklist he'd been using. He could think of no reason to not do this.

"Rick? Any questions?"

"Sorry. I was just trying to figure out how to phrase this."

"Do it the easy way. Just ask." Lydia arched her brows and watched Rick closely.

"How would you like to work for me for the next few weeks?"

Lydia's jaw dropped. "You're offering me a job? At the B&B?"

"It would only be temporary. As you know, Marquetta and I are getting married, and I feel like it would take a lot of pressure off her if we had someone to help out."

"Yes!" Lydia blurted, then threw her arms around Rick's neck. "Thank you, thank you, thank you!"

Adam chuckled. "Looks like you have a new employee, buddy. Congratulations."

On the way back into town, Rick asked Adam to drop him off at the B&B. "I need to break the news to Marquetta that she's getting some help."

"Glad to do it. This is one piece of news I'll bet Markie's happy to hear. It will also give me a few minutes to go by the Bee's Knees and let Traci know I'm running late."

Adam parked behind a truck Rick knew well. "Looks like Devon's working. I gave him a list of things to do before the wedding and he's been chipping away at it."

"Devon might be getting a little slow, but he'll get it done. Pick you up in twenty minutes?"

Rick was about to close the passenger's door when he saw Devon walking toward him carrying a can of paint. "Make it thirty. It takes Devon ten minutes to say hello."

Adam gave Rick a thumbs-up and pulled away.

He and Devon exchanged greetings while the handyman placed a paint can in the truck bed. "Working on the last of your list, Rick. I was doing the touchup on the gazebo and the back of the house today. Gotta tell you, though, my back's starting to act up. I'm taking the rest of the day off and will finish up tomorrow."

"Take care of yourself, Devon. You're the only handyman I've got."

Devon stroked his chin and gazed at Rick. "About that. You know, you're my last client. I've been thinking for a few years now about retiring. I almost did, but then Captain Jack upped and died." He gazed up at the three-story house. "I couldn't let the old girl fall into disrepair, though. But now, with you here and the business doing so well, I think you might want to be looking for someone else."

Why was it life always made a mockery of plans? Rick was just sure Devon would have been around for a few more years. Even though the man knew this house better than anyone, it didn't mean someone else couldn't take over. "It's odd you should mention retiring, Devon. Adam and I interviewed Lydia Smith, and Adam was telling me her husband is a handyman, too."

"Don't sell Matteo short. He's a lot more than just a handyman. But that's actually the reason I brought it up. I heard they were having some hard times lately and, to be honest, I don't need the money. But they do. What I'm saying is, if you want to turn the old girl over to someone else, Matteo's your man. I'd be around and would gladly share what I know about the house. No need to make any decisions today. I'm going home and resting up. See you tomorrow."

Rick said goodbye, then climbed the front steps. Devon wanted to retire? Seriously? Talk about things working out. And Marquetta, what did he tell her about Lydia? He didn't think him hiring help without talking to her would be a problem, but they'd never even discussed the option.

He checked the time. Almost four. Marquetta was probably back in the kitchen. Her domain. Her little spot of heaven. Most likely planning something spectacular for dinner. It was worth checking. With Alex out of the house for the next few hours, this was the perfect time to break the news about Lydia. He was approaching the dining room when he heard Tara Amengual's voice.

"The man was so deceitful, I can't believe I fell for it."

"You were just lonely, and he was there at the right time."

The other voice. It was Marquetta. Rick stood stock still, not wanting to make a sound.

"I never would have known if it wasn't for Alex. I'm so happy she said something when she did."

"We don't usually like to interfere like that."

"It's fine. Totally fine. In fact, I was so mad I called his wife."

"Really?" Marquetta gasped. "Did you tell her who you were?"

Marquetta was quizzing a guest? About her personal life? Rick pushed his jaw up with his fingers. He was beyond shocked. And, in a way, relieved.

"I certainly did," Tara said. "She was devastated. Apparently, she thought everything was fine. Henry always told me they were separated. He led me to believe his wife was torn between him and her ex. According to her, there is no ex. Now I feel terrible about getting involved with Henry and for being the one to tell his wife."

"I tell you what, Tara. If you need anything, you let me know. Okay?"

"I will. Thanks, Marquetta."

Rick peeked around the corner, saw the two women embrace, and quietly retreated a few steps. He retraced his path, this time, calling out, "Marquetta? Are you back here?"

"In the dining room!"

Tara came out, gave Rick a small wave, then pointed behind her. "She's restocking the tea supply. I felt like I had to talk to someone, and she was a great listener."

Rick thanked Tara, then looked at Marquetta. She waved for him to meet her in the kitchen. He hurried and caught up to her just as she pushed the supply cart through the butler door. On the other side, she spun around and whispered, "Oh, Rick, did I get an earful."

18

RICK

RICK KNEW HE SHOULDN'T FEEL guilty over hiring Lydia, but now that he was looking Marquetta in the eye, he was. Or was it the fact that he'd been listening in on her conversation with Tara? "I hired someone to help around the B&B," he blurted.

Marquetta gaped at him for a few seconds, then she stepped back, held out her hand with her palm up, and wiggled her fingers. "Help beats out gossip. What? Who? Why?"

He explained to her about Lydia, and at the end, brought up the wedding. "I just figured that the universe was lining up and telling me to do something nice for you. I hope you don't mind."

"Mind?" Marquetta laughed. "Why would I mind getting extra time each day to plan my wedding? The only one I ever intend to have, by the way." Her gaze bounced over at the butler door. "Unlike some people."

"Let's come back to other people's drama in a minute. So you're okay with me hiring Lydia?"

"Absolutely. Captain Jack wanted to hire her at one point, but he could never do it because he didn't have the money. We're actually busy enough now. We should be able to afford someone."

"That was exactly my thought. Would you mind making the arrangements to get her started?"

"I'll call her this afternoon. By the way, Devon's starting to talk again about wanting to retire."

"I just saw him. He told me he was considering this back before Captain Jack died."

"Devon was pretty serious about it then. I guess he's decided it's finally time."

"What about Lydia's husband?" Rick asked.

"I'll bet he'd jump at the chance. I can ask Lydia when I call her."

Leaning against the kitchen island, Rick gazed at Marquetta. "Sometimes, I guess things just work out. You said you got an earful? The truth is, I heard the last part of it."

"My, my, Mr. Atwood. Spying on your future wife?"

A flush of warmth flooded Rick's face. Why was he so embarrassed? He stammered, "No. It just...happened. I didn't want to interrupt."

"Don't worry, I'll still marry you. And yes, Tara was telling me her woes. It sounds like Henry really pulled the wool over her eyes. She thought he was Mr. Wonderful, but he turned out to be more wanderer than anything." She went on to recap more of what Rick had overheard. When she finished, she said, "I feel like there are two Taras. One is the shy lady who runs a bookstore, and the other is...well..."

Rick recalled Ray Villari's description of Tara. Maybe the man hadn't been so far off after all. "Brazen?"

"I don't think so. She strikes me as more volatile. On the one hand, she falls for a guy because they meet in his bakery and he's nice to her, then she gets angry at him."

"Because she let herself get talked into running away for a few days to play house."

Marquetta cocked one hip and crossed her arms over her chest. "Something like that. Do you know how long they've known each other?"

"I have a feeling you're about to tell me."

"Two months. She told me she never ate baked goods until Henry came into her store. They got to talking and discovered they had a mutual interest in history."

"Wait. She told me she's the one with the interest in history. She said Henry was more into sunken treasure. He also wanted to get away."

Marquetta gazed off to the side. She seemed lost in thought and rubbed her neck with her fingers. "Fascinating. Now she's saying that when she told him about the *San Mañuel*, he got very interested. He invited her to visit his shop. It took her a few days to work up the courage, but she went in and things just developed from there."

"I guess people make crazy decisions when they're in love... or at least when they think they're in love."

"She's really feeling hurt, Rick."

"Or is she doing a good job of making it appear that she is?" Rick raised his eyebrows and gazed at Marquetta.

"It could be. But think about it. She's divorced, runs a small bookstore, and is probably lonely. Here's this guy who says he likes some of the same things she does, is going through the same stuff she is, and so she lets him in."

The way Marquetta described the situation, Tara was a victim of her own emotions. Which might mean she wanted to lash out when she learned the truth about the man who deceived her.

"Congratulations, Counselor. I think you just made the case for Tara having a huge motive to commit murder."

"I guess I did. Didn't I?" Marquetta leaned back against the counter. "It's hard to know what to believe. I suppose Adam's waiting for you?"

"He is. I have to go...again. I'd better get out of here before Alex sees me."

Rick made it out the front door without encountering anyone. He hurried to Adam's 4x4 and hopped in. No sooner had he belted himself into the passenger's seat than Adam said, "Guess what? Henry Nicholas? He was not only cheating on his wife, but he also had a DUI. According to the report, there were injuries in both vehicles, but no deaths."

It took a few seconds for the news to sink in. After all, Rick had started out knowing the man as a gentle baker, and now he was learning there was a whole different side to him. "I'll bet that's something else Tara didn't know about him. When did this happen?"

"About ten years ago. We may not even want to tell her about it."

Rick nodded and thought about the dilemma while Adam drove. When they parked in front of the Inn's lobby entrance a few minutes later, Adam had a wicked grin on his face. He said, "Parking out here on the street is going to irritate the crap out of Ray, but it gives me some leverage."

Inside, the lobby was empty and the front desk unmanned. Adam strode to the bell on the counter and gave it a good rap. The ding pierced the air with its sharp edge.

"Hold on! Hold on!" Ray stormed out of his office. As usual, he had a bad case of bedhead. With dark, full eyebrows and a three-day shadow, he looked like he hadn't slept recently. When he saw who was waiting for him, he barked, "What do you want, Adam?"

"To finish our conversation. Remember? I said we'd have more questions. Well, it looks like you've been holding out on me." Adam pulled his keys from his pocket and held them out for Rick. "Would you do me a favor and go turn the lights on? I want the whole display. Let's light up the entire block."

Rick's face lit up. "Seriously? I've always wanted to do that." He reached for the keys, but Adam snatched them back.

"Try not to hit the siren by mistake. We wouldn't want to have all the guests panic."

Ray rushed from behind the counter and peered out to the street. He held up both hands in surrender. "Okay, Adam. You win. There's no need to scare off my customers."

"In that case, let's just get this done." Adam pocketed the keys and sighed. "Sorry, buddy. Maybe I'll let you play with the lights another day."

"No worries." But in a way, Rick really was disappointed. It wasn't very often a civilian had the chance to hop behind the wheel of a police vehicle, and better yet, turn on the lights and siren—by accident, of course.

Adam pulled out his notepad and flipped it open. "Tell us again about Tara Amengual."

"I told you. She was here and was headed up to 210 when I saw her."

"Did you see her leave?" Rick asked.

Ray's jaw muscles were working overtime, and Rick thought for a second that Ray might actually try to lie or not answer. "Yes," he huffed. "It was ten or fifteen minutes later. She looked pretty upset."

Given the situation, Rick felt that description covered the gamut from having had another argument to full-blown remorse after committing murder. "Can you be more specific?"

"I don't know. Her eyes were red, and she was crying."

"How close were you to her?"

Ray jabbed his finger at the doorway to the inner courtyard. "She came through that door when I was restocking some of the travel brochures." He pointed at the wall on the far side of the room. "I heard her walk in and turned around. There she was, crying her eyes out. She didn't notice me, so I went back to what I was doing."

"Did you see what time this was?" Adam asked.

"I didn't think I was going to be called as a witness in a murder. Otherwise, I could have made a few notes. Taken a video."

"Do you have security cameras?" Rick asked.

"Only out in the back parking lot. Why should I have them here? You don't have any in your B&B, right?"

Ouch. That hit close to home, especially given the coffee-salting incident. It was one of those times when Rick wished they did have security footage. It would have made it easy to find the culprit. "Fair point, Ray."

"Anything else you recall about her?" Adam asked.

"She was in an all-fired big hurry when she left. Rushed right out without even a sideways glance."

"Did Mr. Nicholas interact with anyone else while he was here?"

"How should I know? Wait. Yeah. That morning, after he checked in, there were three of them here in the lobby. One of them was the guy who's staying in...104. Yeah, that's it. Max Rado. They were acting all buddy-buddy. Later in the day, I saw them coming back from somewhere."

Adam lowered his notepad and gazed at Ray. "Do you know where they'd been?"

"Crusty Buns. They had cups from there."

Well, at least that was an easy statement to verify. Mary O'Donnell was a much more willing source of information than Ray, even though Ray was on his best behavior. How long that would last was anyone's guess. Most likely, he was cooperating to avoid testing Adam's patience. And while Ray wasn't being a jerk, Rick wanted to take advantage of the situation. He asked, "Has Max Rado checked out?"

Ray looked at his computer screen and shook his head. "He's been here since Friday. Supposed to check out this coming Friday. Don't bother going to his room. He's probably out to dinner."

"He's alone?"

"Yeah. Although he's also been kind of friendly with the guy who's staying in 111." Ray tapped his finger against one of his teeth, then nodded to himself. "That's right, he was the third one. Kiernan Walsh. Those two have been down here getting coffee a couple of times. They talk a little."

Kiernan Walsh? He was the other diver from the accident. Walsh knew this Max Rado? And the three of them had been together? Apparently, Henry Nicholas had known more people in town than they'd thought. Their suspect pool was growing rapidly.

19

ALEX

WHEN I WALK INTO THE kitchen, Marquetta's got ground turkey, onion, and garlic out on the countertop. "Oh good, Sweetie. You can get out the rest of the ingredients, okay?"

"What are we having?"

"Tamale Pie."

"Awesome." It only takes me a couple minutes to get out the rest of what we'll need. When I'm done, I stand in front of the kitchen window. The fog is coming in off the ocean. Today there are a lot of wisps. The kind of stuff you see in a ghost movie. That's unusual for Seaside Cove. Ours is usually higher up. And now that I know my dad won't be back until later tonight, it's kinda depressing, too.

"Sweetie? How about if I put you in charge of the skillet?"

"Okay." I get Marquetta's big skillet in place and turn the heat on medium. Once I have some onions sautéing, the gloominess from all the fog goes away. "Marquetta?"

"Yes, Sweetie?"

"I love cooking with you."

She kisses me on the top of my head and gives me a hug. "I love cooking with you, too. Tamale Pie isn't a huge challenge, though."

"It was for me when we moved here."

"I remember," she says with a laugh. "Extra crispy. I believe those were the words your dad used to describe your first grilled cheese sandwich."

I turn up the heat and add ground turkey to the skillet. As I'm breaking up the meat, I say, "He had to be nice 'cause he's my dad."

Marquetta bumps her hip against mine. "To be honest, he wasn't very good in the kitchen, either."

"I know." I take another look out the bank of windows over the sink. This is all so much different from where we lived in New York. We never saw the ocean there. Here, we see it all the time. Of course, with the fog moving in, it won't be long before it disappears. The surface is what Marquetta calls choppy. To me, it just looks super rough. But it's still a pretty view. "I know why you love this kitchen so much."

"Why's that?" Marquetta asks as I turn off the heat.

"Because it's so bright and cheery. All the white counters and cabinets. Even when it's gloomy outside, it's cheerful in here."

"My, my. You are growing up." Marquetta gazes around. "I'm so thankful to Captain Jack because when he remodeled the B&B, he let me do whatever I wanted in the kitchen."

"This room is totally you, and it always makes me feel happy to be here with you."

"Thank you, Sweetie. This is my dream kitchen. I never want to have to give it up."

We chitchat while we add the shredded cheese to the skillet and stir it in. The pan is super heavy now, so Marquetta lifts it for me and pours the mixture into the baking dish. We add the cornmeal topping, then put the dish in the oven and start on the cleanup. While Marquetta's adding hot water and soap to soak the skillet, I decide it's time to lead into my questions. "I heard Mr. Gray fell and got hurt, so I called him."

"Oh? What did he say?"

Marquetta's on alert. She's trying to sound way too casual. But she's not so good at pretending to be what she's not. "He was telling me how he thinks Mr. Pallett got mad at him and tripped him on purpose."

"Alex, you can't repeat that outside of this room." Marquetta gives me what I call her stern mom look. "I'd hate to think of how tense things would get around here if Mr. Pallett heard you were talking about him behind his back. Do you understand?"

I nod. "Totally. But what if he did trip Mr. Gray on purpose? Maybe he salted our coffee, too."

"And maybe you're stirring up rumors based on Joe Gray's anger. I agree—Mr. Pallett isn't the nicest man. But what if Joe is simply looking for a scapegoat? Did you ever think of that?"

Uh...no. And now I'm in trouble. Marquetta doesn't get angry very often, but she's getting close. It's not so much the way she's talking, but that she's still giving me the mom stare. I look across the room at the rack filled with antique plates. Most of them are like almost a hundred years old 'cause they were in the attic when Captain Jack bought the house. That was way before Marquetta started living here with her mom.

"You must have a lot of memories of what the house was like before. Right, Marquetta?"

"I do. I practically grew up in this old house. And you know what's amazing? Now I get to watch you grow up here."

Wow. I never thought about that. "Growing up is super hard. There are so many things to learn."

She gives me another hug. "I know, Sweetie. I know."

"Can I ask you a question about Mr. Gray?"

"Sure."

"Mr. Gray's our friend. Shouldn't we take his side?"

Marquetta pulls me close and wraps her arms around me. "Sweetie, what if you got into an argument with Sasha? Would you want Robbie to have to choose between you and her?"

"But me and Sasha wouldn't fight. We're best friends."

"Even best friends can have a falling out. What if you both decided you liked Billy Thornton?"

"No way...ewww."

Marquetta laughs. "Okay. You're right. Billy Thornton's not a good example, but do you see what I'm saying? What if it meant losing Sasha?"

Oh man, the thought of losing her is enough to make me want to throw up. I scrunch up my face and give Marquetta a hug. "You're right. I'm sorry. I took Mr. Gray's side 'cause he's our friend. I thought about Mr. Pallett being so mean to me, and then the salted coffee, and then Mr. Gray...I get it. He might not be one of those...what do you call them in the movies?"

"A psychopath?" Marquetta asks with a grin.

"Yeah. One of those."

"No, Alex, I don't think Mr. Pallett is a psychopath. It's possible that he does have a problem with anger management. If we're lucky, we'll never find out. Now, let's finish our dishes." She puts on the gloves and starts to wash one of the plates.

Since we're kind of on the subject of our guests, I might as well go for the big question. "Is Tara the main suspect?"

The soapy dish Marquetta is holding slips out of her hand and lands with a thud on top of the mat in the bottom of the sink. She waits a few seconds, then says, "The evidence is pointing in that direction."

If I play it cool, maybe she won't worry so much. "Tara's not a murderer." I don't know for sure, but I like her and can't believe she'd do that.

Marquetta sighs. "Alex. Your dad is helping Adam with the case, but he doesn't want you to get involved. If you've heard rumors..."

"I was thinking somebody should write up the story for the Cove Talkers newsletter. You know, get all the facts so everybody knows the truth."

"An admirable goal, young lady, but somehow I can't help but wonder if you've got more in mind."

I'm so busted. But I gotta go for it. Marquetta's helped me in the past. I wonder if she'll do it again. "Well, I kinda was. You've helped me investigate before, and we made an awesome team."

"Alex, it hasn't even been twenty-four hours. Your dad and Adam have barely gotten started. Besides, we have a wedding coming up. And as my junior bridesmaid, you have responsibilities."

"The only thing left is for me and Grandma Madeline to check out the band. There's nothing else until the rehearsal."

Marquetta hangs up her dishtowel and spends some extra time fussing with it like she's trying to think of what to say. "You can be very exasperating, at times, Alex."

"I know. I'm sorry. But if we checked out Mr. Pallett and Mr. Nicholas, it would totally save Daddy and Chief Cunningham some time. And it would give Daddy more time to spend on the wedding."

Now I'm really in trouble. Marquetta's giving me the mom look again. That's like three times since I walked into the kitchen. It's gotta be a record. Even for me.

20

RICK

RAY BEING BORDERLINE NICE WAS surprising, but Henry Nicholas hanging out with other guests at the Inn could be a real game changer. Both he and Tara had claimed they didn't know anyone in Seaside Cove. If Henry knew these two guys, did Tara? There was something very fishy going on. But what?

"When does Walsh leave?" Rick asked.

"Checks out Saturday," Ray said.

"Did you see Henry Nicholas with anybody else?"

"No. Of course, he was only here the one day. So how come he was here and his wife was staying with you?"

If the argument between Tara and Henry hadn't happened in full view of the other guests, Rick might have given Ray some of his own medicine. But since half the town had probably heard by now—and the other half would hear by breakfast tomorrow— there was no point in playing games. "She was never his wife. They booked their room as a married couple, and it wasn't until they had a big blowout in the living room that anybody was the wiser."

Ray gaped at Rick for several seconds, then screwed up his face. "Why did they bother? Nobody cares who does what anymore."

"I don't know, Ray. Why do people do the things they do?" Why was Ray so difficult? Why did some people enforce the law and others did their best to get around it? "Human nature, I guess. The world would be a very boring place if we all did things the same."

Ray grunted something. Agreement? Disagreement? Who knew? Better yet, who cared? "Thanks for your time."

Another grunt, but a second later, Ray lifted his chin and looked at Adam. "Put in a good word with the mayor, would you? She's been on my case lately."

"About what?" Adam asked.

"She wants me to do a big remodel. Take the place upscale. Make it fit with the rest of the downtown."

"I'll tell her, but you know how Madam Mayor is."

Ray's scowl deepened. "Yeah. Got a pretty good idea."

"We're going to check the rooms for these two before we leave. Come on, Rick." Adam led the way back to the courtyard. They walked past the pool and followed the path to rooms 104 and 111. Neither man answered, so they headed for the exit. When they were approaching Adam's 4x4, his right cheek curled up, and he chuckled quietly.

"What's so funny?" Rick asked.

"You know why Ray got so cooperative, don't you?"

"Because you wanted me to embarrass the crap out of him. Right?"

"That's only part of it. I played dumb in there, but the mayor has threatened to pull his business license if he doesn't start acting more like a reputable hotel and less like a flophouse. She's using the B&B as an example of how he could turn things around."

Rick put his hand to his throat and swallowed hard. "That explains one thing."

Adam looked across the vehicle at Rick as he unlocked it. When they were both inside and had the doors closed, Adam asked, "Explains what?"

"Why Ray Villari hates me so much."

"Truer words were never spoken. Now, let's see if we can find these guys who were hanging out with our victim. I especially want to talk to Walsh."

"You never got to talk to him after the diving accident?"

"Deputy Kama took his initial statement, but your guest got himself killed and put the diving accident on the back burner before I was able to follow up with him. Guy's been around one too many dead bodies. He's moved to the top of my priority list."

Rick and Adam returned to the police station. While Adam ran a background check on Kiernan Walsh, Rick sat in the visitor's chair in front of the desk and texted Marquetta.

—*Worst fears coming true. Looks like I'm going to be late.*

—*Don't worry. I'll save you some dinner.*

When Adam let out a low whistle, Rick sent a final text telling Marquetta that Adam had found something. "What's up?" Rick asked as he pocketed his phone.

"Walsh has a few arrests. Mostly for small-time stuff. Nothing major, but he's no stranger to the system." Adam turned the monitor around. "This is who we're looking for. Thirty-two years old. Five-eleven. A hundred and seventy pounds. Brown eyes, and as you can see, bald."

The man in the picture had an almond-shaped face and a wide nose. He had olive skin and wore glasses with a thin frame. "He doesn't look dangerous. If I met this guy on the street, I'd probably think he was some sort of techie."

"He's got computer fraud listed on his...uh...resume."

Rick snickered. "Resume? Huh?"

"Traci keeps telling me I need to be less cynical."

"I see. Far be it from me to stand in the way of a man who's trying to improve himself. What about Max Rado?"

After a few minutes, Adam shook his head. "It looks like we're dealing with the cream of the crop. Rado's got his own 'bio' in the system." He made air-quotes, then turned the screen so Rick could see it.

"His...uh...resume isn't as impressive as Walsh's."

"The good news is neither of them has any violent crime in their backgrounds. These two are more like a couple of grifters with bad luck than they are hard-core criminals."

Rick read through the statistics—six-foot, a hundred and eighty-five pounds, brown eyes and brown hair. "At least we won't confuse them. Do you want to go looking for them?"

"It's about dinner time. Why don't we start casting our net?"

Pushing his chair back, Rick stood. "Let's get going. I'm about ready for dinner myself."

Their first stop was at the Rusty Nail. A wall of sound slammed Rick in the face as he followed Adam through the front door. With tile floors, stacked stone pillars, and an open concept design, the noise from customers could become almost deafening. This evening appeared to be one of those times.

"I can't believe how busy this place gets," Rick said as they waited inside the front door.

"When you've got two restaurants in town, there aren't a lot of options."

Sally Costas, a five-four fireball with the energy of a marathoner, waved to them from across the restaurant. She was seating a couple that had walked in just before Rick and Adam. Less than a minute later, she approached. "Evening, Chief, Rick. Are you two here for dinner?"

"No, Sally. Looks like you don't have any available seats, anyway."

"You're right. I'm actually surprised it's so busy this early on a Tuesday. What can I do for you?"

Adam turned his phone to display the photos of Walsh and Rado. "We're looking for these two men. They may be witnesses in a case."

Sally pursed her lips as she gazed at the photos. "Ah, the murder. Can't say as I've seen either of them. Have you spoken to Ken?"

"No. We thought we'd come here before we went to the Crooked Mast. Give me a call if you see either of these two. Okay?"

"Of course."

Rick suppressed a little laugh. There were eyes everywhere in this town. When he and Alex had first moved here, Marquetta had warned him about the town's gossip mill. He'd soon learned there was no tidbit of information that didn't make the rounds. He was sure Sally would call if the men came in, but he was also sure she'd phone a friend...or maybe two or three to spread the word.

Sally stood on her tiptoes and waved at someone behind them. Rick looked, saw a family of four standing inside the door. He felt a twinge of guilt for holding them up and turned back to Sally. "Our business has been the same way. We're booked all the time. I guess we can't complain. Right?"

"When my husband passed, I wasn't sure I was going to keep this place," Sally said. "Now, I'm glad I did. It keeps me hopping and I get to meet new people all the time. Tell Marquetta I said hello, okay?"

After assuring Sally he would pass along the message, Rick followed Adam and made way for the arrivals. Including the time it took to park, it was a short, three-minute drive to The Crooked Mast. Adam parked in the alley a short distance back from the connection to Main Street. When they entered the front entrance, Cecelia greeted them from behind the reception stand. Adam told her they were there to speak to the owner, Ken Grayson. She scampered off, disappearing around the partition separating the lobby from the main dining area.

At a lanky six-foot-four, Ken towered above her when they returned. Ken greeted Rick and Adam, then shook his head. "Can you tell me what's going on? Why are all these people here? Tuesdays are always slow."

"No idea, Ken," said Adam. "Sally's got the same problem."

"The B&B has been busy, too," Rick added. "Maybe the tourist season is starting earlier."

"Or maybe we've been discovered," Ken grumbled. "Much as I like the money we're making right now, I think everybody's looking for a little downtime." He looked at Cecelia. "Poor Cecelia, she just went on summer break and already I've got her in here most nights."

"It's okay, Mr. Grayson. I'm trying to save money for college. I don't mind."

"Works for me. Right now, I need all the help I can get." A cold rush of air blew in from the open door. Ken cocked his head to one side. "Let's get out of the way so Cecelia can handle these people."

Rick checked to see who had come in. It was John and Sheila Brower. They exchanged a quick hello, then Cecelia took them back to the last open table while Ken watched.

"I'm going to be in a world of hurt when she goes off to college."

"You say the same thing every time one of them leaves." Adam chuckled, then added, "Sometimes I think you just don't like change."

"I don't," Ken said with a snort. "Hate it, actually. Sorry, Adam, but I have to get back to the kitchen. I hear you're looking for a couple of suspects."

Rick held his tongue. It was so tempting to make a comment about the rumor mill being faster than two men in a police car. Then again, the grapevine in this town was faster than almost anything.

"They're not actually suspects, Ken. Did you get a photo, too?"

"Nah. You didn't leave the photos with Sally, you only showed them to her. Besides, we have to let you have something to do, Adam. Right?" Ken's blue eyes sparkled as he grinned at them.

"Suppose so. Here, take a look. And no, I'm not leaving copies. As you say, I have to have something to do."

"Gotcha." Ken studied the photo of Max Rado and shook his head. "No. Never seen him. Show me the other one."

There was a long pause when Adam brought up the second photo. "You've got a funny look on your face, Ken. Like you recognize him. Has he been in here for dinner?"

"Pretty sure. But I don't think it was dinner. Hang on a sec."

21

ALEX

Oh man, Journal, I'm pooped. And stuffed! I had to have two dinners today! Grandma Madeline picked me up for the trip to San Ladron right after me and Marquetta had Tamale Pie. She drove like ten miles-an-hour over the mountain, and I fell asleep a couple times. Then we went to the restaurant where the quartet was supposed to be playing. She had the times all messed up, so we were way early. She made me have a second dinner while we waited! It was totally boring because it was a fancy restaurant and she wanted me to be on my best behavior. Plus, she kept complaining about the cost of everything on the menu.

The quartet was okay, but they were boring. I almost fell asleep once, and I'm sure Grandma Madeline did, too. All they played was classical, and when I asked if they played anything else, they said no. I told Grandma Madeline it wasn't gonna work. Instead of disagreeing with me, she said she knew it, too, and wouldn't interfere in the wedding plans anymore. When I asked her about Traci's gift, she said it was a nice gesture and that she'd realized she was being petty.

We didn't get back until late, so I said goodnight and came up to get ready for bed. Tomorrow, I'm gonna talk to Marquetta and ask her if she said anything to Grandma

Madeline. I kinda think she told her she needed to be on her best behavior!

Xoxo

Alex

I've just put away my journal when there's a knock on the door. I can tell it's Marquetta by the way she knocks. I unlock the door, tell her to come in, and hop back into bed while she sits on the edge.

Marquetta looks at me and strokes my hair. "I'm sorry your trip with Mom was a waste of time."

"I guess it wasn't too bad. It's good you sent me 'cause that band is like totally boring. You and Daddy might have fallen asleep before you could say 'I do.'"

She gives me a small smile. "Could it be you're exaggerating a little, Sweetie?"

"No way. They were like so bad even Grandma Madeline fell asleep for a minute. You didn't hear them! They were awful."

"Were they awful? Or just not the kind of music you like?"

"Well, I guess that's kinda true." I tell Marquetta that Grandma Madeline didn't put up a fuss about the band and ask if she said something to her.

"Wasn't me. I didn't say anything."

Huh. Imagine that. Grandma Madeline must have figured it out on her own. It's time to ask about what I really want to know. "Did Daddy say anything about the murder investigation?"

"There's nothing much to say right now. They have more people to talk to tomorrow. Your dad will probably be out most of the day. I also spoke to Lydia. She'll be here at six. Once we've got her paperwork taken care of, I'd like her to shadow one of us so we can teach her the ropes."

"The ropes?" That sounds kinda weird.

"The way we do things. Which is very different from how she did things at the Inn. Maybe you could let her work with you for the breakfast service. Then we'll figure out the rest of the day."

"Awesome. I get to be in charge of somebody else."

"Don't let it go to your head, Sweetie. It also means you have responsibilities."

"Got it." I like these alone times with Marquetta. She listens to me and understands me. But what will happen if she gets pregnant? Will she still have time for me? My dad listens, but he's stricter and doesn't always understand the difference between boys and girls. Marquetta knows all of that. And that's super awesome. She's gonna be the best mom ever. "Marquetta? When you and Daddy get married, how long will it be before you have a baby?"

Marquetta laughs. "You're pretty anxious for a little brother, aren't you?"

The room gets a little warm 'cause I realize what I'm thinking is kinda selfish. "I was wondering how much time you'll have for me if..."

"Sweetie, I'll always have time for you. I'll be living here and you'll get so sick of me..."

I look away from Marquetta. The room is getting so hot it's making me want to push away the bedcovers. My face feels like it's on fire. "It's just..."

Marquetta lifts my chin so I'm looking at her. "Does this have something to do with your biological mother, Sweetie?"

My throat is all scratchy. "I wanna be sure you haven't changed your mind. You know...about me."

"That is not going to happen." Marquetta takes the covers from my hands and rearranges them. She strokes my hair and kisses me on the forehead. "Don't worry. I've told you I will never do to you what your mother did."

I sit up straight and throw my arms around her neck. She hugs me back, and when she eases me down onto the bed, the heat that was in my face has moved down to my chest. Finally, I'm gonna have a real mom. And we'll be just like a real family— except for all the guests who come and go all the time.

When Marquetta leaves and I'm drifting off to sleep, I also think about how awesome it will be to have a baby brother. Yeah, Operation Baby Brother is totally gonna happen.

22

RICK

KEN GRAYSON DID A VISUAL scan of the back of the restaurant. He must have been looking for Cecelia, because he raised his hand and motioned for her to join them. She finished seating the Browers, then threaded her way through the maze of tables.

"Cecelia? Look at this photo, would you?" He had Adam hold the phone so the girl could see it. "Is this the guy your mom was talking about?"

Cecelia's eyes widened, then she reached into her back pocket and pulled out her phone. She tapped a few times on the screen, then mouthed a quiet 'oh.' "I think so. Here, Chief. My mom told me he was trying to get a job on the *Blue Phoenix*."

She held out her phone and showed Rick and Adam a photo of a man who was standing on the docks in the harbor. The man leaned against one of the pilings, which extended well above the decking, indicating he'd been there at low tide.

"That's Walsh," Rick muttered.

"This guy's really beginning to irritate me. Apparently, he told my deputy the same story your mom heard, Cecelia."

Rick felt his brow furrow as he looked at the photo. "Why would Walsh want a job on Flynn O'Connor's boat? Unless he wants to work on the *San Mañuel* recovery."

"Miss O'Connor told my mom he talked to Captain Struthers about a job as a diver, but Captain Struthers took a dislike to the man. He called him shifty."

And, of course, Cecelia's mother knew all this because this was, well, Seaside Cove. "Flynn's very picky about who she hires. And Struthers told me once before that all of his crew were former SEALS. He's not going to hire some clown who shows up on the docks."

Adam made a quick note, then looked up. "Cecelia, tell your mom Rick and I will be by to see her in the morning."

A heavy mist enveloped Rick and Adam as they left the Crooked Mast. Droplets of moisture clung to everything and had already blanketed Adam's vehicle. Rick shrugged down into his jacket to ward off the chill. "Talk about a change in the weather. I guess I'll adjust, eventually."

Adam nodded absently, then said, "Since these two don't appear to be the restaurant type, we should run by the Seaside Cove Market to see if they've visited the deli."

Oh, the market. Rick realized he'd never made it there. If only he could just go there, do the shopping, then go home and sit next to a warm fire with Marquetta. That would be so much better than interviewing witnesses. "Let's go. We've got a case to solve."

One of the clerks at the deli remembered seeing Max Rado, but didn't recall Kiernan Walsh. By the time they walked out, Rick's frustration level was nearing its limit. "This is ridiculous. Why can't we find these guys?"

"Makes me mighty suspicious about how they're existing without food. There is one place, though. Crusty Buns."

Rick's spirits lifted. Everybody went there. Locals. Tourists. And Ray had mentioned they'd had cups from Crusty Buns. Come to think of it, Rick had never heard of a tourist who hadn't visited at least once. "You're right. Unfortunately, they're closed."

"Got an idea, Rick. Why don't we have coffee there tomorrow morning? My treat."

"Does this mean you're feeling guilty about taking me away from the B&B again?"

"If you'd rather pay for your own..." Adam let the words hang in the air.

"No. That's okay. This may be the only payment I ever see from the Seaside Cove Police Department."

Adam clutched his hand to his heart and stuck out his lower lip. "And here I thought you were doing this because you enjoyed my company more than Marquetta's."

"Right. And I'm going to wave my hand and make this fog disappear in the next ten minutes," Rick scoffed.

Adam tugged absently on his ear as he nodded. "I like that idea. Come on, I'll drive you home."

Rick texted Marquetta on the way. When he walked through the front door, he was amazed at how quiet it was. He found her waiting for him by the fireplace in the lobby, the gas log flickering lazily to the side. By the time he finished dinner, they'd shared their stories about their days. After Marquetta left, Rick went upstairs. He would have checked on Alex on his way, but the lights in her room were out. Not wanting to wake her, he went to bed and fell fast asleep.

At three-sixteen a.m., Rick checked the time on his bedside clock. The faint glow of moonlight created barely discernible shadows on the walls and floor. It was hard to believe that in just a few days, he'd be sharing this room, this bed, with Marquetta.

He rolled onto his back and gazed at the ceiling. Closing his eyes, he took a deep breath and told himself to stop thinking. He mouthed the words, "Quiet your mind." Breathing in slowly and deeply, he concentrated on a steady count of four. After another count of three, he breathed out for four more counts, waited, then repeated the process five more times.

Gradually, his thoughts began to slow. Questions about the wedding, the business, the murder, gradually subsided until the only remaining thought was the slow count of one-two-three... Rick opened his eyes and muttered, "Oh, crap."

He got out of bed, dressed, and quietly went to his office. Sitting at his desk, he pulled up the email Adam had forwarded from Deputy Kama. The email included an inventory of Henry Nicholas's belongings. The one she'd made while taking everything into custody. "Please make me be wrong," Rick whispered as he scanned down the list.

When he got to the last item, he grimaced and shook his head. One very important thing was missing from the list—the pink box Tara had told him she'd found in Henry's belongings the night they checked in. Rick leaned back in his chair and focused on his laptop screen. So far, Tara hadn't even admitted she'd been in the room. What if she had? Would she have taken the baker's box? Talk about an awkward breakfast conversation.

Knowing there was nothing he could do about Tara now, he closed the lid on the laptop, turned off the lights, and returned to bed. He repeated the same process as before, and this time, when he opened his eyes, it was five-fifteen.

Lydia arrived at six. They agreed to get her paperwork taken care of after the breakfast service. She helped Marquetta with some of the prep work, then shadowed Alex at six-thirty when they started taking orders. By seven-thirty, Rick wondered how they'd ever gotten along without the additional help. Lydia was not only able to work tables, but she also assisted Marquetta in the kitchen in between orders.

Tara showed up for breakfast shortly after eight. She had her hair concealed under a silk headscarf. Judging by the flush of her skin, her sweatshirt, and leggings, he was pretty sure she'd gotten out for some exercise.

"I decided to start running again. Today it was just a walk, but Henry's death has made me realize we only get one shot in life. I'm not going to waste another minute of mine."

Rick poured coffee while she talked, overly aware of his middle-of-the-night question. "Good for you. It's important to take care of yourself. How are you holding up?"

"I'm doing great. I'm determined to get back out there."

"Good attitude, Tara."

Rick moved to one side so Alex could slip by him to deliver an order to a nearby table. As he waited for his daughter to finish her delivery, he watched Lydia change out the coffee carafes, a job they normally couldn't get to until after the service ended. She was settling in perfectly. Maybe they'd be able to keep her on longer.

He checked on another of his tables while Alex finished up, but when she headed back to the kitchen, he returned to Tara's table.

"Tara? Didn't you say you and Henry decided to visit Seaside Cove after you talked about the *San Mañuel*?"

"To be truthful, we almost didn't come here at all. I told you how Henry wasn't very interested in the history when I told him about the *San Mañuel*. It was a few days later when he started asking questions. Was there treasure? How much was it worth? The next thing I know, he wants to stay here."

She frowned and gazed down at the floor for a second. "It was like an overnight switch. He said something about talking to a friend. Henry could be very unpredictable—he'd do a one-eighty on the basis of a conversation."

"And that didn't bother you?"

Tara shook her head. "Rick, I told you before. I was being stupid when it came to Henry. Looking back, it would have been a terrible match. I'm a planner. Henry was..." She stopped, screwed up her face, then said, "Stupidly impetuous."

"I can see where that could be difficult for both of you. Would you mind answering one more question?"

She tore the top off of a sugar packet, poured the contents into the mug, then added enough cream to turn the coffee a light tan. "I guess not. What did you want to know?"

"On your first night here, you told me Henry received a phone call and went downstairs to talk. While he was out of the room, you found a pink box. Is that right?"

Tara nodded as she sipped. When she lowered the mug, she said, "Yes. I've been thinking about it. It would have been just like Henry to bake me a special cupcake with an engagement ring inside. Why?"

If Adam were doing this, he would simply ignore Tara's question or tell her he couldn't answer at this time. But Tara was a guest, and Rick wanted to keep the peace, despite the fact that they might be investigating this woman for murder. "When Deputy Kama inventoried Henry's belongings, the box was missing. There's no mention of it. Henry didn't give it to you when you went to see him, did he?"

Her brow furrowed, and she gazed off into space. She shook her head and mumbled a quiet, "No." A few seconds later, her eyes widened, and she looked up at Rick. "You don't think I took it, do you?"

"I'm not sure who did," Rick said. "It just occurred to me in the middle of the night that the box you'd seen was not listed in the inventory. I'm sure it will turn up somewhere."

The furrows in Tara's brow deepened. She narrowed her gaze at Rick. "My God, you do think I took it."

"That's not what I'm saying." He was about to say the missing baker's box was an inconsistency—one they might be able to use to find Henry's killer—when Alex came and stood next to him.

"Daddy, if Tara said she didn't take it, she didn't take it."

"Thank you, Alex," Tara said.

Rick felt as though they'd suddenly become the center of attention. Unless he was mistaken, every eye in the room was now trained on this table. This interaction. And how he handled it. He had to end this, both gracefully and fast. "I'm sure you're right, Alex. Tara, I'm sorry if I upset you. I'm sure we'll figure out who took the box before long. I'll give you a minute to look over the menu...be right back." Rick turned to Alex and reminded her she needed to check on Lydia. She made a face, but appeared to get the message that she should stop interfering and left.

When Rick returned to take Tara's order, she acted as though their earlier interaction had never happened. The dining room slowly cleared out, and when Tara was the last one there, Rick went back one more time and sat opposite her.

"I'm sorry about the misunderstanding. I didn't mean to put you on the spot."

"It's not a problem. I was just surprised, that's all." She scrunched up her nose and added, "I do wish you'd have asked me in private, though. Not in a room full of people."

"Huge mistake on my part. I apologize for doing that to you."

"You know what? What's done is done. Let's move on."

"Sounds good to me," Rick said as he excused himself. The problem was that with an investigation in progress, nothing might be 'done'. It might appear that way now, but the situation could easily change. If that happened, he might have to put more pressure on Tara Amengual.

23

ALEX

AFTER WE OFFICIALLY CLOSE THE dining room for breakfast, me and Lydia pick up the last of the dirty dishes and linens while my dad and Marquetta get the kitchen cleaned up. Lydia's a hard worker and we've been getting along all morning. She's a super good fit. I hope she's gonna be working here for more than just a few weeks. If she is, she might want to do something to help with Operation Honeymoon.

"Lydia? How are you liking the job?"

She stacks a few plates on a tray, then straightens up and arches her back. She takes a deep breath and says, "This is so much better than the Inn. I hated working there, but I think I'm going to love it here."

I bite my lower lip. There might not be another chance. "Awesome. You know my dad and Marquetta are getting married next week. Right?"

"Yes. That's one reason your dad hired me."

"Well, here's what I'm planning."

As I tell her about Operation Honeymoon, her face lights up and she starts to look happier. When I'm done, she hugs me. "Thank you for making me feel like part of the family. I'll do whatever I can to help. And your secret is safe with me."

Wow. That was super easy. When we get all the tables cleared and the dishes bussed into the kitchen, Daddy takes

Lydia upstairs to get her signed up as an employee. Me and Marquetta have breakfast while they're gone. It also gives me a couple minutes to talk to Marquetta alone about what I heard Daddy saying to Tara.

"Marquetta, does my dad still think Tara killed Mr. Nicholas?"

"I don't know, Sweetie. I'm sure he and Adam will get to the bottom of it." She picks up her mug and looks at me over the top of it. "Why are you so certain she didn't do it?"

"She's too nice of a person."

"Even nice people can be driven to do bad things, Alex."

"I know, but when I talked to her on the back patio, she called him a rat, but she was still worried enough to ask if Daddy had found him a room. She was sad, but she didn't act like she was super angry."

"As I said, your dad and Adam will get this all sorted out. Just give them a little time, okay?"

"I'm worried they'll stop looking for the real killer."

Marquetta lets out a little huff. I can tell she's getting frustrated with me. She totally believes in my dad and Chief Cunningham. I do, too, but I also know the mayor hates it when there's a murder. She's gonna want this taken care of faster than Chief Cunningham and my dad like to work.

"What if the mayor puts pressure on Chief Cunningham to wrap up the case and they just stop looking?"

"You're right about Francine. She's not very patient. But I also know your dad and Adam, and neither of them is going to take shortcuts. Now, let's get the dining room set up for the day, and when your dad finishes with Lydia, we'll start with the guest rooms. Okay?"

While we're finishing up, I try again to convince her that we should do some investigating on our own. I give up when Lydia joins us. I get it. Marquetta's not convinced. Okay, fine. I'll just do it on my own.

"All finished, Lydia?" Marquetta asks.

"Yes. All the paperwork's done. Rick said you and Alex will be training me. I've never been trained by someone so young." She puts her hands on her knees, leans over, and looks me in the eye. "Other than my kids, of course."

Me and Marquetta laugh, but it's totally true. My dad didn't have any experience when I was born, but he learned what to do. He turned into an awesome dad, so I guess I did a good job on training him.

Marquetta looks around the room. "We've got all the tables cleared and the chairs are back where they belong. We're almost done here. Why don't you two get the trash taken out while I restock the coffee and tea? Once all that's done, we can clean the guest rooms."

While me and Lydia are working, Marquetta checks the guest list. Most of the guests are easy 'cause they don't even want us to change the towels or bedding. We've only got one checkout today. There's another guest coming in this afternoon, so we only have one full cleaning to do this morning. We also have to do a partial on two other rooms—the Foresail Room where Miss Larkin and Mr. McNasty have been staying, and the Captain's Quarters, which is where the Browers are staying.

"I'll take the room for Mr. Pallett and Miss Larkin, Alex. You and Lydia can work on the Captain's Quarters."

Darn. I was hoping to be able to do some spying. I wanted to see if I could find anything on Mr. McNasty. But that would be totally impossible with Lydia around. I'd get in a lot of trouble if my dad or Marquetta found out. "Why don't me and Lydia do the full cleaning on the Jib Room?"

My dad's message tone rings on Marquetta's phone. She wrinkles her nose when she reads the message. "Rick just texted me. The guests who were supposed to check into the Jib Room are cancelling their stop in Seaside Cove. Some sort of family emergency. Okay, Alex. You two take the full cleaning. I'll do the partials. Let's get busy, shall we?"

I show Lydia where we keep the towels and have her carry the clean ones while I grab a laundry bag. When we get to the door, I knock. "We always knock first. Then we announce ourselves."

"It was the same at the Inn. I can't count the number of times Ray told me a guest had checked out and they were still in the room. There was one time I even caught a couple in bed."

Ewww. That would have been gross. Down the hall, Marquetta has already knocked on the door to the Foresail Room. The door jerks open. Mr. McNasty is standing there looking grumpy. Marquetta apologizes and says she'll come back later, but he grumbles something about having a phone call to make and pushes past her. I duck behind Lydia so he can't see me as he storms by.

There's no answer when we knock, so I try again and wait a few seconds. Down the hall, Marquetta goes into the Foresail Room. Oh, man. I totally wanna hear what that phone call is all about. I slip the master key into the lock and open the door a crack. When I can see there's nobody in the room, we prop the door open.

I shove the laundry bag into Lydia's hands. "Just change out all the towels and put the dirty ones in there. I'll be right back."

Lydia's jaw drops open as I give her a thumbs up and walk away. "You've totally got this, Lydia," I say as I head for the stairs.

When I get to the first floor, I see Miss Jones is still sitting on one of the couches, reading. She looks up at me, rolls her eyes, and stares toward where Mr. McNasty's voice is coming from. I can tell she's not happy about him 'cause we can hear almost every word he's saying. I wave to Miss Jones as I walk past her. At the edge of the living room, it's easy to hear the grump arguing with someone.

"I'm telling you, this is going to be a big moneymaker. This town is a treasure hunter's paradise. When I set up these Joaquin Murrieta tours, the crazy fools who come here will gobble it up. They can't get enough of that crap."

He stops talking and I can hear his footsteps on the hardwood floor. It sounds like he's getting close, but then his footsteps fade. He must be pacing back and forth.

The footsteps stop again and he laughs. "Yeah, yeah. That's it. That's the line. Go on a search for the ghost who's wandering through the hills crying, 'Give me back my head.'" He laughs again. "Brilliant. You got the photo I sent you, right?"

That's the proof I need! He's admitted the business he's setting up really is a scam! The mayor is so not gonna be happy about this. She likes all the tourists, and she hates it when people take advantage of them.

"You got it, bro. Wild, frizzy hair. Floppy hat. Mean look on his face. Perfect. They'll eat it up. I guarantee it. We'll make a fortune off this. Okay. I'd better go. That stupid housekeeper should be done in my room by now. I'll send you a couple more files."

His footsteps get louder and then he's right there in front of me. Glaring at me.

"Hi, Mr. Pallett." My heart is thumping in my chest. I don't want him to know I overheard him talking. "I'm sorry about the other day."

"How long have you been there, kid?" He moves closer, so I back up a little.

"I was on my way to the laundry room. We have a guest checking out today...so we gotta do a full cleaning." Man, my heart is gonna explode. What if he doesn't believe me?

"Oh, and don't forget the extra towel you promised me for my room," Miss Jones says as she joins us. She looks at Mr. Pallett. "I always go through extras when I'm on vacation. I don't know how I do it at home."

Mr. Pallett glares at the both of us, then grunts and walks off. I close my eyes and take a deep breath. When I open them, Miss Jones is smiling at me.

"What a jerk. Don't let him get to you, Alex. He should be ashamed of himself, trying to intimidate a young girl like you."

"Thanks, Miss Jones. Do you really need a towel?"

She wrinkles her nose and shakes her head. "No. I made it up. When you're a spy, you learn to think on your feet."

"What agency do you work for? Are you still a spy?"

Miss Jones laughs, then winks at me. "You know I can't answer your first question. But I can tell you I'm no longer in the business. I just feel like a girl needs to keep up her skills. You never know when they'll come in handy. Right?"

Before I can say anything, I hear Marquetta calling me. She comes into the dining room and has Lydia with her. Uh oh.

"Alex? What are you doing down here? Why did you leave Lydia?"

"Sorry, Marquetta. I just..."

"That's my fault," Miss Jones says. "She was getting me an extra towel. I'm sorry if I pulled her away."

Awesome. I think me and Miss Jones are gonna get along great.

24

RICK

RICK STOOD ON THE CORNER of Whale and Court streets facing the home of Francine Carter. The Seaside Cove Mayor's house, at three stories tall and with a tower on the northwest corner, stood head-and-shoulders above its neighbors. A massive set of stairs climbed to the second-floor main entrance. About the only thing that helped this house blend in was the paint, a sedate yellow with beige, white, and forest green accents.

Meetings with Francine were never part of a social call, at least not in the early mornings. In fact, he'd been summoned to visit, and that could only mean one thing—the mayor wanted to stick her nose where it didn't belong. Most likely, she was also anxious to have them arrest the killer. Fortunately, Francine would have to open Scoops & Scones soon, so this wasn't going to take very long.

Rick opened the elegant wrought-iron gate, admired the perfectly manicured landscaping, then began the climb to the main entrance. He drew a calming breath before using the polished brass knocker to announce his arrival, then checked his watch. One of the things Adam had told him was that the mayor always made visitors wait. After hearing about the tactic, Rick had timed how long it took Francine to answer the door—it was almost always thirty-three seconds.

Right on cue, Francine opened the door and ushered him inside. "How nice to see you, Rick. Thank you for coming."

As if he'd had a choice. However, propriety dictated he say something nice. "It's my pleasure, Madam Mayor. You're looking lovely today."

Francine patted the back of her perfectly coiffed hair and beamed back at him. "Oh, pish tosh. You're just being kind."

Now what? He certainly couldn't agree with her. But he also needed to get this meeting over with. "I'm only being honest, Francine. I'm sure you're in a hurry because you'll have to open soon."

"Yes." She raised her arm and flipped her hand, almost as though she were trying to throw it away. "Follow me!" She trilled in a voice that reminded Rick of a piccolo.

The first time Rick had visited Francine's parlor, the room she used as an unofficial meeting space, he'd considered it gaudily impressive. But after having been here a few times, he saw it for what it was, an ode to generations past—and maybe the color lilac. A grand chandelier hung from the coffered ceiling. The chandelier was bordered north and south by two painted half-umbrellas, lilac, of course. An area rug covered the hardwood floors. But it wasn't just any area rug. This was a black-and-lilac geometric pattern dotted with tan roses. In keeping with the room's theme, ostentatious, everything in between was equally over-the-top—gold, gaudy, lilac, or a combination of all three.

It didn't help that the oil paintings were all straight out of a Renaissance-era castle. So, while the room was impressive at first, Rick had come to realize it could be described in three little words. Way. Too. Much.

"I'm sure you know why I asked you here."

Unfortunately, yes, thought Rick. "You're wondering about the case, aren't you?"

"Yes, yes. How are you doing? When will you nab the killer?" Francine jabbed the air with a punch, emphasizing her words like a prosecutor making a final argument.

"I'm sure Adam filled you in. Has he not?" Although it would make perfect sense if he'd been avoiding this very conversation.

"Well...yes, but I like to hear from the troops. Keep my finger on the pulse of the investigation."

"I see," Rick said. But he didn't, really. Other than the fact that Francine Carter was one of the town's biggest gossips, he couldn't understand the point of this conversation. "There's not much to report yet. Today, we'll be tracking down a couple of key witnesses. In fact, that's where I'm heading now. To the police station. To work the case."

Francine missed—or ignored—the bit of sarcasm. Her hopeful expression slowly fell. "So you have nothing?"

"We have leads."

"Anyone in particular? Not a local, I hope."

Thinking about Walsh, Rick said, "No. Not a local. We're not even sure if he knows anything."

"Aha. A man. Is he a witness to the murder?"

"We don't think so. Let's just say we're getting close." Rick regretted the words the moment he said them. They weren't close. They weren't even sure if there were more witnesses. He'd fallen into the same trap he sometimes did with Alex—trying to give her hope prematurely.

"Very well," Francine sighed. "I'll let you get on with it. Please, keep me informed."

"Of course, Madam Mayor."

On his way to the police station, Rick thought about his interaction with Francine. She was much like the parlor—over the top. And something about her high-pitched voice and gesticulations just made him want to put a positive spin on things. Marquetta had warned him about getting sucked in and making promises he couldn't keep. Perhaps that was part of Francine's political success. Anywhere else, she might not stand a chance, but in Seaside Cove, she fit in perfectly. Probably because she had something on everyone.

Walking along the tree-lined streets, Rick breathed in the cool morning air. It felt fresh and clean. Overhead, birds chirped in branches that were poking through the evaporating gray mist. His footfalls sounded like a metronome beating time to an other worldly experience.

Deputy Kama sat at the front desk when Rick entered the Seaside Cove Police Department. She looked up from her screen, her brown eyes intent and thoughtful. "Good morning, Rick. Chief's on the phone talking to Susan Nicholas."

"Oh." Rick saw that Adam was at his desk, phone to his ear, and elbows on the desktop. "He looks kind of busy. We don't get to talk much, Amy, how are you doing?"

"Feeling better every day. I want to thank you again for being so hospitable when I first got to town. I don't know if I'd have ever recovered this well in LA. You, Marquetta, and Alex all made me feel so welcome at the B&B."

Rick's cheeks warmed as he thought about the circumstances surrounding her first visit to Seaside Cove, the murder she'd stumbled upon, and the events that followed. "We had a bit of a rough start, but it all worked out."

"You guys aren't to blame. After the shooting in LA, I was so closed off I didn't know if I'd ever function normally again."

"And now you are?" Rick raised his eyebrows and watched Amy's face. She did look better. Maybe it was nothing more than a lowered stress level, but Amy looked happier. Of course, she wasn't the type who ever really seemed happy. Even when she smiled, there was a sadness about her.

"I'm getting there. I never realized how much my job as a court officer was wearing on me." Amy cleared her throat and sat a bit straighter. "Anyway, I'm finding my way back to normal. I think the chief's about done. If you want, go on back. He won't mind."

"Thanks, Amy. Oh, by the way, how's the cottage working out?"

For the first time, Amy's face lit up. "It's wonderful. The owner's been great about letting me do little things to make it more my style. Tell Marquetta how grateful I am for lining me up with the owner."

"I will. Looks like Adam's almost off his call. You take care."

Rick started in Adam's direction, but even from across the room, he could see how drawn Adam's face was. Dark circles had formed beneath his green eyes, which weren't as bright as they usually were. Rick took the seat in front of Adam's desk, feeling sorry for him as he ran his hands over his face and let out a deep sigh.

"That's the hardest part of the job."

"Giving people bad news?"

"Susan Nicholas is taking her husband's death pretty hard. She was peppering me with questions about some woman who called her."

"Tara Amengual. She told Marquetta that she was so angry that she called her."

Adam nodded knowingly. "Makes more sense now as to why Susan Nicholas kept asking how come her husband was here. From what she said, Henry kept apologizing for not bringing her on this trip. How the guy would have brought her along also, I have no idea."

Rick winced at the thought of two women, both wronged by the same man. "Sorry. I should have told you about Tara's phone call when I heard about it."

"No worries. I just don't think it's my place to explain that her husband was cheating on her." Adam shook his head. "She did say he'd become more distant lately. What he told her was things were busy at work."

"The cheating spouse's first line of defense."

Adam stared off into space for a few seconds before he responded. "Sorry, I guess you are familiar with that, aren't you?"

"All too well. Giselle had it down to a science. By the time things were over, I really didn't care what she was doing to me. But ignoring your own daughter, that's just unforgivable."

"I hear you, but the munchkin did turn out pretty good, anyway. By the way, Deputy Kama received the phone records for Henry Nicholas. We now know his last call was to his wife at 4:58 pm. She confirmed they spoke at about five o'clock. We have multiple witnesses who put Tara Amengual at the room right about the same time. And our victim was killed sometime Monday evening."

"Which looks bad for Tara."

"Unless we can find somebody else who entered Room 210 after she left. On that bit of good news, how'd your thing with Madam Mayor go this morning?"

"Did she tell you she was going to talk to me?"

"You know Francine. Can't keep anything in."

Rick snickered. "Or away from her. Other than letting it slip that we're looking for witnesses, she got nothing from me. So what's our game plan?"

"We're going to leverage Seaside Cove's finest information source to find Max Rado and Kiernan Walsh."

There was only one place Rick could think of that might fit Adam's description. With a lopsided grin, he said, "Here we come, Crusty Buns. By the way, you are paying, right?"

"Nope. The mayor is. She just doesn't know it yet."

25

ALEX

MARQUETTA DOESN'T LOOK LIKE SHE believes what Miss Jones told her, but I know she won't argue with a guest, either. She turns to Lydia and says, "We're going to get started on the laundry. I'll give Alex the next couple of hours off." She looks at me and adds. "Lunch. Noon. In the kitchen. Don't be late. And don't leave the B&B."

She cuts her eyes to the side like she wants me to leave. Oh yeah, she totally knows all that was bogus. But at least she didn't ground me. "Okay," I say and wave goodbye to Miss Jones.

Marquetta tells Lydia to follow her so she can show her the laundry room. I consider going back to talk to Miss Jones, but if Marquetta finds out, she'll ground me for sure. On my way upstairs, I get another idea. I could check on Tara and see how she's doing. If I'm in her room, Marquetta's not gonna know. I go to the cabinet where we keep a few extra linens and grab a couple of towels, then go to the Port Room and knock on the door.

After a few seconds, I knock again. Rats. She's not here. I put the towels back and head downstairs, hoping I might find her. I check out the foyer, then the living room. I'm about to give up when I hear Tara talking with Miss Jones. OMG. I have to chance it. This could be my best shot at talking to Tara again. Sucking in a breath, I hurry into the dining room.

My jaw drops when I walk into the room. Marquetta's there with both of them. She sees me and crooks her finger. I am so busted. My shoulders kinda slump as I walk toward her. I'm totally getting grounded.

"Lydia's taking a break, Sweetie. She had a few phone calls to make. You can join us. You're not in trouble."

Miss Jones gives me a wink, but Tara looks confused.

"I get in trouble a lot," I sigh.

"Alex has a tendency to...overstep." Marquetta puts her hand on my shoulder and gives it a little shake. "She's very precocious."

"Oh, I see. Kind of like when we were on the patio?" Tara says.

I nod.

"I appreciate your concern. It was helpful to have someone to talk to. And you do seem to understand my situation."

Miss Jones tilts her head to the side and gives me a look like she wants to know what the secret is. When I don't say anything, she says, "Let me see. I'll bet Henry lied to you about his marriage."

"Yes. He lied to both of us."

Wait. How does she know that? Unless... "Did you call his wife?" I ask.

Tara gets all flushed at first, then she huffs. "I told Marquetta before. This whole affair with Henry is just making me sick. I never should have trusted him. But when I realized just how self-centered he'd been, I lost it. I'm ashamed now about how much pain I caused her. The poor woman was crushed when I told her who I was. Neither of us realized he was burning the candle at both ends."

We all turn at the sound of footsteps coming into the room. Lydia stops and takes in a breath. She's just standing there staring at Tara.

"What's wrong, Lydia?" Marquetta asks.

Lydia points at Tara. "You're the woman I saw going to that man's room."

Tara squeezes her eyes shut and her shoulders quiver. A few seconds later, she mumbles, "Oh, God, this is awful." She chews on her lower lip. "I didn't kill him. I swear."

Whoa. Super. Awkward.

"It's okay." Marquetta says. "Nobody's accusing you of anything. Lydia didn't realize you were staying here." She glances at Lydia like she's expecting her to say something. I feel better when she does.

"I'm sorry, ma'am. Marquetta's right. I had no idea you were a guest and was surprised when I walked in and...there you were." Lydia looks like she doesn't know what to do next. She glances at Marquetta and says, "I only came in here to ask about the linens in the dryer. I can wait for you...in the kitchen?"

Oh, man. Tara was starting to open up and now she looks super uncomfortable being here with Lydia. I get that. At least Lydia didn't actually accuse her of murder. That would have been like a huge disaster. I hope this doesn't blow my chance to ask Tara more questions.

"No need to wait for me, Lydia. I'll show you now." Marquetta turns to Tara. "Everything will be okay. Chief Cunningham is very thorough and Rick is helping him. They'll find the person who did this. Come on, Lydia. Let's go see what needs to be done."

Lydia apologizes again, and Tara mutters something about it being okay, but I know it's not. Then Marquetta tells me she thinks we should get back to work.

"I just wanna talk to Tara for a second."

"Alex..."

But Tara cuts her off. "It's okay. I don't mind."

"Don't be too long, Alex," Marquetta says, then turns and leads Lydia away.

I don't want Tara to feel any weirder than she already does, so I say, "Our laundry room is in the back end of the kitchen."

Both Tara and Miss Jones nod, then look at the dining room entrance. I turn to see what's going on now. Dr. Turner is standing in the doorway. She takes one look at me and rushes away.

"That was weird," I say.

"It was like she saw a ghost," Miss Jones says. "She's the coroner, right? Maybe she's worried about a conflict of interest."

Uh oh. That doesn't make Tara feel any better, either. Right now she's gotta be feeling like the world's against her. Maybe I can show her I'm on her side.

"I'll go talk to her." Miss Jones waggles her eyebrows a couple times, then hurries after Dr. Turner.

Tara looks like she's about to have a meltdown. If I'm gonna get her to talk, I have to make her feel better first. I hope I don't mess this up. "Marquetta was right. Chief Cunningham and my dad are working together to solve the case. They'll find the real killer. I'm sure you totally had a reason for going to the Inn. Have they asked you about it?"

"Yes."

"You should think it through before you talk to them anymore."

"Maybe I should have a lawyer present."

"You didn't kill Mr. Nicholas. Right?"

"No! Of course not. I just went there to hash things out and tell him exactly what I thought of him." She stops, squeezes her

160

eyes shut, and her voice cracks. "I didn't want him dead, though."

"How long were you in the room?"

"I was only there for a few minutes when his wife called. There we were with Henry, trying to tell me he loved me and the phone ringing. When I asked him if he'd talked to his wife about leaving her, he told me he hadn't. That's when I realized just how self-centered the man was and left."

"Where'd you go?"

Tara crosses her arms over her chest and her cheeks get real tight. She's looking super uncomfortable again, and I wonder if I'm pushing too hard. "It might give you an alibi," I say. "If they ask you where you were at the time of the murder, it will help if you don't have to think about it."

Tara sighs. "I feel so stupid. I went to the lighthouse to clear my head."

"Was anybody else there? Maybe we can find them."

"There was nobody around. It was dinner time, and the sun was going down. I took a photo or two of the sunset, but the wind was blowing and it was cold. I was only there for a few minutes. I followed the trail up to the parking lot. That only took a little while. Then I turned around and came back. It was just after six when I went up to my room and went straight to bed."

"That's like super early. So nobody saw you?"

"I was just so depressed—Henry made such a fool of me. I'd spent so much time thinking I'd found someone, and he turned out to be worse than my ex." Tara hugs herself and shivers. "I'm sorry, Alex. I can't talk about this anymore. I have to go."

"But..."

But it's too late. She's already on her way out the door when Miss Jones returns. They pass each other, but neither of them says anything.

"What's up with Dr. Turner?" I ask.

Miss Jones gets kinda flustered. She scrunches up her face. "She thought she was interrupting. That's all. Did you learn anything helpful?"

"Tara went to the lighthouse and nobody saw her."

"So, as far as the police are concerned, she doesn't have an alibi. You know what this means, right?"

"She's a strong suspect."

"Exactly. But my spy instincts are telling me she didn't do it."

"What are we gonna do, Miss Jones?"

"The first thing is you can call me Anita. You should know, I'm quite familiar with investigation techniques, and I think there's someone else the police are overlooking."

"Who's that?"

"Victor Pallett."

"Oh man, I would totally love to prove he's the killer. What makes you think he did it?"

"The man exhibits all the signs of a sociopath. My guess is he felt slighted at breakfast for some petty reason. I'm sure he's the one who salted your coffee, probably because your dad stood up to him. No offense, Alex, but he picked a fight with a child."

"It's okay. I get it." For once, I didn't mind someone saying that 'cause it was true. "But how did he know where Mr. Nicholas was staying?"

"What if he followed Tara to the room? You may not have noticed it, but he couldn't take his eyes off her during breakfast. So what if he was following her, went in after Tara left, and killed Henry Nicholas?"

Okay. That kinda makes sense. But I still have one big question. "Why? What's his motive?"

Anita shrugs, then takes a deep breath. "Why do bullies do anything? Maybe he didn't intend to commit murder, but flew off into a rage. He could have left and been in the clear because all the evidence points to Tara. For all we know, you and I may be the only ones who can save her. We should go check out that room for ourselves. Maybe the police missed something."

Oh man, Marquetta is so not gonna like this.

26

RICK

RICK STOOD NEXT TO ADAM at the entrance of Crusty Buns, listening to the hum of happy customers. Whether it was a table for two, four, or the big one for ten, most were taken. There were empty chairs scattered here and there, but the place was a madhouse. At the large table, a group of older men, mostly locals, clucked like old hens as they sipped coffee and munched on delectable desserts.

"As usual, this place is packed. And noisy," Rick said. "Even if we find this guy, it's going to be tough talking to him. What do you want to do?"

Adam inclined his chin at the line of people waiting to place an order. "Let's get in line."

"Okay." Rick followed in Adam's wake, letting the man in uniform blaze the trail through the maze of customers and tables.

By the end of the five minutes it took to work their way to the front of the line, Rick had spotted three people he thought might be Max Rado. When Adam nudged him, Rick realized he hadn't even thought about what he wanted.

Mary O'Donnell seemed to know Rick wasn't prepared to order. Perhaps it was because she saw the same thing ten times a day. Or maybe it was something akin to a grandmother's intuition with a young child. Either way, her Irish brogue made

Rick feel at home and relaxed when she made a suggestion. "How about a nice mug of today's blend and a blueberry muffin?"

"You know me too well, Mary."

"I know all my regulars. How's that lovely lass of yours?"

"Alex is doing just fine. Curious. Mischievous. Too smart for her own good."

"She's a smart one, she is."

Adam handed Mary a credit card. As she ran the transaction, he showed her a photo of Max Rado. "Have you seen this man?"

"Aye, Chief. Max was sitting at one of the back tables. I think he's still there. Was all by himself today now that his friend is dead."

"You know him by name?" Rick blurted.

"It's my superpower," Mary tittered.

Adam thumbed through to another photo and showed it to Mary. "This man?"

"Henry Nicholas. That's the one."

"Thanks, Mary. We'll take a look for Mr. Rado."

"I'll bring your order to you, Chief. I think there might be an open seat at his table."

Adam peered at the rear of the store, then took back his credit card and slipped it into his wallet. "It looks like most of the tables back there are filled."

"Aye, but you can just pull a chair over from another one." Mary wrinkled her nose. "You have my permission."

As they walked away from the counter, Rick whispered. "She knows Rado by his first name?"

Adam held up his receipt. 'Chief Cunningham' was printed at the top. "Haven't you ever looked at your receipt before? She gets everybody's name when they order."

"I never really looked closely. I'll have to do that the next time I'm in. I'm curious to see what she calls me." Adam ducked between a couple of tables, nodding as he did so. "There he is."

Just as Mary had said, Max Rado sat alone at a table for two. He had short-cropped dark hair, a scruffy beard, and wore a blue-and-red plaid shirt. There was an empty plate in front of him, along with a mug that was also empty. When he spotted them, his dark eyes flitted involuntarily to the open seat at his table. Even with a few vacant spots at the surrounding tables, Rado was basically penned in by other customers.

Rick recognized two men sitting nearby, the remnants of their visit—a few wadded up napkins and a pair of empty mugs —before them. They were B&B guests from Portland and had arrived three days ago. Tomorrow, they would leave. One of them saw Rick, nodded enthusiastically, and gave him a thumbs-up. Rick responded with one of his own.

Rado focused on Adam and asked, "Looking for a place to sit, Officer?"

"It's Chief. Cunningham. You mind if we join you?"

"You're welcome to the table. I've finished." He started to push his chair back.

"Actually, we'd like to talk to you for a few minutes." Adam's voice was stern, the implication clear—you don't have a choice.

"Me?" Rado's hand went to his chest. "What did I do?"

"This is more about what you saw."

Rado gestured at the empty chair, then reached out and grabbed another from a table for four. He caught the eye of one of the men sitting at the table. "You mind?"

The man raised his hand with his palm up. "It's all yours."

"So what did I see?" Rado asked as he positioned the chair he'd borrowed.

"This has to do with the murder of Henry Nicholas. By the way, this is Rick Atwood. He's a consultant for the Seaside Cove Police."

"Seriously?" Rado asked with the hint of a sneer. "The cops in this town hire consultants?"

"For murder investigations," Adam said matter-of-factly.

The smugness on Rado's face fell away. "Yeah, I guess so. Tough situation for a small-town PD."

"Exactly. You knew Mr. Nicholas?"

"We met at the Inn at their funky breakfast bar. Coffee there tastes like day-old swill. Food here's a lot better, too. So we came over to kill a little time." Rado winced. "Sorry. Bad choice of words."

Rick wanted to feel sorry for Ray, but he couldn't. There was only one person to blame for the Inn's poor reputation, and that was Ray. Except for the incident with the salted coffee, the B&B had never had a complaint. When there were times Marquetta couldn't make loaves of quick bread for the next day, they ordered muffins from Crusty Buns. The solution was more expensive than cardboard hockey pucks, but the guests never complained.

"Mr. Rado, were you in the courtyard of the Seaside Cove Inn on Monday at about five p.m.?" Adam asked.

"I was. Oh. You want to know about the woman. Well, Chief, the lady who runs this place had told me I should check out the sunset. I thought I might get some photos, so I grabbed my camera to go down to the harbor. As I was walking through the pool area, I heard a door slam. I looked up and saw this woman leaving Henry's room. I didn't pay her any more attention and went out the front entrance. When I went to take my first picture, I discovered the battery in my camera was dead."

Rick's stomach tightened. Now they had another witness who placed Tara at the scene. She'd been seen on her way in and out. How could she not have been in the room? "Had you ever seen the woman before, Mr. Rado?"

"Please, call me Max. No. Henry told me he'd come here with some woman, but she kicked him out of the hoity-toity B&B they were staying at."

Rick spotted another table where his guests were enjoying muffins and coffee. He knew for a fact that they'd come here based on his recommendation. Maybe this guy didn't appreciate what the B&B offered, but the ones who actually stayed at the B&B did. "That's my hoity-toity B&B," he said coolly.

Max made a face. "Sorry. That's what he called it. I'm sure it's a nice place."

"No problem. It's not for everyone. What did he tell you about this woman?"

"Not much. He said this trip was her idea. And that she was wound a little tight."

"Did the woman you see look upset?" Rick asked.

"She slammed the door pretty hard. I'd say that was upset."

"What's your line of work, Mr. Rado?" Adam asked.

"I'm an importer. I find rare items from overseas and match them up with buyers."

"Seaside Cove isn't exactly an international port. What brings you here?"

"I'm hoping to strike up a deal with the woman in charge of the *San Mañuel* recovery. Her name's Flynn O'Connor."

"Oh?" Rick raised his eyebrows. "Could be a hard sell."

"I'm a good salesman," Max said confidently.

And Flynn was fanatical about ethics. Rick had learned how dedicated she was during her stay at the B&B. There was no way she'd make any sort of deal with someone who wanted to sell artifacts from the *San Mañuel*. "Good luck with that. Did you meet anyone else at the Inn?"

Max frowned and stroked his scruffy chin. "Um...there were other people around, sure. Just people I ran into, you know? Like Henry."

"Do you recall a conversation between you, Henry Nicholas, and another man?"

"Oh, sure. Kiernan. Nice guy. Me and Henry were talking about the *San Mañuel* and Kiernan joined us. He said he was a diver. He's trying to get a job on the *Blue Phoenix*. You're probably familiar with it. Right?"

"It's Flynn O'Connor's boat," Rick said. "We know her quite well."

"Really?" Max's face lit up. "Can you put in a good word?"

Wow. This guy really was a salesman. Expecting an introduction or a recommendation after one meeting—and while they were doing a police investigation, no less. Rick shook his head. "I'm sorry, but I can't really recommend someone I don't know."

"No worries. Had to ask, you know?"

"Where might we find Mr. Walsh?" Adam asked.

"I've got no idea. He did say he was spending some time down at the harbor. I guess you could try there."

The *Blue Phoenix* had been docked when Rick walked by. Flynn was scheduled for at least one meeting today with one of the B&B's guests worked for a museum. She and her crew typically spent four days at the dive site, then returned to send artifacts to the lab and stock up on supplies. The question was, did Kiernan Walsh know their schedule? Or was he simply hanging around the harbor, hoping for the boat to return?

There was only one way to find out.

27

ALEX

ANITA CRANES HER NECK AND looks around the room. I think she's checking to see if we're alone. There's nobody here except the two of us. "Well, Alex?"

She looks impatient, like she's expecting me to agree to investigate with her right now. But I don't know that much about her. Anita's the one who reported the salt in the coffee, and then she pointed the finger at Mr. Pallett. All of a sudden, I'm not so sure he's the one who's responsible. What if Anita's the one behind all this? I could be talking to a killer right now.

"I dunno. I better talk to Marquetta."

"Why? All she'll say is you can't leave the B&B, right?"

Uh...yeah. But why is Anita so interested? If she is who she says she is, she should know the cops have already been over the room. There won't be anything left. "Why do you wanna go there?"

"The police miss things all the time. You know that, right?"

I try to swallow, but my throat is dry. I'm getting super uncomfortable talking to her like this. I back away, but almost trip when I bump into a chair. Anita grabs my arm. Before I can call for help, Marquetta rushes to my side.

"Alex, are you okay?" Marquetta pulls me close.

I wrap my arms around her. My heart is pounding like crazy. I nod and give her another hug.

Marquetta looks straight at Anita and asks, "What's going on here?"

"She bumped into the chair. I thought she was going to fall." Anita gives me a little smile. "Are you okay?"

Now that Marquetta's here, I feel a lot safer. I swallow and my throat's not so dry. "I just tripped. That's all. I'm fine, Marquetta."

"Alex, you're coming with me. We've got things to do in the kitchen." Marquetta puts a firm hand at my back to guide me away. She looks Anita in the eye and adds, "If you'll excuse us, I have to put Alex back to work."

I've never been so happy to hear Marquetta say those words. When we get into the kitchen, she guides me to the island and points at my stool.

"Sit. Now, what really happened out there?"

I check the room to see if we're alone. "Where's Lydia?"

"She's upstairs preparing the Mainsail Room. We were walking by the dining room when I heard you talking. Right now, I want to know what happened between you and Miss Jones."

The truth is, I can trust Marquetta and my dad, but I don't really know any of the guests...or Lydia. Maybe I should be more careful. Guess I should've thought of that before. "Me and Anita were talking with Tara and when Tara left, Anita said Mr. Pallett might have been the one who killed Mr. Nicholas."

"Wait. What?" Marquetta stares at me like I'm crazy. "That makes no sense."

"Anita thinks Mr. Pallett is one of those social...pathics. She was a spy, and she said he shows all the signs."

"Are you referring to a sociopath, Alex?"

"That was it! Is that the same thing as a psychopath?"

"Not exactly. One big difference is that sociopaths are more impulsive. Does this have something to do with the salted coffee?"

"Totally."

Marquetta blows out a long breath. "That is antisocial behavior, but this is the problem with jumping to conclusions about people, Sweetie. Was Mr. Pallett unkind to you when he tore into you? Yes. That doesn't necessarily make him the person who salted our coffee...or a killer. I think it would be best if you kept some distance from Miss Jones. I'm not saying you need to avoid her, just don't involve her in one of your investigations."

I avoid Marquetta's gaze by watching my shoes. What am I supposed to say? I like Anita. And I've never known a spy before. But what if she's not what she seems? Oh, wait, isn't that what a spy does? Ugh.

Marquetta lifts my chin and studies my face. "Are you not looking at me because you're going to ignore my instructions?"

"No." Marquetta's eyes are kinda sad, and that makes me sad, too. "I'm sorry I disappointed you, Marquetta."

She tilts her head to the side. Her forehead is puckered. "Why do you think that, Alex?"

"I thought she wanted to help Tara, but now I think maybe she tricked me."

Marquetta kisses my forehead, then pulls me in for another hug. "Sweetie, you've never disappointed me, and I doubt if you ever will. You do, however, worry me sometimes. You're too trusting."

I scrunch up my face. My dad says the same thing. I don't mean to worry them. I don't do it on purpose. And not telling Marquetta what I know about Mr. Pallett feels like I'm hiding something on purpose.

"What Anita said about Mr. Pallett? It kinda makes sense."

"Why's that?" Marquetta asks as she hops up on the stool next to mine.

"Because I heard him on the phone talking to someone he does business with. It sounds like this whole treasure hunting thing is a big scam. He's gonna tell people there's treasure out there and charge them to look for it. But he doesn't even have any idea where it is."

"I see." Marquetta blows out a long breath. "You know how much I hate it when people get scammed, but he hasn't done anything illegal yet. We can't stop him from planning something like that. If he does go into business, we can have Adam keep tabs on him. And besides, most of the treasure hunters come to town hoping to strike it rich, but knowing the odds are against them."

"So there's nothing we can do to stop him?"

"I think you should tell Adam what you overheard. It will be up to him to decide what he wants to do about it. But, speaking of Mr. Pallett, the reason Lydia's upstairs is that the young couple staying in the Mainsail Room caught me in the hallway. They have to leave because she's going into labor early and they want to get home so she can see her regular doctor. Kathryn Larkin wants to take the room."

"Why would they want to switch rooms? The Foresail Room and the Mainsail Room are exactly the same."

Marquetta looks at the butler door, then lowers her voice. "Miss Larkin wants to move into her own room. She's breaking up with Mr. Pallett."

My jaw drops and I blink hard. "For real?"

"It appears you're not the only one with doubts about the man."

"So I was right?" This is awesome. I so wanna do a little happy dance.

"I don't know. She didn't tell me why she wanted to end things, and she hasn't told him yet. But we can help her by getting the room ready and letting her know she can have it. What happens after that is up to her."

That's when it hits me. If Miss Larkin breaks up with Mr. Pallett, he's not gonna be happy. And he might wanna take it out on us...or her. "Marquetta?"

"I'm way ahead of you, Sweetie. If she's really taking the room, I'll call Adam and tell him to be on alert."

I just hope that'll be enough. Especially if he's the one who killed Mr. Nicholas.

28

RICK

RICK LOOKED UP TO HIS right as he and Adam approached the entrance to the Seaside Cove Marina. The B&B stood proud and tall on a small bluff looking out to sea. When they'd first arrived, Marquetta had given Rick and Alex a tour. She'd taken them to the back patio and pointed out the small maze of docks. Rick chuckled at the memory of Alex's reaction.

"What's so funny?" Adam asked.

"I was thinking about the first time Alex and I saw this marina. She called it tiny."

"It might be that. But back when Seaside Cove was nothing more than a fishing village, this little marina was a busy place and helped support the people who lived here." Adam waved to Joe Gray, who was sitting on the rear deck of his houseboat. "Be back to see you on our way out, Joe."

Joe waved with his left hand and shifted position in his chair, but didn't say a word.

Rick's and Adam's footsteps thudded on the wooden planks. Below those planks, water lapped against the dock pilings, creating a soothing rhythmic melody. Listening to the natural rhythms, Rick said, "He looks positively miserable."

"That he does. I think his broken arm has really set him back."

They continued on toward Jennifer Martin's bait and tackle shop. The Ugly Worm was located in an old shack she'd leased from the town and renovated. With its bright blue-and-white color scheme, the onetime eyesore the town council had wanted to tear down now drew a steady stream of customers from the local fishermen needing supplies and tourists in search of ocean-themed trinkets.

"She's really turned the place around. When we first got here, I'd look down at the marina and shudder at the sight of that shack. It was like a festering boil in the middle of all this serenity. Now we tell all our guests to stop by and check it out."

Adam paused before opening the door. "There's no question everything has changed over the years. The old-timers have a love-hate relationship with the tourists. They know we need them, but they hate the crowds. They miss the quiet of the old days, but in my opinion, it was being discovered as a destination that helped save the town."

"We all work together. That's how we survive."

"Exactly. Enough about that. Let's see if Jennifer has a minute to talk."

Jennifer Martin sat behind the counter, her elbows resting on the glass top, her gaze fixed on a point in space. Her red hair was parted on the left and cut straight a few inches above the shoulder. She wore a blue Ugly Worm Bait and Tackle tee shirt. After greeting Rick and Adam with a wide grin, she got up off her stool. "Thank goodness, a couple of live bodies."

"Slow today, Jennifer?" Adam asked.

"Today's been one of those days when even the worms are bored. I think my regulars are taking the day off. I got no idea why. But I'm pretty sure I know why you two are here."

"Why would that be?"

Jennifer glanced over her shoulder at the open window she used as an exterior service counter. "Well, Chief, when I get a visit from Seaside Cove's top cop and his sidekick consultant, it can only mean one thing. You're here to ask questions about a murder. Am I right, or am I right?"

"As usual, Jennifer, nothing gets past you. I'll bet you can even tell me what I'm going to be asking about."

"Well…" Jennifer stretched out the word, then stood and went to the window. "I have a great view from this spot. My money's on you being here to ask me about that guy I reported— the one who was hanging around Flynn's berth. What I don't understand is why. I already talked to your deputy. She's not exactly a perky thing, but she does get the job done."

Having been the subject of Jennifer's sharp tongue himself, Rick felt a little sorry for Amy. Here she was, trying to reboot her life after a severe trauma, and Jennifer was making snide comments about her. "Be nice. She came from a tough situation in LA."

Jennifer rubbed her chin as she contemplated Rick's comment, then her cheeks brightened. "Actually, I like Amy a lot. She helped my daughter when she had a flat tire on the way home from work one night. She's always polite, and she patrols through here on a regular basis. You got yourself a good one there, Chief. But you know me, Rick, they don't call me Sharp Tongue Jenny for nothing." She stopped for a beat, then asked, "So, what do you two want to know?"

"Is this the man you reported?" Adam held out the photo.

"That's the one. Kiernan Walsh, right?"

"What was he doing?"

"Nothing illegal. He was hanging out by Flynn's berth. But I got suspicious when Amy came through on patrol and he skedaddled. Something about him just wasn't quite right. I told Amy about it and she said she'd keep an eye out for him."

"I'll talk to her and see if she came up with anything. What else can you tell us about him?"

"I know he tried to talk to Captain Struthers at one point. I saw the captain getting off the *Blue Phoenix,* and this guy waltzed over and started chatting him up. Guy looked bold as could be when he went over there. When he left, he had his tail between his legs." Jennifer laughed. "Captain Struthers is nobody's fool, and I'm sure he saw through whatever smoke this Walsh guy was blowing."

They thanked Jennifer for her time and were on the way out when she called after them.

"Hey, Chief, did Joe Gray ever talk to you about his fall?"

"He did. He believes he was tripped on purpose. So far, it's his word against the man he's accusing. Why? Do you know something?"

Jennifer came around from the back of the counter. She stuck her hands in her pockets and her normal lighthearted attitude faded. "In all seriousness, I saw what happened. At least part of it. Looked like Joe got suspicious because there were three of them hanging around. From what I could see, it didn't look like that conversation went very well, either. Those three started laughing and Joe stormed off."

"So there were two other men hanging out with Walsh?"

"That's right. One of them called after Joe and then jogged over to talk to him. When the guy got close, it looked like Joe tripped. But I'm almost positive the guy bumped him on purpose. Walsh didn't do anything, but the third man went over to help Joe up."

Rick's eyes widened. Did this mean what he thought it meant? "Adam? Have you got Pallett's photo, too?"

"Sure do." He brought up a photo, then turned his phone around. "Is this one of the men, Jennifer?"

She snapped her fingers and pointed at the image. "That's him. He's the one who bumped Joe."

"His name is Victor Pallett. If you see him down here, let me know." Adam scrolled to another photo, then showed it to Jennifer. "Is this the other one?"

"That's him. What's his name?"

"Max Rado. We suspected he was connected to Walsh, but we weren't a hundred percent on it."

"I'm impressed," Jennifer said with a laugh. "You two are cleaning up crime all over this town. Anyway, I went over to help, too. Joe was pretty dazed because he hit so hard. I think he's losing his balance, but he was definitely upright and stable when that Pallett guy hit him."

Adam sighed, then looked at Rick. "Sorry, buddy, but I'm going to have questions for Mr. Pallett."

"No worries. If this guy did bump Joe on purpose, he needs to be held accountable. Jennifer, if it came to it, would you testify about what you saw?"

"Of course. I hate the idea of someone getting away with bullying a sweet old guy like Joe."

Rick did his best to avoid laughing. As he'd quickly learned, 'sweet' was not one of the adjectives typically used to describe Joe Gray.

"Thanks, Jennifer. Let's go, Rick."

When they were out of earshot of Jennifer's bait shop, Rick said, "She'd make a terrible witness. Wouldn't she?"

Adam screwed up one cheek and nodded. "I'm afraid so. She's way too biased. But it sounds like we've now got a link between all four of them."

Indeed they did. And that made Rick nervous because Victor Pallett had already demonstrated he had a temper.

Joe Gray was still sitting on the back deck of his houseboat as they walked by. He still looked miserable. "Hang in there, Joe. We'll be back in a bit," Adam called out.

"I'll be here. Got nowhere else to go," he grumbled.

They followed the dock to the right, went all the way to the end, and took another turn to where the *Blue Phoenix* was moored. Captain Struthers stood on deck watching Rick and Adam approach. Stern-faced, he showed no indication of emotion as he acknowledged them with a curt nod. He maintained an erect bearing as he came down the ramp to meet them.

"Morning, Chief. Morning, Rick. What can I do for you two today?"

"Looks like you're all alone, Captain," Rick said.

"Not quite. Most of the crew is in town. We'll be stocking supplies and heading back to the *San Mañuel* tomorrow. I've got a man coming back to relieve me in a couple of hours. As you both probably know, we can no longer leave the *Blue Phoenix* unguarded."

"I didn't realize there had been more sabotage attempts after those treasure thieves tried to sink her."

Struthers continually scanned the marina as he replied. "There haven't."

"Are you expecting another sabotage attempt?" Adam asked.

"We're not, Chief. But I don't take any chances." The captain gazed across the marina in the direction Rick and Adam had come. "I noticed you made a stop at the bait shop. Are you inquiring about Kiernan Walsh?"

"We are," Adam said. "We understand you had a conversation with him."

"He was waiting for us when we docked. Claimed he was a diver. Produced no credentials, but did say he was certified for scuba."

"What was your impression of him?"

The captain snorted. "Unreliable. Undisciplined. Not the sort of man I want on my team. I asked him about his certification, and he said he'd taken lessons down in LA. As you both know, every one of my team has military training. I'm not bringing on some weekend scuba warrior who thinks he can just walk on and go diving for four-hundred-year-old treasure."

"Did he leave after your interaction?"

"Yes. Although I did see him hanging around the marina this morning. That's one of the reasons we're taking turns standing watch. If he tries to come back and force his way on board, he's going to get a surprise. I've got a man in the cockpit who's armed. Hope you don't mind, Chief."

"Same crew? No changes?"

"No changes. I'd notify you if there were."

"Then I have no problem. We've checked out all your crew members."

"Captain, where was Walsh when you docked?" Rick asked.

"Sitting on that piling over there." Struthers pointed at a piling on the outside of the pier. "He was just sitting there like he didn't have a care in the world."

"Were you docked when Joe Gray fell and broke his arm?"

Struthers shook his head. "That happened before we got here. Ms. O'Connor told me the story. Apparently, she heard about it while she was in town. She also heard this Walsh might be linked to the death of that scuba diver. Yet another reason I wouldn't want to hire him. You think he somehow contributed to that diver's death?"

"All we have for the time being is what he told us in his initial statement. He was nearby when the incident occurred, but lost track of his friend," Adam said.

"Pure negligence, in my opinion. Keep me advised, gentlemen. Just say the word if there's anything you want me to do the next time he shows up. I have to say, it's a real shame about Mr. Gray. I have a lot of respect for him. If this joker had something to do with what happened to him, we'd be happy to detain him for you."

It was one of the few times Rick had seen Captain Struthers smile.

29

ALEX

IT ONLY TAKES ABOUT TEN minutes to finish getting the Mainsail Room ready. While Lydia does the vacuuming and I take out the trash, Marquetta goes to talk to Miss Larkin. When I get back to the room, Marquetta's got the door propped open and is helping hang clothes in the closet.

Marquetta sees me when I walk in and says, "Alex, stay here while I help Kathryn get the last of her things."

Miss Larkin's jaw tightens. She looks worried as she glances at the open door. "I can do it on my own."

"No. Not only will it go faster if I help, but it will also provide you with a little more protection. Let's go."

I'm still waiting alone in the room when Lydia walks in. She gives me a little nudge with her elbow. "I'll keep you company."

"Sorry. Leaving you alone wasn't very nice."

"Don't worry about it." She nudges me again. "Just don't run out on me again."

Waiting for Marquetta, I start to get kinda worried. Mr. Pallett scares me. Who knows what he'll do when he finds out he's being dumped. That's why I'm so relieved when Marquetta and Miss Larkin come back. With all of us working together, we get everything taken care of super fast.

"All right," Marquetta says. "Kathryn, why don't we go downstairs? We'll take care of your paperwork to get you checked in and then you can join us for lunch. While we're doing that, I'll call Chief Cunningham and tell him he should be on alert in case Mr. Pallett doesn't take this well."

Miss Larkin leans against the wall and lets out a long breath. "Thank you. I need some time to settle down. I'm way too keyed up to think about dealing with Victor. And please, all of you, call me Kathryn. You're the closest thing to friends I have right now. In fact, I'm not even sure my friends would have helped me as much as you three did."

While Marquetta gets Kathryn checked in, me and Lydia start making four salads. We put together bowls with a little spinach and some romaine lettuce, tomato, celery, and cucumber. Then we dice up some leftover chicken. When Marquetta and Kathryn join us, Marquetta takes over for me and asks me to tell Kathryn about the conversation I overheard.

Kathryn has a mug of tea in front of her. She keeps her hands wrapped around it. Her fingernails are painted a pretty red. She's pulled her white sweater around her, and she looks kinda cold.

"Are you worried about Mr. Pallett?" I ask.

"I shouldn't be. I deal with all kinds of people in my work."

"What do you do?"

"I'm a locksmith. It's the family business. When my dad retires, I'll be taking it over."

"We're kinda the same. Me and my dad moved here when he inherited the B&B."

Kathryn gives me a nervous smile. She's pretty when she smiles. That's when her dimples come out. Her teeth are a little crooked, and that makes her look like someone you'd just want to know. She turns to look at the kitchen door. "Are you sure he won't find us here?"

The truth is, maybe. That could totally be a problem. But I think she wants someone to tell her it's gonna be okay. Kinda like when my dad tries to make me feel better when something bad happens.

"Nah. He'll never come in here. Just like he didn't expect anyone to be listening in on his phone call."

Kathryn stares off into space for a minute, then looks at me. "So, what did you hear?"

I tell her about the tour business he wants to set up and how he doesn't know where the treasure is, but he's gonna make people think his tours will help them find it. "Marquetta says we can't do anything unless he breaks the law. But there's something else. He might have tripped someone down at the docks and caused him to break his arm."

She stares down at her mug. Her forehead's all puckered. "What exactly do you mean? Do you think Victor deliberately pushed this person?"

"We're not sure," Marquetta says as she puts down the salad plates.

Lydia's laying out the silverware, and Kathryn is looking super depressed. She sighs and her shoulders slump a little. After a few seconds, she swallows hard and looks at me.

"Do you have any proof that Victor did this?"

"Let's back up for a second." Marquetta sits on the other side of the island from Kathryn. "Joe Gray runs a charter service out of his houseboat in the marina. He just turned seventy, and he's generally in good shape, but his balance has been suffering lately. Apparently, he'd been talking to Victor and a couple of other men. Joe claims that when he walked away, Victor deliberately bumped into him. Joe lost his balance and fell. He landed hard and broke his right arm."

Kathryn's face has turned a pasty white. She's all fidgety now, too. "Joe Gray? That's the man Victor was complaining about. He said this local practically called him an idiot because of the business he wants to start here. Victor hates it when people think he's stupid. He can't stand it. As Alex found out firsthand, he's also got a temper. I hate to say it, but it's possible he did bump that poor man on purpose."

"Kinda like the guy at Halloween?" I ask.

"Yes. When I get home, I'm going to make sure I stay well away from Victor Pallett. Unfortunately, we drove here together, and I'm not sure how I'm going to make it back. To be honest, I'm afraid to be alone with him now."

"I don't blame you," Lydia says.

Marquetta reaches across the table and takes Kathryn's hand. "I agree with Lydia. You could get a rental car. We have an office here in town."

Lydia clucks a couple of times and puts her hand over her heart. "They're so expensive here. My husband had to rent a car when ours broke down. It was outrageous."

"How about if we drive you to San Ladron?" Marquetta says. "Once you're there, you should be able to rent a car at a reasonable rate. If you leave the day after Victor checks out, you shouldn't have to worry about running into him."

Kathryn blows out a long breath. "That would be wonderful. Getting away from him is going to cost me a fortune, but it will be worth it."

Marquetta looks up at the ceiling for a second, then at Kathryn. "You said you're a locksmith?"

"Yes. Licensed, bonded, and insured. Why?"

"Rick ordered some new hardware for the master bedroom, his office, and Alex's room. Let's talk to him about giving you a free night or two in exchange for having you replace those. Are you interested?"

Kathryn's jaw drops. "Of course. I can't believe you'd do that for me."

Marquetta's cheeks get a little pink. "Don't mention it. You're in a pretty tough spot. And because of circumstances beyond your control, you'll be stuck here for an extra day or two."

"I can't thank you enough, Marquetta. I just hope Victor doesn't do any damage once he finds out how nice you're being to me."

"Don't you worry about that. One of the nice things about a small town is the police can be very responsive. And Chief Cunningham will deal with any problems swiftly."

Marquetta's right, but if Mr. Pallett is a killer, I wanna be sure we put him away before he has a chance to hurt someone else. I'd especially hate to see something happen to Kathryn. I really like her. Plus, I feel kinda responsible for putting her in this situation.

We finish our salads without anymore talk about Mr. Pallett. Instead, Kathryn wants to know all about the wedding and how Marquetta and my dad met.

As we're cleaning up, Marquetta says, "Kathryn, I have a few things I want to show Lydia, but you're welcome to hang out here for a while if you don't want to go up to your room."

She looks at the clock. It's barely noon. She scrunches up her nose. "Actually, what I'd like to do is get out for a walk. This whole thing with Victor has me on edge. Isn't there a lighthouse around here?"

I point out the back toward the coast. "There's a path that goes to it over there. I can show you where it is if you want."

Kathryn looks at Marquetta. "If it's okay with you."

"Sure. I think it's a great idea. Alex, why don't you take Kathryn to the lighthouse and we'll tie up some of the wedding details when you get back."

While Marquetta and Lydia go upstairs, I show Kathryn the French doors at the far end of the kitchen. The view from the patio is awesome today. Blue sky. Some little puffy clouds on the horizon. The worry on her face seems to melt away as she takes it all in. "It feels so good to be rid of that man. I feel like a weight's been lifted."

I hope she's right, but I'm afraid things are gonna get worse before they get better. "Come on. It's this way."

Our feet crunch on the decomposed granite as I lead her toward the trail that winds along the coast.

30

RICK

AFTER TALKING TO CAPTAIN STRUTHERS, Rick and Adam returned to Joe Gray's houseboat. Joe was still sitting in the same place, looking just as miserable as when they'd first seen him. Rick couldn't remember ever seeing Joe sit for so long at one stretch. Normally, when Joe wasn't booking a charter for a customer, he was puttering around the two-story houseboat. If he wasn't sanding and painting the wood siding or trim, he was cleaning one of the large windows or tending to the plants on the fantail. But today, in a most uncharacteristic manner, he was doing none of those things.

"Permission to board?" Adam called out.

"Sure thing. Come on." Joe stood, winced as he straightened up, then went into the cabin and met them at the counter where he normally dealt with customers.

A sign for Gray's Sailing Charters, the letters painted in a pale green script that matched the trim of the houseboat, hung on the wall behind the counter.

"Hey, Joe. I haven't seen you since the accident. How are you doing?" Rick said.

"Never felt so useless in my life. Doc wants me to take it easy. Angela's on my case all the time. This whole mess is driving me crazy. So, what brings you two here?"

"Deputy Kama tells me you think Victor Pallett bumped into you on purpose. Do you still feel that way?"

"Of course I do, Adam. The man's an egotistical moron. He's a crook, too. When I saw him out there on the dock talking to those two others, I was sure he was up to no good. I went out to see what I could find out and..."

"Why?" Adam asked abruptly.

"Why what?"

"If you thought the man was a crook, and that he was 'up to no good,' why would you go out there alone?"

Joe's jaw muscles worked for a few seconds. He took a deep breath. "I probably shouldn't have, but after what he pulled at Crusty Buns, I figured he was trying to poach some of my customers. I wasn't about to let him get away with that."

In all the different versions Rick had heard about Joe's accident, Crusty Buns had never come up. "I haven't heard what happened there. Were you and Victor Pallett in some sort of altercation?"

"Well..." Joe avoided Rick's gaze, then rubbed the stubble on his chin. "I was talking to Devon and a few of the other guys. We meet there every morning. Mary calls us her most regular regulars." Joe's mouth curved into a sheepish grin. "Anyway, this guy came over and introduced himself. He asked if he could sit with us. Right after his butt hits the chair, he starts in about Joaquin Murrieta. He's selling us on his idea of running tours and maybe expanding into some charters. He even asked if anyone was interested in booking one."

"Did he know who you were at the time?"

"Probably not," Joe admitted. "It's not like we all did introductions or anything. Anyway, I made the mistake of telling him all those stories about old Joaquin hiding gold in the hills were false. He didn't appreciate my comments one bit. Got sort of obnoxious afterwards, so I reminded him he was the one who asked to sit with us and suggested he might want to find another table."

"Really know how to make friends, don't you, Joe?" Adam snickered as he jotted a note.

"Don't get smart with me, Adam. I can remember when you were just running around town in knickers."

Adam snorted. "Joe, you know as well as I do that I've never worn knickers. Come to think of it, I don't have a clue what they even look like."

"Well..." Joe huffed and waved his good hand in the air. "You know what I meant."

"I do. What made you think this guy was trying to poach your customers? The *Blue Phoenix* is on the opposite side of the marina from you. If those guys he was talking to on the docks were going to be booking tours with you, they would have stopped here on their way in. Right?"

Joe's expression turned all squirmy. To Rick, he looked like a man who quite literally had ants in his pants. "Fine. I didn't think they were customers. You happy?"

"Almost. You were being nosey, weren't you?"

"Adam, you're really trying my patience," Joe said as he scowled from behind the counter.

"Only doing the job you and the other fine folks in this town hired me to do."

"All right. I was curious. I knew that guy was trouble, but when I went out there, he apologized. I think he expected me to do the same, but I didn't. His friends got a kick out of it and were ribbing him about losing his touch. I got about halfway back here when he came running after me. That's when he bumped into me and knocked me down."

"Did any of his friends help you up?"

"One of them. Dark hair. Scruffy beard. Wore a red-and-blue plaid shirt."

Rick looked at Adam. "Sounds like Max Rado. Right?"

"Yep," Adam said absently as he flipped back a couple of pages and underlined Rado's name. He pulled out his phone and showed Joe the same photos he'd shown Jennifer. Joe agreed that the two men in the photos were the ones on the dock.

"So what's it mean, Adam?" Joe asked.

"We don't know yet. But there's a curious connection between these three men. And we're going to find out what it is. Now, do me a favor. If you see any one of these three, do not approach them. You call me if you think you're in any danger. In fact, call me if you see them at all. Okay?"

"Yeah. I can do that," Joe grumbled. "Can't do much else."

"Ah, Joe, you could do plenty if you set your mind to it. I think you just want to be miserable for a while. That's all."

Joe scowled at Adam, then said, "You can be a real pain sometimes, Adam."

"Part of my job description," Adam said with a wink. He looked at Rick. "You ready to go?"

"I guess so." Rick's phone pinged with a message from Marquetta. He felt his eyebrows rise as he read the screen.

"Something interesting?" Adam asked.

"It appears that Kathryn Larkin is splitting up with Victor Pallett. She wants to move to a different room."

Joe nodded and grinned. "Good. Getting what he deserves. Smart girl."

"You could be right." Rick acknowledged Marquetta's message with a reply that also told her he wasn't going to make it to the market.

They turned to leave, but when they got to the door, Joe called after them. "Hey, Adam? Thanks for taking an interest and for putting up with a cranky old man."

"No problem. You just remember what I told you. I don't want to hear you've had another accident at the hands of Victor Pallett or his friends."

Once they were on the dock and had a bit of distance between themselves and Joe's houseboat, Rick said, "What next? Lunch, maybe?"

Adam checked his phone and nodded. "I can drop you off at the B&B, if you'd like. Give you some time to make sure everything's okay. Maybe check out your Victor Pallett situation. I'm going to grab a sandwich at the market and go back to my desk. Kama's got the phone records for Henry Nicholas. I'll call you if I come across anything interesting."

"That's okay. I'd like to walk." Rick turned to leave, then stopped. "Adam? There is one piece of physical evidence that should help convict our killer."

"What's that?"

"The baker's box Tara saw in Henry's things. She's just sure it contains cupcakes and an engagement ring."

"You can't be serious."

"What do you mean?"

"You want me to get a search warrant for some cupcakes?" Adam snickered and held Rick's gaze. "Judge would love that one."

Rick's cheeks warmed at how ridiculous his idea now sounded. He averted his gaze and muttered, "Yeah. Guess so. I'll just head home now."

"Hey," Adam said and winked. "You sure you don't just need another trip to Crusty Buns?"

"Joe was right. You can be a real pain sometimes. See you later." Rick waved to Adam as he walked away. He definitely did not want to stick around to hear Adam's retort.

Adam's 4x4 followed the roundabout on Front Street to the second exit and turned up Main Street. While Rick was anxious to get back to the B&B, he also knew Marquetta had things under control. The real problem was Alex. The longer it took to wrap up this case, the higher the odds were that she'd decide to investigate on her own.

Rick stopped, looked in the direction Adam had gone, then did an about-face so he was facing the B&B. After a few seconds of internal debate, he did another about-face and went the same direction as Adam. He had one stop to make before he went home.

Keeping to the north side of Main Street, Rick walked quickly, scanning the south side, specifically focusing on Scoops & Scones. To his relief, the mayor was not out sweeping the sidewalk in front of her store. Once he knew he wasn't going to run into Francine, he darted over to the other side and continued on to Crusty Buns.

He surveyed the tables when he entered the store. Neither Rado, Walsh, nor Victor Pallett were here, but Mary O'Donnell was, as usual, hard at work. He meandered through the maze of tables, chairs, and people to where she was wiping down a table for two.

Mary saw him, gave her handiwork a final inspection, and welcomed Rick with an upbeat lilt in her voice. "Twice in one day. I'm honored."

"I wish I was here for another muffin, Mary, but I'm not. Have you seen Max Rado again?"

"Not so far. He might be in this afternoon. He does have a wee bit of an afternoon sweet tooth."

"He's got a couple of friends. Kiernan Walsh and Victor Pallett. Have you seen either of them?"

"Hmmm...Kiernan and Victor...not ringing any bells. He was with a couple of other men that one time, but Henry Nicholas is the only one whose name I know. Max usually bought for his friends. Maybe if you had a photo, I could help you more. Jog the old memory." Mary tapped her temple with her finger.

"I should get those from Adam. Tell you what, if Max Rado comes in, would you call me?"

"Of course."

"I have one more question for you. If Max bought for his friends, why do you know Henry Nicholas's name?"

"Ah, simple. Max didn't buy for him." Mary's attention was suddenly pulled across the room to the counter. "Oh no. Angus is taking an order. My husband is good in the kitchen, but I don't dare trust him with the cash. I've got to go, Love."

Mary tossed Rick an exaggerated wink, grabbed her towel and the tray with the dirty dishes, and bustled away. Making his way back to the front door, Rick scanned the store's interior. Mary was still as sharp as could be, but Angus was becoming more forgetful. Someday, the two of them would be forced to retire and sell Crusty Buns. He just hoped it wouldn't undergo too many changes.

Rick chuckled as he walked out. Oh great. He was starting to sound like a local.

31

ALEX

IT'S NOT FAR TO THE lighthouse from the B&B. My dad says it's less than a half mile. On a nice day, it's a fun walk, but when the wind picks up or it's foggy, it can get super cold. Today it's not bad, and the walk goes fast with Kathryn. She tells me about Mr. Pallett, and it's so obvious she's totally done with him.

It only takes us about ten minutes to get to the lighthouse. When we come around the turn and she sees it, Kathryn stops and stares. "It's like something straight out of the past! It's gorgeous."

"It doesn't work anymore. My teacher told us they turned it off in the eighties."

Kathryn pulls out her phone and takes a picture. "That must seem like ancient history to you. Even to me it does, and I'm probably fifteen years older than you."

"I'm eleven." I don't mention the 'and a half.'

"Okay, fourteen." Kathryn chuckles. "Hey, let's take a selfie!"

"Okay."

We get closer to the lighthouse and find a spot on the trail where Kathryn can get some of the ocean, too. "One, two, three." She gets the photo. "Again, funny faces this time."

Kathryn takes three more shots. We both stuck out our tongues on the first one. Then she made an angry face while I kept my eyes closed. On the third one, we both did a zombie imitation.

"You gotta send those to me."

"I'm texting them right now."

My phone pings a few seconds later. I check the message. "Awesome! I got all four. I gotta show these photos to my dad and Marquetta." I close the last photo and take another look at the message. "Holy moley."

Kathryn pulls back and looks at me. "What, Alex?"

"The photo Tara took. I bet that would prove she was here when the murder took place! I need to get back."

"Oh. Okay." Kathryn looks around the area. It's only us out here. Today, there are no other tourists. "Go ahead. I think I'll walk a little further."

"The trail goes up to the parking lot. It's not even half the distance we already walked."

"What if I get lost?"

"You won't. Just follow this trail. There's another one not far from here, but you don't wanna take that. Nobody uses it."

"One thing I can tell you, Victor would never walk all the way out here. And he doesn't do tourist things. God only knows why he's starting a business that involves anything to do with nature."

"I don't think he's gonna be going out with his customers. It sounded like he was gonna give them a map. You know, like an old-time treasure map."

"Classic Victor. Do the minimum, but charge the maximum. It's so peaceful out here. I'd like to spend a little more time. Why don't you go do what you need to do?"

"You sure you'll be okay?"

"Positive. Thank you for showing me the way out here." Kathryn gives me a hug, then turns and heads over to the lighthouse.

I start to walk back, but when I get to the bend in the trail, I stop and look for her. She's standing next to the fence along the cliff. She looks kinda lonely.

I don't like the idea of leaving her alone out here, but I need to check that photo. I look both ways on the trail again. We haven't seen another person since we left the B&B. Kathryn's gonna be totally fine. I turn around and start walking home.

I keep checking over my shoulder all the way back, but she's never there. Even when I go through the French doors to the kitchen, she still hasn't caught up. I guess she stayed to hang out and enjoy the view.

There are noises coming from the laundry room. It sounds like Marquetta might be doing laundry, but when I look in, it's Lydia. She's just pulling a sheet out of the dryer. "Do you want help folding?"

"Sure. If you have time. They get a little awkward."

"How are you liking working here so far?"

Lydia laughs, then looks at the open doorway to make sure we're alone. "This is so much better than working for Ray. He's just so grumpy all the time."

"That's what my dad says."

We each grab an end of the sheet and fold it in half, then fold it again. When the sheet gets smaller, Lydia takes my end and finishes the folding. The bottom sheet and the pillowcases are already done and sitting on the work table.

"Do you know where Marquetta is?"

"She said she was going to take care of the bookings so your dad doesn't have to do it when he gets home. It's nice they can help each other out."

"Marquetta's awesome. She practically ran the place by herself when Captain Jack died."

Lydia's mouth opens a little. She sounds amazed when she says, "Wow. That must have been hard for her. I saw her a few times at the market and she always looked so determined. I didn't realize she was doing this all on her own."

"Her friend Traci helped out when things got super busy, but most of the time, she did it all. Of course, the place wasn't that busy then, either. Hey, I have to go tell her something."

Lydia's putting the final load from the washer into the dryer when I leave. On my way out the butler door and to the dining room, I see Dr. Turner. She's dipping a tea bag in a mug of hot water. I bet she'd know if Tara's photo would help prove her alibi.

"Hey, Dr. Turner."

She whirls around, takes one look at me, and her eyes get real wide. There's a splash when she drops the tea bag in the mug. She holds up her hand like she's warning me to stay back. "I have to go, Alex." She bumps into one of the tables as she rushes out of the room. Her mug is still sitting where she left it, a small puddle next to it on the counter.

I'm so shocked that I stand there gaping at the empty doorway. "Totally weird," I whisper, then wipe up the mess and go looking for Marquetta.

Lydia was right. Marquetta is at my dad's desk working on the bookings. I sit in one of the visitor's chairs. She holds up a finger, but doesn't look up at me. "Hang on, Sweetie. I'm almost done." A few seconds later, she clicks the mouse and closes the laptop. "There. We're all caught up. What's going on? Did you get Kathryn to the lighthouse?"

I tell her about our walk and how we didn't see anybody else. Then I bring up the photos. "Tara told me she took one when she was out there. On my way in, I saw Dr. Turner getting some tea. I was gonna ask her if Tara's photo might help prove her alibi for the time of the murder, but she ran away from me."

Marquetta puts her hand over her mouth and starts to laugh. What's up with that? My face gets hot. This totally sucks. Marquetta doesn't make fun of people.

"I'm sorry, Sweetie. I think I know what happened. It's a bit of a misunderstanding. Dr. Turner's just trying to honor your dad's wishes."

I scrunch up my face and stare at Marquetta. "What wishes?"

"He was hoping to keep you from getting involved in the murder investigation. He asked her to not talk to you about the case. I'll straighten things out for you." Marquetta taps her chin with her finger and looks up at the ceiling. "In fact, let me see if I can deal with this right now. I don't want her feeling like she can't walk around freely."

Marquetta calls Dr. Turner. She asks if they could meet in the living room. Then she hangs up. "Let's go. She said they were getting ready to go out for a while."

Dr. Turner and her husband are sitting on the couch when we get downstairs. When the doc sees me, she stiffens and looks at her husband. "We were going to go walk around downtown."

"This will only take a few minutes," Marquetta says. "I think there's been a bit of a misunderstanding. Rick asked you to not talk to Alex about Mr. Nicholas. Right?"

The doc presses her lips together, then takes a quick look at me. "Yes."

"I don't think Rick fully thought through what he was doing when he made that request," Marquetta says. "He put you in a terrible position. I'm sorry about that."

Dr. Turner lets out a big sigh and leans into her husband. It's one of the few times I've seen her actually be anything other than serious. "Oh, good. That's a relief."

I feel kinda silly. Here I am, the one they're talking about, and all I wanted to do was ask a question. It wasn't even about the murder. At least, not directly.

"I'm sorry I scared you, Dr. Turner."

"And I'm sorry I ran away. It wasn't your fault. You just startled me, that's all."

"Can I ask you a question?"

Dr. Turner sits up straighter. She looks at Marquetta.

"It's fine," Marquetta says. "Alex is very...persistent."

At least she didn't say annoying. "It's about a photo someone took."

The doc's eyebrows go up and she mouths a silent 'oh'. "I see. What about it?"

"Could a photo be used to prove someone was in a place when they said they were?"

"It depends. If it was taken with a device that's GPS equipped, the coordinates would be embedded in the metadata."

"So it would work!"

"Not necessarily. The timestamp might not be reliable depending on the type of device. Basically, it all comes down to whether or not the time could be changed. A phone's timestamp would be almost irrefutable. The timestamp on a camera, however, can be changed by the user. That means someone could set a different time on the camera before the picture was taken. Forensics would be able to determine if the metadata— oh, sorry." All of a sudden, she stops and her cheeks get a little pink. "I'm a bit of a techno nerd. Professional hazard. What's this for?"

"Tara told me she went to the lighthouse after she was at the Inn. She took a picture while she was there. That would prove she was somewhere else when the murder happened. Right?"

The doc shakes her head. "Not until there's a firm time of death. Our office has been busy, but my boss wants me to start the autopsy tomorrow. Even if I come up with something, the police would still need some physical evidence to establish the exact time of death. Without that, there's no way to help Tara."

My shoulders slump. I hadn't thought of that.

Dr. Turner winces when she sees my reaction. She tries to sound hopeful when she says, "I'm sure the chief is trying to get the phone records, but that's not really my area."

Ugh. Even if they already have those records, my dad's never gonna let me see them. I gotta figure something else out.

32

RICK

RICK CLOSED THE FRONT DOOR to the B&B and immediately heard voices coming from the living room. He recognized Dr. Turner's voice, which was followed by one he didn't expect to hear— Alex's.

His temper rose at the thought of how quickly Dr. Turner had ignored his request to avoid discussing the case with Alex. He entered the living room, prepared, but not for what he found. Marquetta and Alex stood a few feet away from the couch where the Turners sat. Flames from the gas log in the fireplace licked at the air, casting the room in a cozy atmosphere. They all looked fully at ease.

"Rick..." Dr. Turner said when she saw him. The color in her cheeks blanched and she shot a worried glance at Marquetta.

"You're home. Good," Marquetta said. "I was just telling Dr. Turner it's okay for her to talk to Alex. I explained how you were trying to keep Alex away from the murder investigation, but that you also wouldn't want to make a guest uncomfortable by forcing her to avoid one of us. Are you okay with that, Rick?"

The heat in Rick's cheeks was still there, but for a completely different reason now. What had he been thinking? Putting the onus to avoid his daughter on a guest? He stepped forward and rested his hands on Alex's shoulders.

"Dr. Turner, I'm so sorry. Marquetta's right. I never realized what I was asking of you. My apologies if that caused you to be uncomfortable."

Alex stepped back, planted her feet, and put her hands on her hips. "You made her run away from me, Daddy!"

The four adults burst into laughter. The doctor's brown eyes crinkled as she leaned into her husband. Greg Turner gave his wife a hug and chuckled.

"I haven't seen Patty so panicked in all the time I've known her. When I asked what was bothering her and she told me she was trying to avoid your daughter, I almost fell on the floor laughing."

Giving her husband a solid whack on the shoulder, his wife added, "I have to admit, it is pretty funny—now that it's all straightened out." She stood. Her long, dark hair cascaded over her shoulders. "If you'll excuse me, I'm going to get that cup of tea I wanted. I might also need one final cookie."

"Well, I never miss out on an opportunity for a sugar break." Greg stood, looked around, and sighed. "I'm going to miss this place. And your baking." He winked, then followed his wife.

Rick peered at Marquetta. "What just happened?"

"They have to leave in the morning, but we have something else to talk about upstairs. Your office, boss. Now."

As they climbed the stairs, Rick said, "Somehow I have a feeling I'm the boss in name only."

Once they were in Rick's office with the door closed, Marquetta and Alex sat on the couch and Rick pulled over one of the visitor chairs. Marquetta told him about what Dr. Turner had gone through to avoid Alex, then asked her to explain about Tara's photo and how the timestamp might eventually clear her.

"I guess this means until we can find some proof of exactly when Henry Nicholas died, Tara's still a suspect."

"Daddy, she didn't do it."

"I want to believe you, kiddo, but you know Adam and I can only go by the facts. Let me call him. Susan Nicholas did say she spoke to Henry at about five. If we get the exact time of that one telephone call, maybe it will help clear things up."

Rick dialed Adam's cell. He picked up on the third ring. "You're missing me already?" Adam chuckled.

"Actually, I was wondering if you'd checked those phone records?"

"I'm looking at them as we speak. Why?"

"Tara Amengual took a photo at the lighthouse sometime around five. I haven't seen the timestamp, but depending on the time of that call, it could put her in the clear."

"Let me look." Other than the sounds of paper rustling, there was silence for about ten seconds. "Henry Nicholas called his wife at 4:58 pm on Monday. The call lasted twelve minutes."

"That's a long time for two people to talk when one of them wants to get out of the relationship," Rick said.

"The wife did say she was trying to persuade him to come home. I'm guessing that's the truth. Hey, gotta go, Deputy Kama says I have an important call on the other line."

Rick relayed the information to Marquetta and Alex. "We have an exact time for when we know Henry Nicholas was alive. If Tara's photo was taken after 5:10 pm, she's in the clear."

Beaming, Alex sat up straight. "I'll ask her."

"You'd better let me do it, kiddo."

"But it was my idea!"

Raising a precocious child like Alex was always a challenge. She'd want to see the timestamp for herself, and short of locking her in her room, there was no way he could stop her. He sighed in resignation, knowing he needed to pick his battles. "How about if we ask her together?"

"Okay. I'm good with that. Daddy, since Tara's gonna be in the clear, you're gonna need another suspect."

Marquetta's eyes cut back-and-forth from Alex to Rick several times. He could tell she was struggling to hold back her amusement.

"What?" Rick asked.

"She's right, you know."

Rick leaned his head back and sighed at the ceiling. "Not you, too." He held up his hands in surrender. "Okay, who's this new suspect?"

"Mr. Pallett," Alex said proudly.

It took a moment for Rick to think of what to say. Pallett was probably the worst possible suspect. If he found out he was under investigation, who knows what he'd do? "You can't be serious. Have you got any proof?"

"He's running a scam."

"Alex overheard him talking to a business associate about selling Joaquin Murrieta buried treasure tours," Marquetta added.

"Being a tour operator isn't much of a crime in this town. Alex, just because you don't like the man, doesn't mean he's a killer."

Alex shook her head. She held his gaze and spoke defiantly. "That's not why I think he's the killer. Dr. Turner says he's a sociopath. He doesn't have a conscience."

"Why not look at him, Rick? Kathryn was telling us the same sort of thing. It was the reason she moved to the Mainsail Room."

"How's you move her there? That room's already occupied."

Marquetta explained about the cancellation and the deal she'd made with Kathryn Larkin.

"The things I missed this morning. Tell you what. I'll be working with Adam again this afternoon and I'll pass along all of this. If he thinks Pallett's worth looking into, we'll do it. Until then, let's all keep a low profile around him. We don't need him pulling another stunt. For now, I could really use some lunch."

"We already ate, but I can put something together for you in no time," Marquetta said. "Come on."

Walking through the living room, Rick noticed a paperback novel, a mystery from the B&B's small library, on the coffee table. He wasn't surprised. Guests had a tendency to leave books all the time. The odd thing was, it hadn't been there when he'd been talking with the Turners. And now, whoever had been reading that book wasn't here.

If it was still there later, they could always shelve it where it belonged. Just as they reached the dining room, though, Tara Amengual appeared in the doorway. She held a steaming mug in her hands. She glanced down at the mug, then back to Rick.

"Is it okay to take this to the living room? I thought I'd read for a little bit."

"Of course," Marquetta said.

Rick nodded his agreement, saw that Alex was watching him expectantly. If he didn't ask within about the next five seconds, he knew Alex would. "Tara, I understand you took a photo while you were at the lighthouse on Monday evening."

She raised her eyebrows. "Yes. I told Alex about it. Why?"

"It'll prove you couldn't have murdered Mr. Nicholas," Alex said.

"I actually took several photos while I was there. A couple of selfies and a couple of the lighthouse itself. Let me show them to you." Tara set down the mug, pulled out her phone, and brought up the first image. She shoved the phone at Rick.

While Rick would have liked to have phrased Alex's statement a bit more diplomatically, he couldn't disagree with the intended purpose. "Just tap the little information icon at the bottom, please."

Tara turned the phone so she could see the screen, tapped the icon, then showed it to Rick. Sure enough, the first photo had been taken at 5:14 pm. There was no way she could have gotten to the lighthouse in the four minutes from the time Henry's call ended until the timestamp in the photo.

"You said you took other photos, too?" Rick said.

"Yes! Look!" She scrolled to the next one.

The timestamp was 5:22 pm. There were two others, one at 5:26 and another at 5:32. The final photo Tara had taken was of the B&B. Rick recognized the location. Tara had taken it from the trail at the edge of their property, looking toward the house.

"Congratulations, Tara. It looks like you have a rock-solid alibi. I'll call Chief Cunningham. He may want to stop by and document those photos himself."

Rick called Adam, told him what he'd discovered, then asked if he'd had lunch. "No? Well, then come on over. You can talk to Tara and then Marquetta will save you from a deli sandwich."

"Does Marquetta have any of those chocolate chip cookies around?"

"Only if you hurry," Rick said.

33

ALEX

Hey Journal,

I did it! I got Chief Cunningham to look at Tara's photos and say she's not a suspect anymore. Once he saw the proof, he realized she couldn't have been the killer. Now that Tara's in the clear, I feel lots better. I still want to prove Mr. McNasty did it, but that could be super hard to do, but I'll find a way.

My dad and the chief are having lunch in the kitchen. It's nothing fancy, just a couple of salads and turkey sandwiches that me and Marquetta put together. Marquetta gave Lydia the grocery list so she could do the shopping while we go to Crusty Buns to talk with Traci and Grandma Madeline about the wedding. It's gonna be here in a week and she wants to make sure everything's ready.

I'm gonna do some research before we go. Bye for now,
Alex

I sit on the edge of the bed and open up my laptop. Leaning over the keyboard, I do a search for 'Victor Pallett.' I'm hoping there's something on social media about him, but when I find his profile, I see he doesn't post much. He's only got a few friends, too. That figures. This has been a huge waste of time and now I have to go. I totally don't wanna miss a trip to Crusty Buns. Mrs. O'Donnell's chocolate chip muffins are awesome!

On my way downstairs, I knock on the door to Kathryn's room. She doesn't answer. Maybe she's in the kitchen? When I get down there, my dad and Chief Cunningham are finishing their sandwiches.

"Has anybody seen Kathryn?" I ask.

They all just shake their heads. Marquetta suggests I text her to see how she's doing. I tell her that's a great idea, send the message, and get a response a few seconds later, telling me she's still wandering around the lighthouse. Now that I know she's okay, I feel better. Marquetta gives a cookie to my dad and Chief Cunningham. She also puts one in a baggie, and when she hands it to the chief, she almost scolds him.

"I've known you since fourth grade, Adam Cunningham. I know what a sweet tooth you have. I've texted Traci and told her I'm sending a cookie home with you. This is for her. If you cheat on me and eat this, I will cut you off."

The chief looks at the baggie for a second, then screws up his cheeks and asks, "For how long?"

"As long as it takes to make you regret your decision."

"Fine. I'll see that she gets it."

Marquetta wrinkles her nose at him. "You'd better. I'm a lot tougher than I was in grammar school."

The chief blows out a long breath and whispers, "Don't I know it!"

"Rick, Alex and I are going to Crusty Buns. We're meeting with Traci and Mom to make final preparations for the wedding. And Lydia's got the grocery list, so you're off the hook."

My dad grins at Marquetta. "Meeting on neutral territory?"

"Something like that. Are you going to be around?"

"He's busy," the chief says. "We'll be out looking for Walsh and Pallett. I'd also like to talk to Rado again. I've got questions for all of them." The chief looks at my dad. "If you're up for it."

My dad looks at Marquetta before he answers. "What about Lydia? Are you sure she'll be okay?"

"She'll be fine. I've also told her to call me if she has any questions."

"Then I guess my honey-do-list has been taken away. I suppose I'm with you, Adam."

Me and Marquetta say goodbye and walk to Crusty Buns. The mayor is busy serving customers at Scoops & Scones, but she waves to us as we pass. On the opposite side of the street, Laurel, the lady who runs Hot Feet, has put out some shoes that she's selling at half price. I peer into Isabella's Pet Shoppe as we pass. I'd love to have a dog, but both my dad and Marquetta say it would be a problem with all the guests we have. The message on the sandwich board in front of Crusty Buns reads, 'Do something to sweeten your day!'

Traci and Grandma Madeline are already at one of the small round tables for four near the front of the store, so me and Marquetta go to the counter and order. I get my usual chocolate chip muffin and then Mrs. O'Donnell beams at Marquetta.

"Well, Marquetta, how's the bride-to-be? Have you and Rick made plans yet for a honeymoon?" Mrs. O'Donnell looks at me and winks.

Uh oh. I hope Marquetta doesn't catch on that I've been in here talking to Mrs. O'Donnell about that.

"I've been swamped, but Rick just hired Lydia after she quit the Inn. I have time now to get some actual wedding planning done."

Mrs. O'Donnell laughs, then says, "Ah. The planning's fun, but it's nothing compared to the sweetness that comes on a good honeymoon."

Marquetta's cheeks get all pink and she stammers, "Well... um, Mary, I don't know if we'll be able to leave right now."

"Don't worry, lass. Where there's a will, there's a way. And sometimes, those ways are smaller than you think."

OMG. I better get Marquetta away from Mrs. O'Donnell before she totally blows Operation Honeymoon! "Thanks, Mrs. O'Donnell! Marquetta, I don't think Grandma Madeline has much time."

"You're right."

I tug on her hand and pull her toward the table up front, but as we walk, she keeps glancing back over her shoulder at Mrs. O'Donnell. When she asks me if I have any idea what that was all about, I shrug my shoulders and try to sound surprised. "Nah. You know how she is. She likes to embarrass people."

Marquetta shoots a last look at the counter, then huffs. "Maybe you're right, Sweetie."

I get us to the table before Marquetta starts asking more questions and gives Grandma Madeline a big hug.

"How's my favorite granddaughter?" Grandma Madeline asks.

I'm like her only granddaughter. And I'm not official yet, either. But it's awesome to hear it since I've never met any of my real grandparents. "I'm good, Grandma. This is totally gonna be the best wedding ever!"

"I'm sure it will be, dear. Marquetta, you are planning to do something more with your hair than just a ponytail, aren't you?"

"Yes, Mom. Abby Grayson is going to style it. She's quite talented."

"Ken Grayson's wife? Where does she work? Are you sure she's any good?"

Oh, brother. I hope Marquetta's not gonna be like this with me when I grow up.

"She had her own salon in San Ladron before she married Ken. She's working part-time out of their home, but she's thinking of opening a spa here."

"Oh." Grandma Madeline makes a face. "She works out of her home? Are you sure about this?"

"She's coming to the B&B Wednesday morning. Rick's already agreed I can use the master bedroom to get ready and he'll use his office. It's all settled. Stop worrying, Mom."

Mrs. O'Donnell shows up with our order. Marquetta got a Coconut Macaroon Muffin. It looks pretty good, but I still love my chocolate chip. Marquetta takes a bite of her muffin, moans like she's in heaven, then looks up at Mrs. O'Donnell.

"You've outdone yourself, Mary. These are wonderful."

"Thank you, love. How sweet of you to say, but it's Angus who deserves the credit." Mrs. O'Donnell winks at Marquetta. "I know if you're happy, that's a true compliment."

Marquetta looks at me. "You don't know what you're missing, Alex."

I've already taken one bite of my muffin, and I'm totally in heaven. "No way. These are my favorite."

"Aye, lassie. You and Angus are much the same. He won't give up his chocolate chip muffins for anything. That's why they're on the menu every single day." She stops, looks toward the back of the store, then leans in closer. "Looks like trouble a'brewing."

We all turn to see what she's talking about. There's a woman with blonde hair at the back of the store. It's Flynn O'Connor. She's wearing a dark blue camp shirt, one of her favorites, and she's standing next to a table talking to a man I don't recognize. "Who's that with Flynn?"

"His name's Max Rado."

"He's the man Daddy's looking for!"

Mary slaps herself on the forehead. "Ah. I've been so busy with customers that I forgot to text your father. He wanted to know when Max came back. I'm suspecting he's a bit of a shyster. He's been trying to put the pressure on Flynn. Poor man doesn't realize what stern stuff we Irish girls are made of. She'll make mincemeat of him."

Now that I know what's going on, it all makes a lot more sense. Flynn's jabbing her finger at the guy like she's super angry. Then she turns to leave. As she's coming toward us, I wave a couple of times. She doesn't see me until she's near the front of the store, but then she changes direction so she can join us.

Mrs. O'Donnell clucks a couple times, then laughs. "Did you give him what for, Flynn?"

Flynn growls and glares in the direction she came from. "That man is impossible. He actually thought I was going to let him sell artifacts from the San Mañuel. I got his attention when I told him if he ever set foot on the Blue Phoenix, I'd have one of Captain Struthers' men shoot him on sight."

"You can do that?" I ask, my eyes wide.

Flynn puts her hand over her mouth and laughs quietly. "No. But it did seem to scare the pants off him!"

Everybody laughs except for Grandma Madeline, She's looking kinda grumpy. I gotta admit, we're not getting much done on the wedding, but we are having fun—well, most of us. "Marquetta, we should text Daddy and tell him one of the men he's looking for is here."

"I'm ahead of you, Sweetie. It's already done."

Across the table, Traci's also sending a text. "And I've sent Adam the same message. I hope they get here before this guy leaves."

Grandma Madeline huffs. "Really, ladies. All this murder folderol. I thought we were here to talk about the wedding."

Oh well, I guess she's right. If we don't do that, Marquetta might never become my mom.

34

RICK

RETURNING TO THE SEASIDE COVE Inn wasn't what Rick had expected to do next, but Adam wanted to see if Walsh and Rado were in their rooms. He said he 'had a feeling' they might get lucky and find one of them.

"Now you're sounding like Alex," Rick said as the 4x4 pulled into the parking lot behind the Inn.

"What about Nancy Drew? You think she'll stay out of this?"

Rick gazed out the side window, trying to focus on the faded white line of the parking space rather than the truth. "I don't think so. She's convinced Victor Pallett is the killer. In my opinion, the guy is nothing more than a jerk, but if it keeps Alex away from danger and he doesn't find out, I'm okay with her spending time on him."

Adam turned off the ignition, released his seatbelt, and twisted so he could face Rick. "She thinks it's Pallett?"

"Oh, no. Let's not go down that path."

"I'm just saying, she's had some pretty good hunches in the past."

"I don't think this is one of them. She's convinced he's the one who salted our coffee because he felt slighted. With no proof whatsoever, she extended that to committing murder. It's a big leap, Adam."

Adam sat quietly for several seconds, and when he spoke, his tone was upbeat. "Far be it from me to tell you how to handle the munchkin, but let's just keep tabs on what she does. You never know what she might turn up."

"Like I said. If we can keep her out of danger, I'm happy. By the way, we did have another problem with Pallett you should know about. I'm surprised Marquetta didn't say something at lunch."

He told Adam about the room swap and how Kathryn Larkin was splitting up with Victor. "Just an FYI in case he tries to do something."

"I'll pass this along to Deputy Kama. If Pallett gets the least bit unruly, we'll be there in no time. Let's go see if either of these guys are in their rooms."

They crossed the parking lot, doing a quick scan for the men's cars as they walked. Max Rado's was parked in the lot, but they didn't see Walsh's. They went to Room 104 first. Adam knocked firmly, but there was no answer.

"He must be walking around town or something," Rick said.

"Or he's out with Walsh. We still don't know how well these two know each other. Let's check Walsh's room."

At Room 111, it went the same. A knock. No answer. But while Adam was busy knocking, Rick's phone pinged. A couple of seconds later, Adam's did the same.

"Marquetta just sent me a message that Rado's at Crusty Buns," Rick said.

Adam nodded. "Traci sent me the same thing. Let's go."

By taking a shortcut and parking in the back alley, they were walking in the door in less than five minutes. Marquetta, Alex, Traci, Madeline Weiss, and Flynn O'Connor were all crowded around a table near the front. Traci saw them first and motioned for them to join the group.

"Let's go see what's up," Adam said as he strode to the table.

They exchanged greetings all the way around, and then Traci looked at Flynn. "Tell Adam what you told us."

"Chief, I don't know if it's anything or not, but Max Rado was trying to talk me into letting him sell some of the recovered artifacts."

Adam snorted. "He told us that the first time we talked to him. The guy obviously doesn't know who he's dealing with, but he hasn't actually done anything, right?"

"No, but there was something he said when he was trying to butter me up in the beginning. He compared Crusty Buns to a bakery he went to in LA. Chief, wasn't your victim a baker?"

"He sure was. But Flynn, there's probably thousands of bakeries in LA. What makes you think it's the same one?"

Flynn screwed up her cheek. The crows-feet around her eyes crinkled, and she let out an exasperated sigh. "I don't know. It just struck me as too coincidental, you know?"

"Gotcha. We wanted to talk to him anyway, so we can ask. Anything else?"

Madeline was looking decidedly unhappy about this discussion. Rick knew how much she hated being involved in anything to do with crime—that included Alex trying to investigate or his own work with Adam. "Let's go find out," he said.

Max Rado sat at a table near where he'd been earlier in the day. He was alone, dressed the same as on their previous visit, and was scrolling down the screen of his phone. They split up, and both wove a path through the maze of customers. Rick acknowledged those who looked up and said hello with a polite thank you. Some simply made way without even a glance, but there was one man whose chair was blocking Adam's path. Rick noted the look of annoyance on the man's face when he was forced to move his chair.

All the commotion caught Rado's attention. He watched, obviously curious, as they made their way closer. When they were a few tables away, he gave an indifferent shrug of his shoulders and returned his attention to his phone. It wasn't until they stood next to his table that he gave them both a polite wave and said, "You two look serious. What's up?"

"Afternoon, Mr. Rado," Adam said. "How did your conversation with Ms. O'Connor go?"

"Oh. That's why you're here? Okay, okay. She explained the facts of life to me. I wasn't proposing anything illegal. I thought about how people collect everything. Figured maybe she had some discards that might have some commercial value. I'm sorry if I overstepped."

"Good to know," Adam said. "That's not the reason why we're here. She didn't say anything about you doing something illegal, which means your business with her is between the two of you. The reason we wanted to talk to you again has to do with the case we're working—and a comment you made to Ms. O'Connor."

"So she did complain about me."

"No. That's not it at all."

"What then?"

"When we were talking to you earlier, you indicated you met Henry Nicholas at the Seaside Cove Inn. Is that correct?"

"Yeah," Rado said with a nod. "We met at the coffee station. Crap coffee compared to here, but it's free."

"Had you ever met him before?" Adam pressed.

"No. He was waiting for this couple who couldn't decide what kind of donut they wanted. While we were standing there, we started talking."

"Ms. O'Connor mentioned that you have a favorite bakery in LA. We wouldn't by any chance be referring to the one owned by Henry Nicholas, would we?"

Rado snorted. He eyeballed the front of the store for a moment, then said, "Oh. So you think because Henry was a baker, and I went to a bakery in LA, that was the one I was talking about? Sorry, Chief, wrong conclusion."

"Why don't you enlighten us?" Rick asked.

"So Henry told me he was a baker when we met, but I live in Burbank and his store was in West Covina. That's like thirty miles. Don't have much cause to get out there. The bakery I was talking about is a little Italian place near where I live. They make the best cannolis."

Adam made a note and, without looking up, asked, "This place got a name?"

"Rossi's Italian Bakery." Rado shrugged and held Adam's gaze. "Check them out if you want."

Rick was sure Adam would do exactly that. Perhaps this bakery did explain the relationship with Henry Nicholas, but that was only one of the connections. "What about Kiernan Walsh?" Rick asked. "When we spoke to you before, you said the two of you were talking to Mr. Nicholas."

"Same sort of thing. Met him over coffee at the Inn."

"And why were you talking to Kiernan Walsh at the docks?"

"We both had the same idea. He wanted a job on the *Blue Phoenix* and I was hoping to do business with the owner. Didn't work out for either of us." Rado crossed his arms over his chest and made a face. "Win some, lose some, I guess."

"Was Henry Nicholas there?" Adam asked.

"Where?"

"The marina."

"No. There was a guy named Victor. Kind of a jerk, actually. Picking on an old man like he did. Bad form, man. Bad form."

Rick peered at Rado closely. So many things happened after Joe's fall. Was it possible that all these other events were somehow tied to the murder? "Why didn't you tell us about that incident before?"

Rado frowned and shook his head. "Why? What's that got to do with Henry's death?"

"So you didn't think it was relevant?" Adam pressed.

"Can't say as I see a connection."

Just because Rado didn't see a connection didn't mean there wasn't one, thought Rick. "What else can you tell us about the incident between Victor Pallett and Joe Gray?"

After an exaggerated sigh, Rado said, "That the old guy's name? Didn't know. Anyway, I'm sure I can't tell you much you haven't already heard."

He recapped the incident. His description matched closely to what Jennifer Martin had said. By the time he was done, Rick was sure Victor had assaulted Joe, but still couldn't see a connection to Henry Nicholas. Unless it was Kiernan Walsh.

"How well do you think Walsh knew Henry Nicholas?" Rick asked.

"You mean, do I think they were friends or something from before the meeting at the coffee station?"

"Yes. Could there have been a previous connection of some sort?"

Stretching out his legs, Rado leaned back in his chair. "I never really thought about it. Afraid I can't help you there. You'd have to talk to him."

"We will, but were they talking before you met Henry?"

"Hmmm...yeah, come to think of it, they were. I walked in, and they were having some sort of conversation. Like I said, they were waiting for the couple to finish up. Then...I guess it was Henry who let Kiernan go first, and that's when we started talking. I don't know. Is that any help?"

At this point, Rick wasn't sure what was important and what wasn't, but he was willing to take any bits of information he could get.

35

RICK

AFTER FINISHING WITH RADO, RICK asked if they could stop at the wedding planning table.

Adam laughed and looked across the room. "Yup. Exactly what it is, isn't it? Maybe Mary could offer a new service."

"All this place needs is more customers. Let's keep this little idea to ourselves, okay?"

After getting a thumbs-up from Adam, Rick led the way. Alex watched them expectantly as they approached. "Did you get anything, Daddy?"

"Not much, kiddo. Other than maybe it's looking a lot like you were right about Victor Pallett. At least where Joe Gray is concerned. Rado's description matches up with what Jennifer Martin told us."

"Awesome. Are we gonna kick him out?"

"No, we're not. Unless he's charged with a crime, we have no reason to take that kind of action."

Marquetta stood, a look of concern on her face. "There's something I have to tell you, Rick."

Alex eagerly tugged on Rick's shirt. "Did you get any new leads on the murder?"

"Afraid not. We're now also looking at Kiernan Walsh. His name is cropping up a little too often."

"What about...?"

Rick put his finger to his lips. "Shhh...let me talk to Marquetta for a minute."

Marquetta pulled Rick to one side, the concern on her face still there. "Before we came here, Kathryn said she wanted to go for a walk. I had Alex show her the way to the lighthouse. Kathryn stayed behind when Alex came back. Lydia called me just a minute ago. Apparently Kathryn hasn't returned yet. That has me concerned, but the bigger problem is Mr. Pallett. He's back, and when he saw Kathryn's things weren't in the room, he tracked down Lydia. He confronted her, and she told him she didn't know anything, but that I'd be returning in a few minutes to clear it all up."

"Why'd she put you in the middle of it?" Rick snapped.

"Don't be mad at Lydia, she was just buying time and giving me a heads up. You and Adam should go there right now."

"We're on our way." He gave Marquetta a quick kiss, then motioned for Adam to join him. "We have to get to the B&B pronto. Victor Pallett is turning into a problem."

Adam pulled out his keys and waved goodbye. On the way to his vehicle, he radioed Deputy Kama and told her to meet him at the B&B. The whole trip took only a few minutes, but it felt like an hour. Rick jumped out of the 4x4 as it rolled to a stop. He was halfway to the front door when Deputy Kama's vehicle pulled up and parked. He cringed at what was about to happen —a full-scale police intervention. It was all he needed to ruin their business.

He had to nip this in the bud before Pallett started disturbing the other guests, or worse, hurt someone. He burst through the front door and left it ajar for Adam and Deputy Kama. Victor Pallett's voice was the first thing he heard. It sounded like he was unloading on some poor soul upstairs. Rick climbed the stairs two at a time. Adam and his deputy appeared at the bottom of the stairs at about the same time Rick got to the second-floor landing. He held up his hand with his fingers splayed. With luck, he could defuse the situation before the law had to intervene.

Pallett stood in the middle of the hallway. He towered over poor Lydia. His voice boomed again, "Where is she?"

"Enough!" Rick barked. "Mr. Pallett, step away from her."

The man whirled around. He faced Rick, but rather than continuing his tirade, he took a step back. Rick caught a look of terror in Lydia's eyes, but Pallett's changed, too. His snarl fell away, and the color drained from his face. He pointed at Lydia.

"She told me Marquetta was coming back in a few minutes, but she hasn't shown up. I'm...I'm worried about Kathryn. Where is she?"

"Save it," Rick snapped. He looked at Lydia, who'd moved off to the side and had been watching the interaction. "Are you okay?"

A nod. A mumbled, "Yes." But it was obvious she'd been terrified.

"Go downstairs. Chief Cunningham and Deputy Kama are there. I'm sorry this happened to you."

Pallett bristled as Lydia hurried past him, but at the mention of the police waiting downstairs, his shoulders slumped. Once Lydia was out of sight, Rick fixed the man with a determined stare. "You have caused enough trouble in my B&B, Mr. Pallett. I don't know who you think you are, but you cannot intimidate other people while you are in this establishment. That goes for my daughter, my employees, and the guests. Do you understand?"

"I just wanted to know where..."

"Do you understand?" Rick demanded.

Pallett swallowed hard and cleared his throat. "Yes. But..."

"There are no buts, Mr. Pallett. You either act like a civilized human being, or you get out. Right now, I have several options open to me. Quite frankly, the most appealing is to have you arrested for assaulting my employee. Or perhaps for vandalism. You are the one who salted our coffee. Aren't you?"

"You can't talk to me like this." Pallett stiffened and set his jaw. "You're not going to turn this around and make wild accusations at me. Your employees are the ones who turned my girlfriend against me!"

Rick took a deep breath and called over his shoulder. "Adam, would you come up here for a minute?"

"Sure thing." A few seconds later, Adam stood next to Rick.

"Would you explain to Mr. Pallett what we've been doing today?" Rick asked.

Adam's green eyes zeroed in on Pallett. "Of course. You, sir, are a person of interest in a homicide investigation."

"What?" Pallett exploded. "I had nothing to do with that!"

"You'd better hope so. Because if you did, we will find out. Your other problem is, quite honestly, your behavior. Since you've been here in town, it's been questionable at best. If it were up to me, I'd be happy to let you cool your heels in the county jail for the night. Do you have an arrest record, Mr. Pallett? Because you're about this far away from adding to it." Adam held up his hand, his thumb and forefinger about an inch apart.

"Look, guys. I...apologize for what's happened. This is all just a big misunderstanding."

Adam took two slow steps forward. "The misunderstanding is yours, Mr. Pallett. You appear to be under the impression you can do whatever you want while you are in this town. You might get away with that in the big city, but here, we don't appreciate bad behavior. Now, I'm going to ask you the same question Rick did. Do you understand, or would you like to discuss this further on the way to the county jail?"

Pallett's nostrils flared. Rick could see the anger boiling underneath, but he also noticed that the man's gaze ping-ponged between them. Finally, he clenched his teeth and grumbled, "I understand."

The question was, if Rick let the man stay, what would happen? The answer was obvious. Something bad. "Mr. Pallett, I think it would be best if you left. I'll refund your unused nights."

The color returned to Pallett's cheeks. With his eyes bulging, he said, "You can't do that! I have a reservation. I've paid for my room. Besides, I have nowhere to go."

"Actually, the Inn has at least one opening. I can get you booked in there without any problem."

"I demand to stay." Pallett looked at Adam. "Chief? You're not going to let him do this to me, are you?"

"Do what? Protect his family and his business? Mr. Pallett, it sounds to me like you're still having a problem understanding the gravity of this situation."

Pallett raised his hands with his fingers splayed. "Okay, okay. I'm sorry. I guess I got...carried away. I won't give you anymore problems. I swear."

Rick weighed his options. He could force the man out and quite possibly make an enemy out of a guest. He'd never let Pallett back in the house again anyway, so what did that matter? But if he was tied to the killing, would it be better to keep him close or further away? Close. And on a tight leash.

"Very well, Mr. Pallett. You can stay—for the time being. But if you get out of line again or if anything unusual happens around here...like someone salts the coffee or attempts to sabotage my business in any way, you will be out. Believe me, I would be happy to have Adam come back here and lock you up."

"You won't have any problems from me," Pallett said earnestly.

Right. And the Queen of England was coming to stay next week. Rick nodded to Adam. "He can stay, but I'd like periodic checks from you or Deputy Kama."

"No problem." Adam fixed Pallett with another stare. "Don't make me regret my decision to not lock you up. Oh, and if I were you, I'd keep my distance from Ms. Larkin when she shows up. Got it?"

Pallett huffed, then gave a curt nod. "Excuse me, I need to get some air." He pushed past Rick and Adam and disappeared down the stairs.

"Are you sure you want to let him stay?"

"No. But I'm even more concerned about him being out of my sight. Alex already has instructions to give him a wide berth, but I'll talk to both Marquetta and Lydia. Oh my gosh! Lydia. I need to see how she's doing."

Deputy Kama was still standing at the bottom of the stairs. She cocked her head toward the back of the house. "Lydia went into the kitchen. She said she was worried about Ms. Larkin. Pallett caught her knocking on the door and she let it slip that Ms. Larkin had gone to the lighthouse."

"Oh no. Let me check her room." Rick ran up the stairs, knocked on the door, and when he got no answer, used his key. The room was empty, so he hurried downstairs.

"She's not in her room. I need to talk to Lydia. Which way did Pallett go?"

The deputy hooked her thumb over her shoulder. "Out the front door. It looked like he was headed toward the backyard. Chief, do you want me to follow him?"

"I don't want you right on his tail, but yes. I'll drive up to the parking lot at the lighthouse and check things out from the other end."

Rick's stomach did a quick flip-flop. "If he finds her..."

"Yeah. I know," Adam said.

Standing alone in the lobby, Rick wondered if Lydia really was doing as well as Deputy Kama had indicated. He hurried to the kitchen, just sure he needed to do more damage control. But before that, he'd better text Marquetta.

36

ALEX

ON OUR WAY BACK FROM Crusty Buns, I can tell Marquetta is worried about something, but she won't tell me what it is. Because she's keeping it all secret, it's probably got something to do with my dad and Chief Cunningham. When I try to ask, she ignores my question and says we need to inspect the gazebo. She's sure Grandma Madeline will be checking it out and wants to be extra sure there's no painting or other work it needs before it will be ready.

I know that's not really what she's thinking about, so I just stay quiet until we've passed the roundabout. "Since I'm a junior bridesmaid and I don't have a lot of other responsibilities like Traci or Grandma Madeline, maybe I should take care of the gazebo for you, Marquetta."

"That's a great idea, Sweetie. After you do that, why don't you get together with Robbie and Sasha? If you want, they could...what in the world's going on?" Marquetta stops and stares down the street. There are two Seaside Cove police cars in front of the B&B. Chief Cunningham is getting in his. He makes a U-turn and drives away.

"What's going on, Marquetta? Why are the cops here?"

"I don't know, but I'm going to text your dad and find out." She pulls out her phone, but before she can send a text, a message comes through. "Oh no. Your dad says Mr. Pallett had a meltdown. He started harassing Lydia, but your dad and Adam stopped him. Alex, I'm sorry, but I think you need to stay home this afternoon. When we get there, I want you to go straight up to your room. Okay?"

Bummer. I miss all the good stuff. My dad's message tone goes off on her phone again. She reads the screen.

"Everything's under control. We can go in," she says.

Marquetta's super tense on the rest of the walk to the B&B. It's like she's watching for someone. When we walk in the front door, she tells me again to go to my room and wait for her. This is so unfair. What am I? Four? I start up the stairs, but by the time I get to the top, Marquetta's already on her way to the kitchen. I hurry back down and rush out the front door.

I'm coming down the porch steps when Deputy Kama hurries by. I ask her what's going on and she tells me she was following Mr. Pallett and that he might be headed to the lighthouse.

"Go back inside," she says and jogs to her 4x4.

No, no, no. This can't be happening. He's on his way to the lighthouse? Kathryn said he hates nature. But if he's looking for her...maybe he wants revenge for leaving him. And I left her out there all alone.

This is all my fault. She's probably got her phone with her. I start a text, then stop. If she's hiding when I call her, it would be like in the movies and could give away her position. Calls and texts are out, but there's a way to get there first.

I cram my phone in my pocket and run around the house to an opening in the trees. The opening leads to a small path through the woods. It's a shortcut to the lighthouse. It's the same path I told Kathryn about. The one that nobody ever uses. What I didn't tell her is it doesn't get used 'cause it's such a spooky way to go. But if Mr. McNasty's on the main trail, this will totally get me there first.

I duck into the brush behind the shed where the trail begins.

37

RICK

WHITEWATER RAPIDS. IT'S THE ONLY way Rick could describe the barrage of thoughts crashing through his mind as he pushed open the butler door. The chaos subsided when he saw Lydia sitting at the kitchen island with Kathryn Larkin. They each had a Seaside Cove mug in front of them and were sharing a saucer. On it, two tea balls lay on their sides. So intent were they on their conversation that neither of them glanced in his direction until he stepped into the room.

"I'm so glad you're both okay," Rick said.

Lydia started at the sound of his voice, but when she saw it was Rick, seemed to relax. "We're fine. Thank you for getting there when you did."

"I'm just sorry you got caught like that. It must have been a terrifying experience for you."

Lydia averted her gaze for a moment, then pulled in a deep breath and regarded Rick. "I've been through worse."

Of course. She'd seen combat. How could he have forgotten? "I guess you have."

Kathryn shook her head. "I can't believe I was ever attracted to that man. He's awful."

"He's definitely one of the frogs." Lydia raised her mug and watched Kathryn over the rim. "Put him behind you."

"You're right." Kathryn's right cheek curled up, revealing an amused dimple. "He is a frog."

Rick backed away from the conversation. "Chief Cunningham and his deputy are looking for you, Kathryn. I'll let them know you're okay." He sent a quick text and had a reply within a few seconds.

—*I'll tell Kama to stand down. Do you want to press charges against Pallett?*

Rick took a long breath. What did he want to do? Just because Pallett was a jerk didn't mean he was a killer. He also didn't deserve a free pass. But having a guest arrested? That was extreme.

—*Not sure about arrest, but I think we need to take a closer look at him.*

—*Works for me. Headed back to the station to run a background check on him and check out Rossi's Bakery. Why don't you dig up what you can on your end?*

—*Will do. Going to stay here in case he comes back and starts causing problems.*

Kathryn picked up her mug and rotated it in her hands. "What was that all about?"

"At this point, there's enough to arrest Victor for assaulting Lydia. But that's only going to make him angrier. We'll investigate him as a suspect in the murder."

"So he's staying here?" She curled her fingers into a fist and covered her mouth. "What about me? What should I do?"

"If he approaches you, tell him to back off," Rick said.

"And if he doesn't?" Kathryn set her mug down with a determined thump. She winced at the sound. "Sorry."

"Don't be. Call for help if you need it. For the time being, there will always be one of us here. This is terrible timing,

Kathryn, but I have a couple of questions for you about Victor. Do you mind?"

"Ask away."

"When you two checked in, he listed his occupation as 'entrepreneur.' Do you know what business he's in?"

Kathryn snickered. "Is that what he said? What a liar. Victor hasn't held a steady job since I've known him. He starts somewhere, then something happens and a few months later, he quits. He's always had a good reason for leaving, and I never really caught on until we came here. I'm just sure he pulled that stunt with the coffee."

"Did he tell you about it?" Rick asked, almost incredulous.

"No. It was his face. He was smirking while you guys were scrambling around trying to figure out what was wrong."

"What about Joe Gray's accident? Did he give you any indication of that?"

Kathryn twirled a strand of hair between her fingers, a worried look coming over her face. "All I heard was that one of the locals had fallen and broken his arm. When I asked Victor if he'd heard anything, he said 'that old geezer got what he deserved'. He complained about how the man had wronged him. I couldn't believe it, but that's when it hit me—all the jobs...the friends of mine he hated...everything. It all suddenly made sense."

Rick held her gaze. Gone was the sparkle in her brown eyes. Gone were the dimples. Tension lined her features, and Rick had no doubts she'd remember this breakup for a very long time. "Meaning?"

"He's unemployable and antisocial. I don't know how I missed that before. For a while now, he's been talking about starting his own business. He said he wanted to run a tour company. At first, I thought he was joking because Victor hates anything to do with nature. But when he was so serious, I thought maybe he'd found his passion. It was why he was so anxious to come here. The entire trip was supposed to help him lay the groundwork."

Rick peered at Kathryn. "Do you know what he meant by that?"

"Something about connections he needed to make. He would never say exactly." Kathryn paused, then added, "There is one other thing. I could never tell if Victor was serious or not, but a month or so ago, he started talking about Joaquin Murrieta. It was all so weird."

"How so?"

"He came into the shop and was bragging about how he was related to one of the state's most famous bandits. He said he was a great-great-grandson or something like that. That's when he got more serious about having his own business. He claimed he was going to make the most of his family heritage."

Rick rubbed his forehead as he gazed across the room. There were plenty of opinions about Joaquin Murrieta around Seaside Cove. Some of the old-timers said he'd once buried treasure in the mountains. Others refuted those claims and insisted the man had never been in this part of California. The question was, how well known was all this controversy outside of town?

"How do you think he came to the conclusion he was related to Murrieta?"

"I don't know. When I asked him about it, he told me he'd done a DNA test. I got really excited because I'd been thinking of doing one myself, but when I told him that, he just got angry and said I was trying to outdo him. I dropped the whole thing." Kathryn stared at her mug, once again rotating it in her fingers. "I should have seen the signs then, but I was in denial over what Victor was really like. I see him very clearly now."

"I'm sorry. At least you found out before things got too serious." The words felt stupid. Apparently, their relationship had been very serious. He pulled in a short breath. "Do you think Victor's capable of physically hurting someone?"

"You mean, could he have committed murder?"

Rick grimaced. He hated to admit it, but that's exactly what he'd meant. "Yes."

"Maybe. I don't know. Victor was getting more and more controlling the longer we were together."

The butler's door swished open. All three of them turned to see who had entered. The last of the rapids calmed in Rick's mind at the sight of Marquetta. "Thank goodness you're home. Where's Alex?"

"I sent her up to her room. I wanted to talk to you about Victor Pallett. Rick, I don't think it's safe having him in the house. I know what you're going to say—he's a guest and we can't simply send him away because he's obnoxious, but he threatened Alex and now Lydia. I feel very strongly we should get that man out of our home."

Rick fell silent. The rapids were making a return. And with good reason. "Marquetta, this is a tough decision. We could be opening ourselves up to…"

"What if he does something to Alex, Rick?" Marquetta sucked in a ragged breath and her voice rose in pitch. "It will be too late and you'll hate yourself for being more concerned about the business than your daughter."

Watching Marquetta's face, seeing the tears form in her eyes, he knew she was right. There was no hard decision here. His family was his first priority. And when it came down to it, the only one that mattered in this case. "You're right. Pallett has to go. I'll text Adam so he can be here when I tell Pallett he's gone too far. Before I do that, I want to check on Alex. Be back in a minute."

He left the three women alone and deliberately wound his way through the house. The dining room was empty, as was the living area. There was nobody in the lobby and the stairway was clear.

At the top of the stairs, he debated on checking Pallett's room. Why bother? If the man was in, it would only lead to another confrontation. It would be better to leave that step until he had Adam as his backup.

He went to Alex's room and knocked gently. No answer. He waited a few seconds and knocked again. When his daughter still didn't respond, he used his master key to unlock the door.

Rick's heart pounded in his chest as he stared at the empty room. He called Alex's name, knowing there would be no answer, but somehow hoping for one.

He closed the door, locked it, and went to his office. Again, no sign of Alex. He retraced his steps along the hallway to Pallett's room. He rapped twice on the door and used his key when he didn't get an immediate response. His throat went dry as he looked around. Empty. No Pallett. No Alex.

Rick hurried downstairs. Frantically, he again checked each area on his way through the house. He pushed through the door, hoping beyond hope that Alex would be sitting there chatting it up with the women. Instead, it was just Marquetta and Kathryn.

"I sent Lydia home," Marquetta said. "She'll start at six tomorrow. She and Kathryn filled me in on everything that happened. Thank goodness you got here when you did." She suddenly stopped, looked closely at him, and stammered, "What's wrong?"

"Alex is missing."

38

ALEX

YEESH. THE WOODS GIVE ME the creeps. I'm surrounded by trees. They're thick and when the wind whistles through, it sounds like ghosts talking all around me. It makes my skin crawl. I get too close to one and it brushes my arm. It feels like a hand reaching out from the sides of the trail to grab me. I swipe it away, but it's like the touch is still there.

If McNasty's on the main trail, he's not gonna have any of this, but he also won't know I'm out here. As long as I'm careful, I'm totally safe. A small branch almost slaps me in the face and I wanna cry out, but I don't. The trail's getting narrower. I bite my lip hard to remind myself to be extra quiet. I stop when I think I hear a voice.

There it is again. It's a man. McNasty. And he's calling Kathryn's name! I suck in a breath and hold it. Wait! If he's yelling for her, then he hasn't found her yet! I follow the sound and tiptoe forward. If I look real close through the trees, every once in a while, I can see him walking. He doesn't even slow down to enjoy the view. Man, he must be super angry.

Ahead of me, there's a big, old tree across the path. It's covered in moss. There's no way around without going into the woods. I have to go over. I swing one leg up and over to scoot across, but my jeans catch. Crap! I'm stuck with my butt on the tree trunk. Oh man, this is so not cool. If I can't get off this stupid thing and have to call my dad for help, he'll kill me. I force myself up and over to the other side.

I crouch and look for Mr. Pallett. But finding someone when you're looking through a forest is almost impossible. I've lost him. Rats!

I take off, running as fast as I can to catch up. The trail is getting super twisty, but at least there are no other branches in the way. The further I go, the closer this trail gets to the main one. The two of them will meet soon. What do I do then? I might be all on my own out here. My heart is pounding in my chest and I wonder if anybody else can hear it. I have to find Kathryn first. Once we're together, we'll hide in the trees. He'll never find us.

She's gotta be on the main trail...but what if she's not? My throat is totally dry now. It's so bad I just wanna cough it out. But when I hear his voice again, I know I can't. I swallow. Again and again and again.

It doesn't do any good. I squeeze my eyes tight and listen hard so I'll forget the scratchiness. His voice is still there, but he's not calling Kathryn's name anymore. He's talking on the phone. That means she's still safe. Right?

My heart thumps in my chest because I can't stop myself from inching closer to the sound. Ahead of me is the lighthouse. Beyond that, there's a rocky cliff. It goes straight down to the crashing waves. The old-timers in town say the fence was built after a young couple fell off the cliff and died. I don't know if it's true or not, but the kids at school say their ghosts haunt the lighthouse.

I hear his voice again. It's clear now. He's saying something about things heating up. Maybe not working out the way they planned. Whatever he's up to, while he's busy, I have to find

Kathryn. I follow my trail to the main one. Before I step out into the open, I check one last time. There's no sign of him.

The best thing for me to do is to keep watching behind me while I search for Kathryn. The wind whistles through the trees. It sends a shiver down my back. I totally wish I'd told Marquetta what I was doing. She would've talked me out of it. But I didn't tell her. So she couldn't. Where's Kathryn?

There's a noise over in the brush. It makes me stop and look to see if someone...or something...is watching me. "Who's there?" I hiss.

Only the wind answers me. I don't know whether to run toward the parking lot or go back into the bushes. I'm like frozen in place. The leaves to my right rustle again. There's gotta be someone hiding in there. It's probably him.

This has always been a fun walk. Now, it's super creepy. What am I gonna do? I pull my phone from my back pocket to call for help. My dad can ground me. I don't care! I just wanna get home!

A bunny rabbit hops out of the bushes. My shoulders slump with relief, but then there are footsteps on the trail behind me.

"You! You little brat! What are you doing out here? Following me?" He comes running toward me.

I turn to run, but my foot hits a rock next to the trail. My other foot catches and when I hit the ground, my phone flips out of my hand. I can't catch my breath to get up. All I can do is hold my side where it hurts. The tears are pressing against my eyes, but I won't let him see me cry.

"Yeah. You got what you deserved, you little brat. Daddy can't help you now, can he?" He's standing over me. Sucking in deep breaths and grinning like a crazy man. "Maybe you want to go for a little swim, huh? I hear the water's nice this time of year. Just watch the first step. It's a doozy."

He reaches down, grabs my arm, and yanks me to my feet.
I scream as loud as I can.

39

RICK

"SHE'S...GONE?" MARQUETTA CROAKED. "I don't understand. I sent her up to her...oh, my God."

"Her room. I know. I checked. She wasn't there. I looked in my office and the common areas. I even went into Pallett's room. As far as I know, she's not in the house."

Marquetta's hand went to her throat. "Call Adam."

"He'll find her. Right?" Rick said as he pulled out his phone. He watched Marquetta's face, hoping she'd reassure him, but he saw only fear.

Her eyes misted over. "It's my fault. I told her to go up to her room, but I didn't..."

Rick rushed around the island and took Marquetta in his arms. "It's not your fault. We'll find her. I promise." But could they? In time? He dialed Adam's number and told him Alex was missing. When he hung up, he said, "He's notifying Amy. They'll both be looking for her. I'm going to go check the downtown area."

"It would be faster to make a few calls," Marquetta said. "I'll call Traci. You call Francine."

"What can I do?" Kathryn asked, her eyes betraying a deep-seated worry. "I'm the one who brought Victor into your home. I feel terrible about this."

Marquetta reached out to Kathryn and took her hand. "No, it's not your fault, either. But you can help. Call Crusty Buns and ask for Mary O'Donnell. Ask her if she's seen Alex." Marquetta scribbled the phone number on a small piece of paper and gave it to Kathryn.

While waiting for Francine to pick up, Rick went through the butler door to the dining room. He kept glancing outside in hopes that he'd see Alex. His heart sank when Francine answered and told him she hadn't seen her either. She volunteered to call a couple of the other merchants, but to be honest, the mayor seldom missed a thing, so if she hadn't seen Alex... Rick returned to the kitchen. Both Marquetta and Kathryn had just hung up, but neither looked relieved.

"Traci hasn't seen her. She's going to close the store for a few minutes and walk around the block."

"Nothing from Mary O'Donnell," Kathryn offered. "I feel so terrible about this."

"Don't," Marquetta said. "I told you, this isn't your fault."

"Marquetta's right. And right now, we don't know..." Rick's phone rang. He snatched it up and answered on the first ring. "Did you find her?"

"Yes," Adam Cunningham said, his voice somber. "Got there just in time, too. She was with Victor Pallett. I'm charging him with assault. No question."

Rick sank down into the nearest chair. The room felt like it was going to start spinning in crazy circles. His breaths came short. Ragged. What had Pallett done? "Is she...okay?"

A movement outside the nearest window caught Rick's attention. His heart leaped at the wild thought that this was all a crazy dream, but then reality returned. He'd seen the Browers strolling the grounds. Not Alex.

"Tell me, Adam. Did he do something to her?" Rick demanded as the flashing lights disappeared.

A loud hiss, sounding much like wind catching the speaker of his cell phone, filled the background. Adam raised his voice slightly. "The munchkin's a little shaken up, that's all. Deputy Kama is on her way here. I'll have her bring Alex home. We're in the parking lot for the lighthouse trail. She wasn't even a hundred feet from where I'm standing."

"Does she need a doctor?"

"Rick, she's fine. She's got a couple of scrapes and her ego's a little bruised because she tripped over a rock. She knocked the wind out of her lungs, but she's already doing better. You can get her checked out as a precaution, but she's unharmed. I gave her a blanket and have her sitting on the new bench the town put in. She might be the first person to actually use it. Here, say hi."

After a short pause, he heard Alex's voice. Her voice shook as she spoke. Definitely not her usual confident self. "Hey, Daddy. Are you gonna ground me?"

In the background, Rick heard Adam chuckling. If he weren't so mad and worried himself, he might have felt differently. But for now, he was just happy to hear her voice. "We'll talk about it, kiddo. You're not hurt?"

"No. Chief Cunningham heard me scream and got here before..." Alex sniffled and she croaked, "I'm sorry, Daddy."

"Let me talk to Adam again."

"Okay."

"And Alex?"

"Yeah?"

"I love you. More than you'll ever know."

"Love you, too, Daddy."

"Kama's here, so she'll be bringing her home. After what the poor kid just went through, I didn't want her having to walk all the way back. Don't worry, Rick. She's safe with us."

"You're not letting Pallett near her, right?"

"Correct. I don't want Alex in the same vehicle as this guy. That's why I had Kama hightail it up here. By the way, Pallett won't be bothering you, at least for tonight."

"He won't be bothering me again, period," Rick snapped. "I'm definitely kicking him out."

"Good choice, given the circumstances. I think the man has zero impulse control. I'm also going to interrogate him about Henry Nicholas, but if I can't hold him more than tonight, you might want to consider a restraining order."

"That's pretty extreme, but if it will keep him away, I'll do it."

When he hung up, Rick looked at Marquetta and Kathryn, who were standing side-by-side holding hands. He told them Alex had been found, and that she was safe and sound. Marquetta collapsed onto a nearby barstool and whispered, "Thank God."

"Also, Victor's going to be charged with assault and will be spending the night in jail."

The three of them went to the lobby to wait. Within five minutes, Deputy Amy Kama escorted Alex through the front door.

Rick sucked in a breath and opened his arms. Alex ran to him. He closed his eyes and squeezed his daughter tight as he gazed up at Amy. "Thank you," he whispered.

"My pleasure." Amy scanned the room. "Place looks great. I sure do miss staying here."

Marquetta knelt next to Rick. She eased Alex out of Rick's arms and hugged her. "You had me so worried, Sweetie. Don't you ever do that to me again. Come with me. Let's get you cleaned up." She draped her arm over Alex's shoulder and guided her up the stairs.

Rick stepped forward and shook Amy's hand. "Thank you again. And you're welcome back here anytime."

Amy grimaced. "Thanks, but I'm settled in now. And I do love my little cottage. I wish I could stay and talk, but I have to go. The Chief's waiting for the sheriff to pick up Pallett and we just got a call from Dennis Malone. He caught a guy shoplifting."

Rick gaped at Amy for a second, then said, "What is it about Dennis's store? He must get robbed every few months."

"Actually, from what I hear, he gets robbed once or twice a week. But he only catches them every few months. You all take care. He caught this one because there were no other customers in the store. The thief is one of your murder suspects. Kiernan Walsh. I have to go arrest him before Dennis beats him to a pulp."

"Wait, Amy! Dennis has Walsh locked up?"

"More like under intimidation. A couple of Dennis's friends were walking by, and Dennis got them to help him out. Walsh has holed up in one of the changing rooms. Gotta go. Bye." The deputy hurried out the front door and down the steps.

Rick and Kathryn rehashed the situation until Marquetta brought Alex back downstairs. At that point, they agreed to adjourn to the kitchen so they could talk privately about what had happened. "Kathryn, you're welcome to join us. Given your relationship to Victor, you may want to be involved."

Kathryn gripped her sides and bit her lower lip. "I don't know..."

Alex rubbed her shoulder gingerly and said, "You should come with us. You're gonna wanna hear this."

They made their way back to the kitchen, where they all took a seat around the island. With his fears subsiding, Rick felt another emotion rising. Anger at Pallett for being what he was. Anger at Henry Nicholas for being murdered. At Alex for her fearless attitude. Even himself for raising her to be that way. He took a long, slow breath before he spoke.

"Alex, tell us what happened."

It took a few seconds for her to respond, and when she did, her voice cracked. She grimaced as she looked at Marquetta. "Instead of going to my room like you told me to, I went out to the front porch. Deputy Kama said Mr. Pallett had gone to the lighthouse. I thought Kathryn was still there, and I wanted to find her before he did."

Kathryn gasped and whispered, "Oh my God. You went because of me?"

"Why didn't you tell me what you were doing, Sweetie?" Marquetta craned her neck forward, her forehead puckered. "You could have been injured...or worse."

Alex continued to stare at the white granite. Her shoulders rose and fell. "I'm tired of being treated like a little kid."

"Oh, I see." Marquetta reached across the counter, took Alex's hand, and gave it a gentle squeeze. "Hey, look at me."

Alex met her gaze, but for only a second.

"You're eleven, Sweetie. You have a lot of growing up to do." After giving Rick a searching look, she added, "But maybe we could do better about giving you a say in things?"

Rick let out a long sigh. Perhaps he'd just been too protective. Alex would grow up. Whether he wanted her to or not. "Maybe so. How did you get ahead of Mr. Pallett on the trail without him seeing you?"

"I ran through the woods." She went on to describe her trip, even including the log where she'd gotten stuck. She described how she'd passed Pallett, heard a noise once she was on the main trail, and gotten spooked. When she was done, she rolled her eyes and, with a false bravado, said, "Stupid rabbit."

"You're sure that's all it was?" Rick said.

"Totally sure. He jumped out of the bushes when I fell." Alex fixed her gaze on Kathryn, her dark blue eyes suddenly intense. "He was on a phone call when I caught up to him. He was talking to somebody about things not working out the way they planned. When I tripped, he threatened to throw me off the cliff."

"What?" Rick exploded.

Kathryn's hand went to her throat. "That man's just plain evil."

Marquetta got up from her seat and went to Alex. She wrapped her arms around her, and Alex responded by melting into the embrace.

Watching them, seeing how scared Alex had been and what might have happened, Rick thought about what he wanted to do. The obvious, throwing Pallett off that cliff, was not an option. "Did you tell Adam about this, Alex?"

"Nuh-uh. I don't think so. I guess I was still kinda scared."

Rick clenched his teeth, his anger boiling inside. Right now, he was the one who felt capable of committing murder. If Pallett had actually thrown Alex off that cliff, deep in his gut, Rick knew he never would have forgiven himself. The ringing of his cell phone jarred him out of his dark thoughts. He checked the number, saw it was Adam, and pushed aside the last of his anger. "What's up?"

"Can you break away for a bit?"

There was an urgency in Adam's voice that suggested this was less of a request than a demand. Marquetta now stood behind Alex with her arms wrapped around her as though she might never let her go. He desperately wanted to console his daughter, but he could tell from the way she'd responded to Marquetta's touch that what she really needed at this moment was the comfort of a mother-daughter relationship. And even though the two weren't biologically related, they were connected by an invisible bond equally strong.

"Yes. Do you want me to meet you somewhere?"

"At the station? Kama and I are making a prisoner switch. I'd like to interrogate Walsh, but I want you there, too. If you're up for it."

He was so up for it. So tired of these mysterious strangers who had descended on their town. Wreaking chaos. Telling lies. Harboring secrets. Yes, he was ready to send them all to jail. "I'll be there in ten minutes."

40

ALEX

Hey Journal,

This was totally the scariest day of my life. I thought for sure that nasty Mr. Pallett was going to kill me! I'm okay, but now that the whole thing is over, I'm getting mad. When he grabbed me by the arm and threatened to throw me off the cliff, I realized I couldn't fight him off. I'm not like strong enough to arrest him or anything like that. But I've got the power of the pen. I've got the Cove Talkers Newsletter and I'm gonna expose him. I don't know if I wanna become a cop, Journal, but I could be a crime reporter like Daddy was in New York. The power of the press, Journal! I'm gonna use it to bring him down!

Kathryn's been super nice to me, and I feel like we've got something in common. I'm gonna talk with her. Maybe she'll know where he was when the murder happened.

I should've talked to her downstairs, but she left the kitchen before I did. I hope she's back in her room. My dad had to leave. He went to interrogate that guy Walsh with Chief Cunningham. Man, I so wish I could be there!

Marquetta came up here for a while, then she suggested I just rest while she gets started on dinner. I don't wanna rest, Journal. I want to prove McNasty is a killer! I'm gonna see if

Anita's in her room. I owe her an apology. She was just trying to help, and I totally overreacted. Even though Marquetta told me to avoid Anita before, I don't think she feels the same now. Besides, Anita was a spy, so maybe she's got some ideas on how to solve this. Besides, I really do think she's cool. She's not gonna hurt me.

Wish me luck,
Alex

It's four o'clock, and the house feels super quiet. This is the time of day the guests are either getting ready for dinner or relaxing after being out all day. Because Anita's here on her own, I'm hoping she's just hanging out. I knock on the door to the Jib Room. Kinda light at first, but then louder. After a minute or so, there's no answer. Rats! She must be out doing something.

I swallow hard. Should I go for it and try Kathryn? I'm not sure if she'll tell my dad or Marquetta that I came to her, but I'm gonna hope not.

The Mainsail Room is only two doors away. I pad down the hall and it's almost like I can hear my footsteps echo in the quiet. Even though I knock lightly, it sounds like I'm pounding on the door.

Maybe this was a huge mistake. A big one. But then I hear Kathryn's voice. "Be right there."

I can feel my shoulders getting super tense as I wait for her to let me in. If I get caught out here....oh man, I can't...I just can't. But getting grounded is nothing like getting killed, right?

The door opens a crack and Kathryn peeks out at me. "Alex? What are you doing here?" She pulls the door open and eyes me real close.

Oh, no, I didn't think about what I was gonna tell her. "I... wondered if you could talk for a minute?"

"Of course, come in." She pulls the door open the rest of the way.

I duck inside. My heart feels like it's gonna explode. I so should not be doing this. But if I'm gonna write that story, I have to.

Kathryn closes the door and stands with her back to it, still looking at me funny. "What did you want to talk about?"

"Mr. Pallett," I say hesitantly.

She sucks in a breath and I can see the hurt on her face. She pulls me close, wraps her arms around me, and moans. "Oh. You poor thing. You must still be in shock."

Awesome. That's a great idea. It's even sort of true. Maybe more than I think it is. "Kinda." I scrunch up my face and look at her. "Do you mind?"

"No, not at all. To be honest, you and I have both had a bad experience with Victor. Have a seat." She points at the bed.

This just feels so weird. Like I'm invading her privacy...or maybe opening myself up too much. I can't tell which it is. "Can I use the chair?"

Her eyes tear up and she gives me one of those feeling-sorry-for-you smiles. "Of course. I'm sorry." She goes to the little desk and pulls out the chair, then sits on the edge of the bed so she's facing me. "It must have been terrifying out there. Nobody knew where you were. Marquetta was frantic. How are you doing?"

A second ago, I thought I was great. I was ready to take on Mr. McNasty and bring him down...but the red in her eyes makes me wonder if I'm doing what Marquetta says people do all the time. Maybe I'm masking my feelings...from myself. My heart aches at the idea of what could have happened and how sad it would have made my dad and Marquetta. How I never would have seen Marquetta become my mom. I swipe at my cheek to brush away the tear that's trickling down. "I dunno." My cheeks quiver as I try to hold back the fear that's gripping me. "Scared? Mad? I can't...tell."

Kathryn's ragged breath and my pounding heart are the only sounds in the room. Then she nods. "Me, too. But don't be mad at yourself, Alex. You were trying to look out for me. I'm the one who feels guilty because I caused this whole situation."

"But you didn't do anything! You just went for a walk. I should've told Marquetta where I was going. If I had..." My words catch in my throat.

Kathryn lets out kind of a strangled laugh. "Okay, we're both mad at ourselves. We both made mistakes."

"My dad says mistakes are part of growing up."

Her eyes get that faraway look as she rubs her hand across the back of her neck. "At least you have someone to support you. I should have known to not let a man like Victor into my life. And then I brought him here. Into your home."

"But it's not your fault he's nasty."

"I know. That part's all on him, but I should have seen through him."

"How mean is he?"

"I'm sorry. I don't understand."

I bite my lower lip and stare at one of the bedside lamps. I wanna say the words, but they're stuck in my throat. I think about what Marquetta would do. She's strong and determined and I've seen her face down bigger guys than Mr. Pallett. I take a breath and blurt out the words. "I mean, could he have killed Mr. Nicholas?"

Kathryn watches my face for a few seconds. Her eyes get a faraway look, but then she says, "Your dad asked me the same question. Look, I know Victor was horrible to you, but killing

Henry Nicholas is one thing I don't think you can pin on him. We went to the Crooked Mast for Happy Hour. Then we had dinner. As much as I hate to say it, I'm his alibi."

I can feel my jaw drop. Seriously? He's not the killer? "Are you sure?"

She nods. "Yes. I've come to the conclusion that Victor is nothing more than a bully who will go after those who are weaker than him, but wouldn't dare do anything to someone who stands up to him. The next time I see him, I'm going to tell him exactly what I think of him. I'll also tell him that if he comes near me, I'll get a restraining order like the one the Chief talked to your dad about."

Whoa. I was wrong? Now what?

41
RICK

KIERNAN WALSH SAT IN THE 'interview room' alone. A space distinguished by four bland walls, a window that looked out into the main office, and one door, which was currently closed. Once the former chief's office, the room now served multiple purposes, as evidenced by an ancient metal rack with supplies, a small refrigerator, and, of course, a table and chairs. With the department's limited budget, it was used as a space for meetings, lunch, and the occasional criminal interview.

Adam sat at his desk, apparently engrossed by something on his monitor. When he saw Rick, he gestured for him to join him.

"Has he said anything so far?" Rick asked.

"Haven't even tried," Adam said. "I wanted to give him time to cool his heels. Gave us the opportunity to check out Pallett's background and that Italian bakery Rado mentioned."

"And?" Rick asked hopefully.

"Pallett's clean and Rossi's is a real bakery in the same general vicinity of where Rado lives."

"So he could know about it just by having seen it when he drives by."

"Exactly," Adam said. "In the meantime, let's focus on Walsh. He was one unhappy camper when Deputy Kama arrested him. She said he knows some seriously foul language.

And he wasn't happy about being arrested by a woman, especially when he tried to break her hold."

Rick winced. "I hope he's not in too much pain."

Adam rested his elbows on the desktop. The right side of his mouth curled up into a lopsided smile. "She probably cured him of shoplifting for at least a little while. Here's his arrest record. Guy has a prior for shoplifting in LA. He got off easy. I'm convinced the only way to break him is to get a little creative. Make the most of the small-town cop image. Let him think he's facing a murder charge in addition to these others. You ready to talk to him?"

"You really are thinking outside the box, aren't you?" Rick said.

"Desperate times. Let's see how obstinate he is. If he wants to talk, heck, we can get you home before dinner. I'm sure the munchkin will have lots of questions."

"She doesn't know I'm here."

Adam's cheek inched up, and he eyed Rick. "If you say so. Anyway, Kama has Pallett and is waiting for the sheriff. She's also on the lookout for Rado."

"No luck on finding him yet, huh?" Rick asked.

"We'll find him. Unless he's left town, of course. I am very curious about the relationship between these three."

Rick nodded. "Yeah, Me, too."

Adam slid a yellow-lined notepad across the table. On the pad, he'd created two columns—one for Rick, the other for himself. He pointed at the left column. "Here's your part."

Rick read through the notes. When he was done, he pushed the pad back. "You know what? This just might work."

But after two minutes with Kiernan Walsh, Rick was convinced of three things. First, in order to make him talk, Adam really would have to hit him with the murder charge.

Second, the man was a liar through and through. And third, Walsh had been through this drill enough times to know it inside and out.

"So you weren't actually shoplifting—is that what you're claiming, Mr. Walsh?" Adam asked.

"Right. I just wanted to see how the shirt looked in the sunlight."

Adam pursed his lips as he checked his notes. "I see. That's odd, though. How exactly were you going to do that with the shirt under your other clothes?"

Walsh, though handcuffed to his chair, leaned back and gave Adam a happy-go-lucky smile. "I was going to take my jacket off, but the owner jumped the gun and accused me of stealing. Next thing I know, a couple of his overzealous goons were surrounding me and threatening to beat me to a pulp. So I made a break and locked myself in that crappy dressing room."

Rick smacked his palm on the tabletop, Walsh jerked in response and his happy-go-lucky facade faded when Rick barked at him. "Don't be stupid, Walsh. Tell the truth now and this will all go so much better for you."

Inching to one side as though he might put some distance between himself and Rick, Walsh peered across the table. "So, who are you again?"

"I'm a consultant. Working with the Seaside Cove PD. On a murder case."

Like a drunk who'd just seen flashing red lights in his rearview mirror, Walsh was suddenly all business and croaked, "Murder?" He turned his attention to Adam. "You trying to link me to that? I didn't have nothing to do with Henry's murder."

Rather than letting on that he'd caught the reference to Henry Nicholas—almost as though they'd been friends—Rick stuck to Adam's planned script. "According to you, Mr. Walsh, you weren't trying to shoplift, either. If you tell a lie about one crime, how am I supposed to believe you about another?" Looking sideways, Rick noticed that Adam's gaze was cold and betrayed no emotion.

"Oh, I get it." One corner of Walsh's mouth curled up. "You're using the big charge to get me to cop to the smaller one."

"Actually, that's not what we're doing," Rick said. "Let me spell it out for you. First, you were seen talking to Henry Nicholas and Max Rado at the coffee bar late Monday morning. According to our witnesses, you three were quite chummy. Almost as if you all knew each other. Second, Henry Nicholas was killed later the same evening. We suspect the three of you had a falling out sometime during the day. And third, Rado's already given us some information, but we also suspect he conveniently left out your involvement to protect himself. The whole thing's going to come tumbling down, Mr. Walsh. And as you probably know, he who talks first—and tells us the truth— gets the good deal. Everybody else pays...big time."

"You guys always play the same tune." Walsh leaned back in his seat and smirked. "Well, here's my part. I want a lawyer."

"Thought you might say that," Adam said. "Just tell me one thing, Mr. Walsh. Where were you on Monday evening between five and six p.m.?"

Walsh clenched his teeth. His right cheek twitched, and he shook his head. "No, man. I want a lawyer."

"I'll take that as your way of saying you can't account for your whereabouts. Rick, why don't you entertain Mr. Walsh while I call the sheriff and have them send another car. They're gonna love me today."

Walsh's smirk fell, and he sat forward. "Who'd you arrest?"

"We'll let your lawyer sort it out." Adam gave Rick a quick look, then left the room. Rick's cue to lay it on thick.

"Since you're asking for an attorney, this all gets to be very formal now. Shoplifting, first-degree murder, and theft of federal property."

"Wait! What are you talking about?" Walsh stammered. "I didn't steal anything from federal property."

At this stage of the game, it didn't matter much what Walsh had done. It was all about getting him hooked. Unless Rick was mistaken, he'd accomplished that. "You were diving near the *San Mañuel* with the intent to steal artifacts. You probably weren't aware, but diving near a federally protected shipwreck is illegal." Recalling Captain Struthers' comment about the diving accident, he added, "Then there's the crime of nautical negligence."

"What's that?"

Good, thought Rick. The guy had forgotten he wasn't supposed to talk. It was time to do exactly what Walsh would be doing. Twist the truth to his own purposes. "Your dive buddy died, Walsh. The coroner classified the death as preventable, and she believes you are culpable." Stupidity, culpability. whatever. It was all close enough for this conversation. "The bottom line is the shoplifting charge will probably be the least of your worries."

Adam returned to the room and leaned against the doorjamb. He hooked his thumbs in his belt. "Sheriff will be here, but it's going to be a while. You know, Rick, it's possible Mr. Walsh didn't actually commit the murder, so I'm pretty sure the DA will throw in conspiracy just to cover the bases." He stood up straight and started to back out the door. "I hope you explained our closing rate to Mr. Walsh. Hate to have him thinking he can beat these charges."

Rick waited until Adam was gone, then made a face and sighed as though he was completely bored. Making a show of pretending to check and make sure Adam was out of earshot, he lowered his voice. "He's always wanting to brag. You know how small-town cops are. Just because we have a one-hundred percent closing rate doesn't mean somebody's not going to break the streak. Right?" Rick stopped and let the number sink in.

Walsh swallowed hard. "A hundred percent? How many cases?"

"Oh...I don't know. I've lost track." Another lie, but Walsh's earlier confidence was fading.

"Look, what if I change my mind?"

"About what?" Rick asked innocently.

"Talking. You know. Taking the deal."

"Oh. Really? I thought you wanted to protect your friends. Honor among thieves. All for one, and one for all. Until, of course, the law starts putting the pressure on." He waited for a count of five, then added, "Somebody's going to break. It's just a matter of who and when."

A long pall of silence fell over the room. Tempting as it was to fill the void, Rick again waited. Slowly, he saw signs of increasing doubt on Walsh's face. After what felt like minutes, but was really only seconds, Walsh grumbled, "You're right. Max would probably cave and start saying all kinds of things about me."

Rick moved Adam's notepad, which they'd flipped to a fresh page before entering the room in front of him. "You know how these things break down, Walsh. One thing comes out, then another." He paused, doodled on the pad for a moment, then looked across the table. "By the way, how long have you been in Seaside Cove?"

"I got here last Thursday."

"And that's when you checked into the Seaside Cove Inn?"

"Yeah, man. I had a reservation."

"Did Max have a reservation there, too?"

"Not a lot of choices in this town, you know?"

"I certainly do." In Rick's opinion, there was no reason to let Walsh know he owned one of the places to stay. "How well did you know Henry Nicholas?"

It took Walsh a few seconds to answer. He seemed to be contemplating multiple options. As Rick had discovered early on in his days on the crime beat, only one of those options was the truth. The others were various shades of gray, all designed to make finding the bottom line more difficult.

"Well, Walsh? It's a simple question. Were you friends with Henry Nicholas or not?"

"No."

"Really? You were seen talking to him in the lobby of your motel. How did you not know him?"

"We met. Sure. But we weren't like friends or anything. It was just a casual conversation over coffee. Nothing more, man. Nothing more."

"And was it another casual conversation over coffee when you met him later in the day at Crusty Buns? I believe one witness said it was you, Max Rado, and Henry Nicholas. That's an awful lot of casual coffee conversation going on." And a huge leap because Mary hadn't known whether Rado's companion was Walsh or Pallett. But judging by the look on Walsh's face, he'd gotten it right.

"Small towns," Walsh hissed under his breath.

"You're right. It is a small town. And everybody here sticks together. Especially when the police start asking questions. Most of them are all too happy to talk about people they see as causing trouble. And you already had a black mark after that diving accident."

"It was just a casual meet-up," Walsh insisted.

"We have multiple witnesses who will say otherwise." Rick stood, letting a contemptuous scowl paint his face. "You, Mr. Walsh, are lying to me. As a result, you're going to be spending a very long time in prison." Rick spun on his heel and walked out the door, making sure to leave it open so Walsh would overhear the next conversation.

42

RICK

ADAM RAISED BOTH EYEBROWS AS Rick approached his desk, the surface of which was almost perfectly clean, the only items there, a yellow-lined notepad, a pen, and his computer. He whispered, "Ready to do a little more acting?"

Rick clamped his teeth together to keep from laughing. They were hardly seasoned actors, but they did seem to be pulling it off. All those nights of watching the real New York cops work were paying off. He kept his voice low. "Gotcha. Show him who's in control. Ready to go. I gave him something to think about. Small town cops. Gossip. Angry locals. Did you call the sheriff?"

"Not yet. I want to make sure we have plenty of time to finish this little charade. Besides, the longer our Mr. Walsh has to sit there, the more willing he'll be to tell the truth. Here's his arrest record."

Rick sat in the chair in front of Adam's desk. He scanned through the record, then again reviewed Adam's list of new charges. When he was done, he let out a whistle, making sure it was loud enough for Walsh to hear. "Adam, this is enough to put this guy away until he's old and gray. What do you think? Thirty years?"

From the corner of his eye, Rick saw that Walsh was straining against his bonds. He had one ear aimed toward the open doorway and it appeared they had his attention.

"If we get Judge Sumner, it could be longer."

"He doesn't take kindly to strangers coming into his jurisdiction, does he?"

"Not one bit. Hates it, actually." Adam turned suddenly. He slammed his palm on the desktop and bellowed, "Rick! What did you do? You didn't close the door!"

"Sorry." Rick picked up the papers and tried to sound apologetic as he stood. "I guess I forgot." He returned to the interview room, closed the door behind him, and took the seat opposite Walsh. "Hard-nosed cops."

"Was that about me?" Walsh asked. His confidence, which had started to erode earlier, was now in full-blown retreat. His uncertainty was growing rapidly.

"You see anybody else around here who's looking at going to jail?" Rick deliberately focused his attention on the papers in his hand, but held them so Walsh couldn't read the writing. He blew out a long, slow breath. His eyes darted over the page again. "This is serious. Congratulations, Mr. Walsh. You've graduated to the big time."

Walsh's forehead puckered. Beneath the deep furrows, his dark eyes narrowed their gaze. "What are you talking about?"

"The DA wants to make an example of you. He's going to pull out every stop to see that you are convicted. Do you know how long you could get for these charges? I lost count around thirty years. Especially when you throw in conspiracy to commit murder. Man, that's a big one."

"I never did that!"

"It sure looks like you helped conspire to murder Henry Nicholas. Plus, now you're refusing to cooperate. The DA will press this all the way." Rick blew out another breath. "Can you imagine how long the trial's going to take? You could spend years in prison just waiting for motion after motion to be filed.

How's it going to look with all these other charges on top of that? Man, you are so over your head. I hope you have a lot of money for attorneys. Otherwise, you'll be represented by some overworked public defender who just wants your case over."

"What if I want to talk?"

"You know how it works. It depends on what you can tell me."

"What kind of deal am I going to get?" Walsh leaned forward in his chair, his physical discomfort obvious. "Can you make the felonies go away?"

Rick shook his head and chuckled. "Really? Stop wasting my time, Walsh. I'm tired of you."

"Okay, okay. Look, I...uh...me and Henry go back a ways."

Rick felt his brows knitting together. Had they missed an important link between these men? "Are you admitting you lied to me and that you knew Henry Nicholas prior to coming to Seaside Cove?"

"Uh...yeah." Walsh shifted uncomfortably in the chair. His eyes darted around the room.

"How long have you two known each other?" Rick demanded.

"We...uh...went to the same high school."

The hesitancy in Walsh's voice had Rick wondering whether Walsh was making this up on the fly or if they were finally getting down to the truth. He suspected it was the latter. If it wasn't the truth, why reveal it at all? In a way, this was like writing stories under a deadline, just with an audience and immediate feedback. What the heck? He should press hard and force Walsh to make corrections.

"So, why were you both here at the same time?"

"It was just...what do they call it, man, uh..."

"Serendipity?" Rick asked sarcastically.

"Yeah, man. That's it. Serendipity. Neither of us knew the other one was going to be here."

"You know what I call that line? BS." Rick stood, went to the door, and opened it. "Adam, how long before the sheriff gets here? Walsh is just weaving fairy tales."

"Okay, man. Chill. I'll tell you the whole story."

Rick kept one hand on the doorknob as he watched Walsh's face for some sort of tell. Beads of sweat had formed on the man's forehead. Walsh had to be feeling the pressure. He was avoiding eye contact, too. Time for the big push. Make Walsh lie himself into a corner and he might have no other option than to tell the truth.

"Don't waste my time, Walsh. If I think you're lying, your chance at a deal goes down the toilet. You understand?"

"Yeah, man, I understand."

Rick closed the door and returned to his seat. He leaned forward, looked straight at Walsh, and held his gaze until the other man glanced away. "I'm listening."

A purple vein on Walsh's neck pulsed rapidly. "Like I said, me and Henry have been friends since high school. I go to his bakery maybe once a month or so. Last time I went in, he starts telling me about this sunken treasure ship. Me, I'm like a diver. Always looking for cool places to explore. Right? So I'm thinking me and my dive buddy could come up here and check it out. Maybe score a couple things we could sell."

It was time for the litmus test. Was Walsh telling the truth or lying? They already had the name of the diver who had died. If Walsh didn't identify the dead man correctly, there was no point in continuing. "The guy who died in the accident last week. Was he your regular dive buddy? What's his name?"

Walsh groaned, and for once, Rick thought just maybe the man was feeling some remorse. "His name was Tiny Renet."

Rick made a note with the name and placed a check mark next to it. At least Walsh hadn't lied about the obvious. "How long had you two been diving together?"

"Five years. Tiny was a solid diver, man. I don't know what happened to him. He had a heart condition…" Walsh let out a heavy sigh. "Maybe he had a heart attack or something. He was okay one minute and dead the next."

Studying the name he'd written on the paper, a chilling thought occurred to Rick. He wrote Henry Nicholas's name on the same line as Renet's, then connected the two with a line. Could Walsh have killed Nicholas because he knew something about the accident?

Across the table, Walsh fixed his gaze on the two names with the connecting line. His jaw worked from side-to-side. Rick drew another line beneath both names. "You know what I'm thinking. Don't you?"

Walsh shook his head. "No, man. Those two aren't related at all. Tiny and Henry never met."

"They didn't have to. Not if you did something that contributed to Tiny Renet's accident and Henry Nicholas found out about it. Talk about a major problem. You cause one death, tell your friend about it, then have to kill him when he threatens to turn you in."

"No, man. No way. That ain't what happened." Walsh jerked upright in his chair. He cursed his shackles, then focused on Rick. "This is why people say you shouldn't talk to the cops. They twist everything around. I didn't have nothing to do with either of those guys dying. Honest."

Good. Walsh was panicking. All Rick had to do was keep him from demanding a lawyer. "You know, Mr. Walsh, one of the things they teach you in journalism school is that when someone tells you they're being honest, it probably means the opposite. I want to believe there's not a connection, but you've got to give me more."

"Like what?"

"For starters, you still haven't explained to me how you and Henry Nicholas both arrived in Seaside Cove at almost the same time. It wasn't serendipity, was it?" The vein in Walsh's neck throbbed and Rick used it to maintain his focus. If he could stay cool and calm, Walsh's panic would grow. But he still had to make sure the magic words didn't come out.

"Why do you say that?" Walsh asked.

"For starters, Tara Amengual made their reservation at my B&B at the end of April. I'll bet if I check with Ray at the Inn, he'll tell me you made yours right about that same time. That's a little too much coincidence for me. Henry Nicholas knew you were coming here to dive. Didn't he?"

Walsh slumped back in his chair. His voice dripped with resignation. "Yeah. He knew. Henry wanted in. He thought there would be a lot of money to be made, and he was thinking he could sell the stuff me and Tiny brought up. But that wasn't gonna fly, man. Henry didn't have the connections he needed to pull off a gig like that. I told him he wasn't right for it, but he wouldn't let up."

The throbbing vein was settling down. Walsh appeared happy to talk about others, just not himself. "You're telling me a baker was interested in trying to sell stolen artifacts on the black market?"

"It had something to do with Tara, man."

"Really? What?"

"Henry said he was gonna need a lot of cash. He was tired of being a baker. Guy wanted to have some fun for a change. That's why he hooked up with Tara. He was thinking he could keep his family and have her on the side."

"And he wanted you to supply him with stolen goods so he could fund this lifestyle. Sounds like it would have been a nice little arrangement—for him. Was Tiny Renet okay with this?"

"Tiny liked money as much as the next guy, man."

"You didn't answer my question. Did he know about this deal?"

"No. He didn't. All he knew was that we might do a little scavenging. That's all."

If anything, it sounded like there was a possibility Tiny Renet had become a problem. His death could have been a convenient accident, or... "Something's not quite adding up here, Walsh. If you were planning on stealing from the *San Mañuel* directly, why try to get a job working for Flynn O'Connor? You weren't the only two involved in this operation. Were you?"

The look on Kiernan Walsh's face said it all. There was indeed a conspiracy. The extent wasn't clear yet, but Rick was confident he knew who the other players were.

43

ALEX

I CAME TO KATHRYN'S ROOM thinking I was gonna get the proof I'd need for my story about how her ex-boyfriend killed Mr. Nicholas. But I didn't find anything like that. Kathryn even made me see just how crazy it was to go out to the lighthouse all by myself—and what I almost did to my dad and Marquetta.

She's got her head tilted and is looking at me kinda sad-like. "Alex? What's wrong?"

"I...never thought before I ran out there. I was sure Mr. Pallett was the one who killed Mr. Nicholas. But if he was with you, then I was wrong about him. And I could've gotten hurt for nothing."

She combs her fingers through her hair, pulling it away from her face and more to the side. "Are the police considering Victor a suspect?"

"I dunno about the murder, but they wanna talk to a couple of guys they think he knows named Rado and Walsh."

Kathryn gets another funny look on her face. "Rado? Max? Are you sure?"

"Totally. Why?"

"Because he's a friend of Victor's."

Whoa! If McNasty and this Rado guy were friends, maybe he was friends with Walsh, too. And that means they might also have known Mr. Nicholas. "We gotta talk to Tara." On my way to

271

the door, I tell Kathryn we can talk in the kitchen if Tara's in her room.

Because I don't have to worry about McNasty, I totally feel less stressed out. Tara's in her room, and after I spell out the connection me and Kathryn discovered, she's super pumped to talk to both of us. I tell her to meet me in the kitchen and then tell Kathryn that we're gonna talk downstairs.

After that, I run down to see if Marquetta's working on dinner. When I push open the butler door, she sees me right away and waves for me to join her. "Hey, Sweetie, come on in. You can help me."

Uh oh. I knew I was gonna have to explain what I'm doing, but I didn't think about what to say. I let the door close behind me and stuff my hands in the pockets of my jeans. "Marquetta... don't be mad."

Her forehead puckers and she looks at me. "Why would I be mad at you?"

"Because I'm kinda in the middle of something."

Marquetta closes the refrigerator door and comes closer. She gives me the Mom stare. Oh man, I am so busted. But before I can say anything, the butler door opens behind me. Both Tara and Kathryn come in, and when they see us, they stop.

"We're so sorry," Kathryn says. "We didn't realize you were in the middle of—"

Marquetta raises her hand. "It's fine, Kathryn. I gather Alex has dragged you two into her investigation." She stops, gives me the Mom stare again, and clears her throat.

Okay, it's totally my turn to fess up. "I think we discovered something important."

"And that would be..." Marquetta lets the words hang in the air.

"We...me and Kathryn...we think Mr. Nicholas and Mr. Mc
—. Mr. Pallett knew each other before they came here."

Kathryn steps forward and adds, "Tara and I were talking on
our way downstairs, and we both believe Alex is right. There was
something going on between our boyfriends..." She kinda
cringes and looks at Tara. "Sorry. My boyfriend and..."

Tara crosses her arms and smirks. "The rat."

Kathryn laughs at first, then covers her mouth with her
hand. A couple seconds later, she says, "Ouch. Tara, he's dead."

Tara pulls on a strand of hair and nods absently. "I know.
When I found out about his wife, I wished he was dead. Now
that he really is, I honestly do feel terrible."

My dad always says it's not nice to speak ill of the dead, but I
get it. If Daddy broke up with Marquetta, we'd all feel terrible. It
also makes me kinda sorry I've been calling Mr. Pallett a name
like McNasty. If he turned up dead, I'd feel rotten about that,
too.

Tara steps forward and holds out her phone. On the screen
is a picture of Mr. Nicholas standing behind a glass display case
like the ones in Crusty Buns. There's a photo on the wall and
when she blows it up, she says, "After Alex asked me to come
down here, I remembered that there was a picture in Henry's
store of him and three of his friends. Henry only mentioned one
of the men in the photo—Kiernan Walsh. I never knew the
names of the other two until just a few minutes ago."

I can feel my forehead getting all puckery as I stare at the
screen. "No way," I whisper. The guy who was talking to Flynn
O'Connor in Crusty Buns is also in the photo. Holy moley.

"I know, right?" Kathryn's eyes flash with anger as she looks
at the picture again. "Victor and Henry sat at the breakfast table
and pretended they'd never met. What's with that?"

"At the time, I thought Victor looked familiar, but since those two were pretending to be strangers, I just figured my mind was playing tricks on me," Tara says.

"Would you send that to me?" I ask.

"Sure."

It only takes a few seconds and my phone pings. I open the photo and look at the four men. "They had to be hiding something. What'd you think it was?"

Tara shrugs. "I don't know. But it couldn't have been good. Right?"

"So it's Mr. Pallett and Mr. Nicholas." I point at the man on the end. "Is that Kiernan Walsh?"

"That's him," Tara says.

Marquetta points at the one on the other end. "Is that Max Rado, then? They all look so young."

Staring at the photo, I have to wonder. Could my dad and Chief Cunningham have it wrong? Are they even looking at this Kiernan Walsh as a suspect?

"We need to check these guys out," I say.

"Alex, we shouldn't be getting into this. Your dad wants you to stay out of the investigation. Send him the photo."

This is the lead I need for my story. I found it. I wanna follow it. "But I'm not getting into the investigation. I'm just gonna write a story for the Cove Talkers Newsletter. We could expose these guys and what they've been doing."

Marquetta takes a deep breath. She looks at Kathryn, Tara, then me. Her voice is super determined. "Which is?"

"I dunno yet. But we could find out. Right?"

"Wow," Kathryn says. "She is persistent. Marquetta, you have your hands full. Alex, I think Marquetta's right. Your dad probably isn't aware of this connection."

We all look at Tara. She swipes at her cheek and her jaw gets tight. "I agree. I think one of these men killed Henry. I'd bet anything it's Kiernan Walsh. Henry's told me about him before. They went to high school together. He became a diver, and after I told Henry about the *San Mañuel*, he said he couldn't wait to tell Kiernan. That guy's involved in all kinds of sketchy things. I'll bet he and Henry had a falling out."

So the same guy who was involved in the diving accident could be the killer? Whoa. I look at Marquetta, and she's not looking happy with me at all. Uh oh. I'm like on super thin ice. But I can't stop now. The answer to who killed Mr. Nicholas might actually be in his past. I've got a lead. I'm totally on this.

"No, Alex." Marquetta's looking at me like she can read my thoughts. "You, young lady, are not getting involved in this investigation. Send that photo to your dad right this minute."

"But Marquetta…"

"No. This time, I'm very serious. You were already attacked by one of these men. I don't care what you call it, but I will not let you put yourself in danger again."

Rats. There goes my story.

44

RICK

RICK HELD UP A HAND to keep Walsh from saying the words that would stop his questioning in its tracks. He'd spent enough time dealing with unwilling sources on the crime beat to know when he'd pushed too far. Trying to confirm who else was involved in the plan to steal from the *San Mañuel* was apparently the point too far—at least, for now. "Let's back up for a second. I have a couple of questions about..." His phone bleeped with a message from Alex.

—*Urgent. Check this out.*

Short and to the point, but exactly what he needed—a reason to break away.

"Excuse me for a moment." Rick left the room abruptly and pulled up the details of the message. It was a photo. He enlarged it and, as he scrolled across, recognized all the faces—Henry Nicholas, Kiernan Walsh, Max Rado, and Victor Pallett.

He called Alex's number. She answered almost immediately. "Hey, Daddy."

"Interesting photo you sent me, kiddo. Where'd you get it?"

"Tara took it at the bakery Mr. Nicholas owns...owned. It proves Mr. Nicholas and Mr. Pallett knew each other before they came here."

"I can see that. We're talking to Walsh right now. And this photo means we should question Pallett, too." Rick stopped,

276

closed his eyes, and said, "I'll call you back in just a minute, Alex. Nice work."

"Daddy, wait! There's one more thing."

"What's that?"

"Mr. Pallett was with Kathryn when the murder happened."

Tara. Kathryn. Alex was far deeper into her own little investigation than he'd realized. Again. And now Pallett had an alibi. So far, Walsh hadn't alibied out. If Pallett could account for his whereabouts and Walsh couldn't, maybe they really did have the killer in custody. Before they could make that assumption, though, they needed to find Rado. His could be the critical piece of the puzzle that would seal the deal on Walsh.

"Hang on." Rick put the phone on mute, then went to Adam's desk and asked if it was too late to get Pallett back. He kept Alex on mute while Adam called the sheriff, who told him their deputy was at the lighthouse parking lot documenting the scene with Deputy Kama.

Adam raised his eyebrows and looked up at Rick. "You want to talk to him again? Confirm this supposed alibi?"

"Absolutely. I think he's up to his neck in this, too. And this is exactly the leverage I need to get Walsh talking about a conspiracy." He backed away, then returned to the conversation with Alex. "Adam's having Pallett brought in here for questioning. What makes you think he has an alibi for Monday evening at about five?"

Alex told him about her conversations with Kathryn and Tara. When she was done, he felt an odd combination of pride and fear. He'd learned from experience how difficult it was to stifle Alex's interest in crime. Which meant he had to live with his fears. "Nice work, kiddo. Tell Marquetta I'll be home late." Rick pocketed the phone, then looked at Adam and sighed. "What am I ever going to do with her?"

"Nancy Drew comes through again, huh?"

"Looks like it. Right now, I need to ask this joker a few more questions." He turned and stalked back to the interview room.

He was reaching for the doorknob when Adam called to him. "You taught her to be inquisitive, buddy. You should be proud."

Rick nodded. He knew he should be. And he was—but he was also scared to death that Alex's curiosity would someday get the better of her. When there would be nobody around to help.

Pushing open the door to the interview room, Rick shoved the phone in front of Walsh's face. "You've been holding out on me, Walsh. You all knew each other."

The man's eyes widened as he stared at the screen. "I...I can explain."

"That's what most people say when they're about to do some serious time in prison." Rick took another look at the image. "So you, Pallett, Rado, and Henry Nicholas were all in this together. But Henry Nicholas got greedy and someone had to take him out of the picture. Were you the one who did it? Or would you rather point the finger at one of your buddies?"

"It wasn't me, man. I didn't kill Henry. We've been friends for a long time. I liked him. I didn't hurt him."

"What about Victor and Max?"

"Those two were always tight in high school. They played football. Me and Henry, we were into other things."

"Like?"

"Band. We both played music. Victor and Max were all about sports."

Rick looked down at the notes Adam had made. There was something about this foursome that bothered him, but he couldn't put his finger on it. He flipped through the yellow notepad, looking for that elusive key he knew he was missing. "So you and Henry were best buds. You hung out all the time, but you haven't seen either of the other two in ten years? Come on."

"No, man. That ain't what I'm saying. I, um, did some work with Max. He had a couple jobs where he needed someone to help move a shipment he brought in. I helped him out. You know. It was just work."

Jobs? Rado called himself an importer. Or was the term a euphemism for smuggler? "What kind of shipment? Are we talking drugs?"

"No, man. No way. Max didn't do drugs. He's strictly art and that kind of stuff."

Once again, Walsh had settled back in his seat, and he appeared perfectly content to be talking about someone else. But his time to play this little game was running out. "Did Victor help Max out with these jobs?"

"No. Victor's got an MBA. He was like too good for doing grunt work."

"You know what I'm thinking, Walsh? First, you're almost out of time because a sheriff's deputy will be bringing Victor Pallett into the station any minute. Once that happens, we'll ask him the same questions. I'm sure he'll be more interested in saving his skin than you are in saving yours. Second, all of you being here in Seaside Cove at exactly the same time is way too coincidental. If he tells me a different version of why he was here, it means any hope you have of a deal goes down the tubes. One last time, was he in on this *San Mañuel* plan, too?"

"Him and Max stayed friends and they're both kind of entrepreneurs. Those two are the ones who figured out the plan. Handled the organizing end of things."

Still nothing much...unless...there had to have been some kind of falling out. "But everything didn't go as planned. Did it?"

"What do you mean..." Walsh's face turned ashen. He simultaneously tried to shrink down in his seat and peer through the window at what was going on in the front office. "Wait...you really do have Victor?"

Rick turned, saw that Deputy Kama and a sheriff's deputy were escorting Victor Pallett across the room. Pallett spotted Walsh and started to mouth something, but Deputy Kama jerked the handcuffs at his back and forced him to face the other way.

"I told you. You just didn't believe me. Looks like time's up for a deal, Walsh. I'm pretty sure Pallett, once he starts hearing the full list of charges, will be smart enough to cut a deal with us. You said he has an MBA, so the guy's not stupid. Unless you want to correct what I see has happened here. My guess is by the time Mr. Pallett's done singing, you'll be swinging." Rick stopped and sliced his fingers across his throat. "You know, death row."

"Wait, man. I didn't kill nobody."

"Sure you did. You and our victim have been buddies since high school. You decided you could make a ton of money by working together. You were going to insert yourself into the salvage operations and use that to steal artifacts. Rado was approaching it from the business side. He'd fence the artifacts and find other ways to fleece the locals. Unfortunately, Henry Nicholas found out what you two were doing and demanded a cut of the action. When he started making threats, you were the one with the prior record and you stood to lose the most, so you killed him."

"No! That's not it at all!" Walsh licked his lips and squirmed in his chair. "Can you take these things off, man? My hands are killing me."

Rick ignored the plea. Instead, he pressed forward. "Which part was wrong, Mr. Walsh? Did Henry Nicholas come here and change his mind? Is that why you killed him? Because he was going to blow the whole deal?"

"I keep telling you, man. I didn't kill him. You got it all wrong."

"Then enlighten me. Because once we start talking to Mr. Pallett out there, I'm pretty sure you're going to be the one who's left hanging. Pallett will lead us to Rado. The two of them will pin the murder on you. They'll both go free and you'll take the fall."

"No, man. I ain't going down for them. I don't know who killed Henry, but Max has always had big plans for his business. They just never worked out. You know? Good ideas, but some bad luck."

More like bad idea, bad execution, Rick thought. At least, if it involved half the spaghetti he'd thrown on the wall for Walsh. "You said before that he was an importer. Are you telling me the truth?"

Walsh smirked. "I guess you could call it that. Max never liked the nine-to-five routine. You know? He was always looking for ways to work less and make more money."

"And how many times did you work with him on these grand plans?"

"Maybe once or twice a year. If he needed help, he'd call me in."

"What did you do for him?"

Walsh looked away, then fixed his gaze on Rick. "Am I gonna like incriminate myself or something here?"

"I can't tell you that until I know what we're talking about. Can I? But remember, he who is the first to cooperate gets the prize."

"Okay, man, you win. But you gotta promise to get me a good deal."

Rick summoned all the confidence and reassurance he could when he was telling a bald-faced lie. "You cooperate with me and I'll do everything I can to help you."

"Okay. Things didn't go down right on the last deal. Max, um, had this idea for us to bring in these oriental pieces of art and like sell them for a huge profit. He had this client lined up. The guy had buckets of money. Right? But Max decided we could make even more if we made a few copies and sold those after we sold the original."

Rick leaned back in his seat. "I'm listening. What happened?"

"It took a lot of cash to line up a guy who was gonna make the copies. Because Max didn't have that much, we had to find buyers before we, like, had the product. The client found out what we were doing and cancelled the whole deal. Max lost almost everything. I never got paid either."

"That's it? That's all you've got? I hate to tell you this, Mr. Walsh, but bad business sense isn't a crime."

"There were a couple of other deals. Kinda high risk and they fell through."

"As I said, just because Max isn't a good businessman doesn't make him a criminal. We're still looking at you for everything from shoplifting to murder."

"Okay. What if I told you it was Henry who told Max about the *San Mañuel*?"

Rick sat up straight and rested his elbows on the table. "Now you have my attention. So Henry Nicholas was involved in this deal from the beginning?"

"Yeah. It was because of him and Tara that we started this whole thing."

45

ALEX

Hey Journal,

I was super bummed when I came up here. I thought I was gonna have my first big story and be the one to solve the murder case, and then Marquetta made me turn my evidence over to my dad. That really sucks. Marquetta's still down in the kitchen having a glass of wine with Kathryn and Tara. But when I got an email alert on my phone about the mayor wanting to talk to me, I fibbed and told Marquetta I wanted to come up here so I could start on the story.

I wonder why the mayor wants to talk to me? Maybe I can get her to give me a quote for my story. That would be super awesome! I'm gonna call her at Scoops & Scones right now.

Xoxo,

Alex

My phone's already got a contact for the mayor, so I bring up her number and dial. She answers a few seconds later. "Scoops & Scones, the most delicious ice cream in Seaside Cove. Francine speaking."

Wow. That's like a super big mouthful. "Hey, Madame Mayor. It's Alex."

"Oh, Alex dear! My favorite junior detective. I'll come right to the point. I'm concerned about how this murder investigation is going. Do you think Chief Cunningham and your father are up to the task?"

Whoa. She does want my help! Should I tell her I'm just gonna be a reporter now? I guess I don't really wanna be a junior detective anymore. Do I? "They're totally making progress, but neither of them like think outside the box."

"Which is your speciality, my dear." Her voice goes up a little when she asks, "Have they confided in you at all?"

"Nuh uh. You know how my dad is. He totally wants me to stay out of police business."

"Yes...well, I'm not so sure that's the best thing for the town. After all, I'm the mayor and I should be the one to decide what resources this town has at its disposal. Don't you agree?"

"I guess."

"And as the mayor, I'd like to have my best resources working this case. And right now, Alex, the town needs you. I need you."

Holy moley. My dad works with Chief Cunningham 'cause they're friends and they help each other out. But now the mayor thinks they both need my help? Maybe I can't retire.

"I'm sure you agree that those who work for the town should be keeping me, as the mayor, apprised of their progress?"

"Totally." My heart is pounding in my chest so fast I can hardly sit still.

"After all, how can the leader of a town be expected to shine the light forward when she's being kept in the dark by those surrounding her?"

"Uh huh." That's like so over the top, but that's the mayor. Her dial's always like on ten.

"Well, since we're in agreement, I might have a special assignment for you. If you're interested, of course. It's a very big task. Somewhat of an undercover operation."

Oh, wait, that's kinda like reporting. Right? I fist pump the air. Yes! "What do you need done, Madame Mayor? I'm ready to help."

"Excellent, my dear. Excellent." She pauses for a second, then lowers her voice. "Well, what I need is information. I have to find a way to break down the doors of communication resistance and make sure the lines stay open both ways!"

Uh. Okay. That sounds like more over-the-top mayor stuff. Total enthusiasm, but what is she really asking? "What do you need?"

"Wonderful, my young recruit! I knew I could count on you. Now, what can you tell me so far?"

I tell her about the photo of the four men and how they're all friends from high school. By the time I'm done, she's making lots of humming noises. "You said you needed something done undercover. What do you need me to do?"

"Hmmm...let me get back to you on that. Ta ta!"

She hangs up before I can say anything. And that's when it hits me...the mayor is always very pushy and knows what she wants. If she really did want me to do something on the investigation, she would've asked me to do it right now. I scrunch up my cheek and look at myself in the mirror over my dresser.

Instead of a strong, confident investigator like my dad or Chief Cunningham, I see a kid. She's got reddish blonde hair that's pulled back in a ponytail and tied with a purple scrunchy. She's wearing her favorite sweatshirt. It was a present. From her dad. At Christmas. She's me.

The sweatshirt is purple and still kinda big, but it's comfy and when I wear it, it reminds me of how much he loves me. And what have I done? I just sold out him and Chief Cunningham to the mayor. I gotta talk to my journal.

Hey Journal, me again.

I got a problem. The mayor called and asked for my help with the murder investigation. My dad's told me in the past that she's always trying to go behind people's backs. I never thought she'd actually do it to me. Not after I helped solve so many murders. But I think 'cause I was so eager to feel like an important part of this town, I fell into her trap. And it's not like my mistake is gonna go away. As soon as she says something to Chief Cunningham or my dad, they're gonna know exactly who blabbed.

I gotta make this right. Maybe I should talk to Marquetta. She'll know what to do.

Xoxo
Alex

Marquetta, Kathryn, and Tara are all in the kitchen when I get there. They've each got a glass of wine and are putting together a gigantic salad. It looks like Marquetta's changed our dinner plans and we're gonna have a spaghetti feed. Which is cool 'cause I love spaghetti, but my stomach's doing flip-flops and I don't think I can eat.

This is awful. I've screwed up. And now I have to admit it in front of three adults. And if I wait, the mayor will say or do something that might hurt my dad or the chief. That's gonna make things even worse.

"What's the matter, Sweetie?" Marquetta asks as she crosses the room and kneels in front of me. "You look like you've just lost your best friend."

My face feels so hot. And I so don't wanna do this. But I have to. "I think I screwed up." Even my voice sounds like it's not happy with me. Maybe it hates me for what I've done.

Marquetta stands up and looks over at Kathryn and Tara. "Ladies, I think I have an emergency here. Have you got this?"

My jaw drops. Marquetta never lets anyone take over her kitchen. Especially a guest. That, like, never happens. She gets a thumbs-up from Tara and a 'no problem' from Kathryn.

"Come with me." Marquetta rests her hand on my back and guides me to the rear of the kitchen to the small table and chair just inside the French doors. She pulls out one of the chairs. "Sit."

My shoulders slump as I do what I'm told to do.

"What's wrong, Sweetie?"

"I...the mayor called. She told me she needed my help with the investigation. She said she wasn't getting any information from Chief Cunningham or my dad."

Marquetta gets a real serious look on her face and nods. "And she made it sound like you were going to be a huge help to her by serving as her spy."

My face gets even hotter. I wince. "Yeah. I'm worried about what she'll do with the information."

She looks at the clock on the wall and takes a deep breath. "It's going to be tight, but I think we can do this. Put on your shoes, Sweetie. We're paying Francine a visit."

On our way out, Marquetta apologizes for leaving, but tells Kathryn and Tara we'll be back in a half hour. I totally don't know how we're gonna undo what I've done that fast, but if

Marquetta says we can do it, I believe her. We're out the door in a couple minutes.

As we go down the steps, Marquetta says, "We have to walk quickly, Sweetie. We need to make sure we get to Scoops & Scones before Francine locks up."

We're there in like five minutes. So there's twenty to go before the store officially closes. I look up at Marquetta, hoping she's got some magic words she can say to the mayor to fix my mess. "You haven't told me what you're gonna say to her."

Marquetta reaches for the doorknob. She gives my shoulder a gentle squeeze. As she opens the door, she says, "I'm not, Sweetie, you are."

46

RICK

WALSH'S STATEMENT FELT REMINISCENT OF a story Rick had covered about a hit-and-run in New York. Alex had been three at the time, and he could still recall her watching him, fascinated by the pretty lights on the computer screen as he'd poured over record after record about a man who ran down his business partner. The reason, in a true case of convoluted logic, was to hide the embezzlement scheme the victim had uncovered. Even at sentencing, the perpetrator blamed his partner for forcing him to commit murder.

"Are you saying Henry Nicholas caused his own death because he told you about the *San Mañuel*? If that's your story, Mr. Walsh, I think Henry Nicholas would disagree with you."

"That ain't what I'm saying, man. You cops. Always twisting things around. He like heard about this place from Tara. She was telling him what a great piece of history it was. Henry was never a history kind of guy, you know? But when she told him about some wreck in Cartagena and how it was worth billions, Henry started thinking. Just a little portion of that and we'd all be set for life. So he got all excited and called me. Had me make a special trip into the store. He was going on about how much money we could make, so I said I'd talk to Max and see what we could do. Max thought it had potential, so he went to see Henry himself a couple days later."

"When was this?"

"About two months ago. End of April."

"What were your roles in this little endeavor?"

"Max was gonna try to strike a deal with Flynn O'Connor. He's convinced there's a little larceny in everybody, so he offered to help her get some extra cash on the side. I was trying to get on as a diver so I could keep tabs on the good stuff that was being brought up."

"But you got greedy, didn't you? That's why you and Tiny came to Seaside Cove a few days early and tried to grab a few extra pieces just for yourselves."

"I, like, told Tiny we were doing recon, so I'd know what to say when I tried to get hired."

"How did Tiny die?"

Walsh hung his head. "I went in someplace I shouldn't have and got stuck. Tiny was trying to free me. A beam broke away and fouled his line. He got me out, but he got disoriented and took off. My air was about gone, so I had to go up. I found him on the shore. He must've dumped his gear and tried to make the surface. Brutal way to die, man."

It was the first sign of genuine remorse Rick had seen Walsh display. "I'm sorry about your friend."

"Thanks. When I saw his face..." Walsh closed his eyes and shivered. "I couldn't have killed Henry. I'm gonna be seeing Tiny's face for the rest of my life. I couldn't have another one on my conscience."

"You know what, Walsh? I actually believe you." There was a huge problem with the plan that Rick could see—Flynn was passionate about preserving history. She'd no more make a deal to sell artifacts than she would willingly jump in front of a train. Unfortunately, he couldn't let Walsh wallow in his sorrow. They still had a killer to catch. "Things started to fall apart. Didn't they? Flynn turned Max down."

"Yeah, man. Cold. She threatened to call in the cops."

"And you'd already been rejected by Captain Struthers, so you were cut off, too."

Walsh let out a dejected sigh. "Guy told me I wasn't qualified. Plus, he called me reckless."

Rick had to wonder if these guys had any brains at all. Their plan had more holes in it than the *San Mañuel* itself. It was hard to keep a sarcastic edge out of his voice. "Did you ever think that Captain Struthers turned you down because the diving accident you were recently involved in is still under investigation?"

Walsh frowned, then blinked a couple of times as though he'd just come to a major realization. Greg Turner was right— the law might not be able to punish stupidity, but life sure could. Even so, the accident could be the leverage he needed to break Walsh. "So did Henry panic after Tiny Renet died? Things started to fall apart. Henry got worried. Is that why he was here? To back out?"

"You think Henry wanted to—no way, man. He was here because he wanted in. When I told Max about this thing, he was like, we gotta bring in Victor. He'll have connections and be able to move this stuff."

Rick's pulse picked up. So Pallett's part was to traffic the stolen goods? The man was incredibly obnoxious, but Rick had never thought about him having black market connections. Max certainly wouldn't need two people doing the same thing...which meant someone was cut out. A double-cross as a motive for murder? It was certainly possible. "But you said Henry and Max made a deal at the end of April."

"They did, but a few days later, Victor and Max got together and decided to cut Henry out. Max never told me he hadn't talked to Henry. Ain't no surprise Henry tore into me when I told him about the plan and he hadn't heard from Max. I promised to talk to Max for him. When I did, Max promised me he'd take care of it."

"Did he?"

"I don't know, man. I don't think so." Walsh grimaced. He leaned to the side as if trying to get a better view of what was going on in the lobby.

Beads of sweat on Walsh's forehead had gathered like raindrops on glass. Rick felt certain the man was close to giving up. He already knew he'd been seen talking to the police by one of his partners in crime. "Pallett saw you, Mr. Walsh. You're now a liability and your only hope is me. Did Henry know he was out when you were talking to him and Max in the lobby and having coffee?"

"I don't think so. He was acting like everything was all good."

"So Henry must have found out after he talked to you and Max late Monday morning. Which means he might have learned about it that evening."

"Yeah. I think that could be what happened." Walsh collapsed back into his chair, his face carrying the pain of too many mistakes.

Rick stood, gathered up his notepad and pen, and looked down at a broken man. "The good news for you, Mr. Walsh, is that I think the murder charge is off the table. What will happen with the rest of this? I don't know."

"But you said..."

"I said I'd try. I didn't guarantee results."

Rick left Walsh sitting alone, staring through the pane of glass toward the main office where Victor Pallett sat with his back to the room. Clearly, Walsh had finally realized just how much trouble he and his friends were in. The question was, who killed Henry Nicholas? Rather than wasting a lot of time with Victor Pallett, the best solution was to verify his alibi with an unimpeachable source. Rick went to Adam's desk, leaned over, and whispered, "Walsh isn't our guy. It's either Pallett or Rado. I'm sure of it."

"But Pallett has an alibi," Adam whispered back.

"Adam, you know as well as I do that people don't have to lie to be wrong. And that their perception of time can be highly inaccurate. Ten minutes, that's all I need."

Adam nodded. "Go. We'll keep these two under wraps."

Rick went out the front door of the station, took a left, and walked the two blocks to the alley that led to the Crooked Mast. He jogged to the right, then went in through the front door. Cecelia Martin was again at the receptionist's station. After a quick hello, he asked to speak to Ken Grayson.

"Sure, Mr. Atwood. I'll get him." Cecelia darted into the back of the restaurant and returned with her boss in tow.

"What's up, Rick?"

"Do you know who Victor Pallett is?"

Ken huffed. "Everybody knows who he is. Arrogant jerk."

"Lousy tipper, too." Rick and Ken both darted glances at Cecelia, who seemed to realize she'd become the center of attention. She assumed a more defensive posture and blurted, "Well, it's true. The girls have been talking. None of them want his table."

With a wave of his hand, Ken dismissed the apology. "It's okay, Cecelia. I've heard what they say about him." Ken looked at Rick. "What about him?"

"Were he and his girlfriend here for dinner on Monday evening?"

"Yeah, I'm pretty sure." Ken regarded Cecelia and asked, "Who served him?"

"Mary Ellen. She was super upset because he made his date wait for almost an hour."

"Oh yeah. I remember hearing about that. Mary Ellen was madder than a wet hen because she couldn't turn the table." Ken nodded and shook his head. "On top of it all, he was complaining about our limited selection of dinner specials during Happy Hour. Guy walks in with two minutes to spare and thinks he should be able to order filet mignon at half price."

Rick frowned. Two minutes? But Kathryn claimed they'd arrived at five.

Cecelia extended one leg in front of herself and crossed her arms. "Plus, he pulled the old 'forgot my wallet' trick. Seriously? Some guys."

Ken smirked. "You want the dirt? Ask the girls. They know it all."

That's exactly what Rick wanted. The dirt. "Your Happy Hour ends at six. Right?"

"That's right," Ken said.

"Cecelia, do you know exactly what time he got here?"

"Like Ken said, two minutes to six." Cecelia pointed at the receptionist's station. "I remember because I told him Happy Hour was ending, and he made a big stink right over there."

"I heard him all the way in the back, so I came out to see what was going on. It was after six by the time we seated him, but I said we'd honor the specials. His girlfriend was real nice about it and tried to calm him down, but he wouldn't listen to her. Don't know what she sees in that guy."

"Saw," Rick said. "She's leaving him. Rented her own room at the B&B."

"Good for her," Cecelia said smugly. "That'll teach him."

What might teach him even more was a murder charge. "What else can you tell me, Cecelia?"

"Well...Mary Ellen said his date was on her second glass of wine and she was starting to complain about him when he showed up. She claimed this was typical. That he was always inconsiderate. Then he came in all grumpy and she almost walked out on him. They didn't hardly talk during dinner because he was drinking a lot."

Right now, Rick wanted to believe he had everything he needed to put the screws to Pallett. But if he had written proof, that would be perfection. "Ken, can you get me a copy of his receipt?"

"Yeah, sure, but it will take me a while and we're starting to get busy." He raised his hands to his sides. "It is Happy Hour."

"Why don't you ask his date?" Cecelia said. "She used a credit card. He tried to take the receipt, but Mary Ellen handed it directly to her."

"I'll do that. You've both been extremely helpful. Thank you." As Rick walked out the door, he dialed Adam's number. He told him he was on his way to the B&B to talk to Kathryn Larkin and that he might have just cracked Victor Pallett's alibi.

47

ALEX

I can't believe Marquetta is gonna make me face up to the mayor and deal with this. I thought grownups were supposed to fix things when the kid messed up. But Marquetta hasn't failed me yet. She's stood up to protect me in the past, and that makes me wonder why she's forcing me to do this now.

As the door opens and the bell tinkles to announce there's a customer, my insides are cringing. And when the mayor looks up from behind the counter and her pasted-on smile drops, I feel like I wanna throw up. This is awful.

But then Marquetta's hand is there, taking mine, urging me forward. "Come on, Sweetie. You've got this."

I look up at her. She's smiling at me like nothing's wrong. Like she's super proud of me. I can't let her down, so I take one step forward, and then another. Over on the side wall, there's the big aquarium where Homer the turtle lives. Usually, I go over there and watch Homer while my dad chit chats with the mayor. I've never like had to have an actual conversation with her. Even the phone call was just me saying yes when she asked.

The mayor's smile comes back, but it's super forced. "Well, Marquetta, what brings you two in? A scoop or a scone before dinner?"

"No, Francine. I'm sure you know why we're here."

Marquetta lets go of my hand and urges me toward the counter. All the glass on the ice cream cabinets is spotless. Not a single fingerprint or a nose print in sight. I swallow hard. My throat is super dry, and I'm not sure if I can do this. I look up at Marquetta. She gives me a little nod, and I get it.

She's got confidence in me. I should have some, too. I take a deep breath. "Mayor Carter, I think I made a mistake when we were talking on the phone."

Any kind of friendliness is gone now. I can see her eyes getting kinda steely. The mayor doesn't like people saying no to her.

"How so, Alex?"

Might as well just blurt it out and get it over with. "You took advantage of me."

She huffs, then cuts her eyes at Marquetta. "Did you put her up to this? I don't take advantage of children."

I take another step forward. "No," I say firmly. "Marquetta had nothing to do with this. I realized after we spoke that you weren't actually asking me to help, you were asking me to spy so you would know what was going on when the chief isn't ready to share what he has."

Her hand goes to her heart and her jaw drops. "Well, I never!" She turns again on Marquetta. "This is outrageous."

"Oh, cut the act, Francine," Marquetta says. "You and I both know what you've done." She pauses, then quietly adds, "And you know it's not the first time."

Whoa. This has happened before? What's with that? I cross my arms in front of me and look Mayor Carter in the eye. "If you don't back off, I'll write about this in the Cove Talkers Newsletter and then everyone in town will know what you've done."

Her mouth flaps up and down a couple times, but she doesn't say anything. Instead, she straightens up and rolls her shoulders in little circles. After she clears her throat, she looks at me. "Well, Alex. Far be it from me to hold someone to a deal when they don't want any part of it. I'm sorry you felt coerced. I'll remember for the future to be less...forceful...when we speak."

Wow. That was easy.

"Are we done?" Mayor Carter asks.

I'm tempted to say yes and forget about the whole thing, but it wouldn't undo the mess I might have made. "No. We're not done. I can't make you forget what I told you, but I want you to promise me you'll keep it to yourself."

The smile I get from the mayor isn't her fakey kind. It's more like a smirk. Like Billy Thornton's. "Protecting yourself, are you?"

"Nuh uh. I'm telling my dad and Chief Cunningham what I've done. I don't want them getting..." I look up at Marquetta.

"Blindsided?"

"Yeah, that's the word. I don't want them getting blindsided by this. So, you can't use it against them."

The mayor pats the back of her hair and mutters, "Fine. I'm just trying to do my job."

"Then you should let Chief Cunningham do his."

"My, my, sage advice coming from a ten-year-old."

"Eleven." I pull back my shoulders and stand a little taller. "Are we good?"

She scrunches up her face, then gives me a smile that I don't think is fake. "Yes, we are." She looks over at Marquetta. "And you, my dear, are going to make a wonderful mother."

"That's where you're wrong, Mayor Carter. She already is." I grab Marquetta's hand and squeeze it tight. "We can go now."

"Don't you want some chocolate ice cream?" Mayor Carter asks. "On the house."

"Not today. We're having spaghetti for dinner and I don't wanna spoil my appetite."

"My, my. How quickly they grow up. Well then, toodeloo, it's almost time to lock the doors."

We say goodbye to Mayor Carter. When we get out on the sidewalk, I take Marquetta's hand again. "You really are a great mom."

Her eyes get all watery. And then she sniffles a couple times and kisses the top of my head. "I'm proud of you. What you did in there was very brave. You're growing up. Let's go home and see what Kathryn and Tara have done to my kitchen."

"I'd kinda like to tell my dad and Chief Cunningham about this."

"Why don't we wait for your dad to get home? You can tell him then."

"Okay. At least that way, I'll have a few more hours of freedom before I get grounded."

Marquetta puts her arm over my shoulder and gives me a little hug. "Well then, come on. Let's whoop it up for your last hours of freedom."

The second we walk in through the front door, we can smell tomatoes cooking and bread baking. The smells make my stomach growl, so Marquetta tells me to go get ready for dinner while she checks on the kitchen.

I rush upstairs, wash my hands, and hurry back down. When I walk into the kitchen, I'm shocked to see that my dad is here. He holds his arms out. I run to him, and he scoops me up.

He groans as he's holding me. "Oh, you're getting heavy. If you gain one more pound, I won't be able to lift you."

"You're being silly," I tell him. Then I give him a huge hug. "There's something I have to tell you."

"Sounds serious. Do we need some private time for this, or can we talk here?"

I look at Marquetta, Kathryn, and Tara. "Marquetta knows what happened. Kathryn and Tara might as well know, too, 'cause it kinda affects them."

He carries me over to a barstool at the island and puts me down, then pulls another one over and sits next to me. "What's up, then?"

I tell him about Mayor Carter's phone call and how she convinced me to spy for her. While I'm talking, Marquetta walks around behind him. He reaches across to his left shoulder and takes Marquetta's hand in his. When I tell him about the trip to Scoops & Scones, he looks up at her for just a second and they exchange a little smile. It gives me a warm feeling inside 'cause I think they really are proud of me.

"I'm sorry, Daddy. I was being selfish when I talked to the mayor. Are you gonna ground me? I kinda deserve it."

He takes a long breath, and when he lets it out, he looks pleased. "You know, Alex, it takes a lot of courage to confront someone who's taken advantage of you. I'm proud of how you handled it."

"Marquetta's really the one who got me there." I hang my head and confess the truth. "I totally didn't wanna go see Mayor Carter."

Marquetta takes her hands from my dad's shoulders and stands next to me. She holds my hand in hers and gives it a reassuring squeeze. "But you did, Sweetie. It's not easy standing up to someone with a big personality like Francine. I'm proud of you, too."

I sniffle and lean into her. "I couldn't have done it without you."

"You did just fine all on your own."

My dad leans forward. He rests his elbows on his knees and looks at me. "I agree. And I think you've learned a valuable lesson. I have no intention of grounding you."

I suck in a quick breath. "Honest?"

"Honest. You displayed a lot of maturity with what you did. Do you want me to tell Adam?"

"I should do it. Well, then you should call him because the minute I'm done talking to Kathryn, I'm heading back to the station. I think we're getting close."

"Can I stay while you talk? Or do I have to leave?"

"That depends on why you want to stay."

"Because I want to write about it for the Cove Talkers Newsletter. Everybody should know the truth about what you and Chief Cunningham did to solve this murder."

My dad gets a look of surprise on his face. He watches me for a couple seconds, then looks at Marquetta. She looks so happy when she says, "It appears that she's following in her father's footsteps."

"Okay. You get the exclusive on this, kiddo. But you can't print any of it until the case is closed. Do we have a deal?"

"Deal."

He holds out his hand. Wow! He wants to shake on it? A big surge of happiness rushes through me. He's treating me just like I'm a grownup. Or a real reporter. Awesome.

48

RICK

RICK LISTENED PATIENTLY AS ALEX described the events of the past couple of hours, but all the while, he was unable to escape the feeling her confrontation with the mayor might not be the last. Francine was, if anything, determined to do what was best for Seaside Cove. At least, best as she saw it.

"Since we have a deal to give you the exclusive on this, I need to make sure of one more thing."

Alex pulled back and eyed him warily. "What?"

"No more meddling in the investigation. If you do, our deal is null and void." Alex scrunched up her face, so Rick added, "It would be off."

"Oh. I'm cool with that. I think you and Chief Cunningham are gonna figure it out now."

Satisfied Alex would honor her word, and that she'd be much safer reporting the news than being a junior detective, Rick turned his attention back to another doubt he'd been harboring. "Kathryn, I wanted to ask you a few questions about Monday evening. It's my understanding you and Victor went to the Crooked Mast for dinner during Happy Hour."

"Oh God, not Monday night again. Will I ever live this down?" Kathryn's face flushed pink. She averted her gaze, then sucked in a breath and looked sheepishly at Alex. "I'm sorry, Alex. I didn't...tell you the whole truth earlier. If you can be

302

strong enough to face the town's mayor, I should be able to face my own vanity."

"It's okay. If it hadn't been for Marquetta, I wouldn't have done it."

"That's kind of you, but I'm old enough that I should know better. The truth is, Victor and I agreed to meet at the Crooked Mast at five for dinner. He said he had a few things to take care of and promised he wouldn't be late this time. I told him I'd get us a nice table and have a glass of wine while I waited for him."

"Did you tell your server that he'd done this before?" Rick asked.

A soft pink glow crept into Kathryn's cheeks. Rather than answering, she looked away again and nodded.

"What time did you actually arrive?"

"I was there at five. I'm always very punctual. Unlike Victor."

"And what time did he show up?"

Kathryn began fidgeting with the hem of her shirt, and as she did so, her cheeks brightened even more. Finally, she let out a groan. Her shoulders slumped as she spoke. "I'm so pathetic. I waited almost an hour for him. He promised he wouldn't do that to me on our vacation."

Reaching out, Tara squeezed Kathryn's hand and said, "You're free of him now."

"Why I let myself be treated so badly, I don't know. His usual excuse was work. I kept telling myself he was trying to build a business, and I had to be understanding. But we were here on vacation! Deep down, I think I knew what was going to happen. It was two-for-one, so I ordered two glasses of wine. I promised myself that if he didn't show by the time I finished the second glass, I'd walk out and get him out of my life. I made that second glass of wine last as long as I possibly could."

Tara put an arm around Kathryn's shoulders. "Oh, honey. Don't beat yourself up. We all make mistakes."

Kathryn leaned her head against Tara's. She sniffled, then suppressed a frustrated laugh. "We're quite the pair, aren't we?"

Tara's eyes brimmed with tears. She, too, sniffled, then said, "Yes, we are."

"But you're both strong and will get over this," Marquetta said.

"I agree," Alex added.

"I hate to ruin the mood, ladies, but I have a few more questions I need answers to. Kathryn, how did Victor act when he showed up?"

Kathryn combed back her hair with her fingers and gazed at the ceiling. She let out a heavy breath before she began. "That was part of the reason I didn't walk out on him right then and there. He was in a foul mood. I know how nasty he can get when he's angry, so I did what I usually do and put on a good face while he had his little tantrum. He made me promise not to tell anyone he was late." She made a face and sighed. "When you asked me before, I told myself I was protecting Victor's trust. But what I was really doing was avoiding reality. I didn't want you to think I was a loser."

"You're not a loser," Alex said firmly.

"Did you pay for dinner?" Rick pressed.

"You know about that, too? Fine. Yes. Victor claimed he forgot his wallet."

Alex's jaw dropped. "For real? He stuck you with the bill? That's cold."

Kathryn looked up at the ceiling and barked out a laugh. "Yes. And I was fool enough to pay for it. This wasn't the first time it had happened."

"You didn't really have much of a choice, Kathryn. Ken's very hard on people who try to pull a dine-and dash. He would have called the police the minute you walked out the door," Marquetta said.

Tara added, "Hey, think about it, Kathryn. In a small town like this, there's no way to escape."

They both laughed quietly, then Kathryn said, "You're right. Besides, I could never live with myself if I tried that."

"I'm not trying to embarrass you, but if you paid the bill, you should have the receipt. Do you?" Rick said.

"Yes, it's in my purse." Kathryn hung her head and stood. Without waiting to be asked, she crossed the room to the small dining table and picked up one of the two purses. It only took her a few seconds to find the receipt, which she brought to Rick.

He read the timestamp. She'd paid the bill at 6:48 p.m. He took a photo and asked, "How long after you finished dinner did you sit and talk?"

Kathryn put her fingers over her mouth, but she couldn't hide her rueful smile. "With Victor? Are you kidding? Victor's conversations are all about himself, but Monday night, he was not in a talkative mood. I doubt if we said ten words during dinner. And once I found out he was sticking me with the bill, it just killed the evening. I would have requested a different room that night, but I knew you didn't have any available."

It appeared they had reams of circumstantial evidence— plenty to convict a man in the court of popular opinion—but what the law needed was hard proof. And so far, Kathryn had provided nothing substantive. Where did they look? "At breakfast, Victor and Henry were acting like they didn't know each other. Do you know why they were carrying out this charade?"

"I have no idea," Kathryn said. "The entire time, I never had a clue."

Tara shook her head. "I didn't either. I never picked up on them knowing each other until later. I'd seen the picture of the four of them at the bakery, but it was from ten years ago and they'd all changed. After I heard about Henry being murdered, I...blanked out. It wasn't until I was talking to Alex that the lightbulb went on."

"So were they acting like strangers 'cause they wanted to hide what they were doing?" Alex asked.

Rick nodded. "I think so, kiddo. Tara, did Henry display any signs to indicate he might have been in danger?"

"No. He was always enthusiastic about things. He was the happy-go-lucky guy. You know, the one who constantly believes life will work out. It was strange, though. He had kind of lost some of the enthusiasm for his baking recently."

"How so?" Rick asked.

"He started talking about other ways to make more money. He'd say things weren't going his way at the bakery, but he was never specific. When I asked, he just said he was working on something big. A big change in his life. That's what he called it. I thought he was thinking about expanding. I kept expecting him to get over whatever was bothering him because I'd never seen him with anything but a positive attitude."

"Would you say he was worried about something?"

"Not worried. More like, annoyed." She paused and nodded to herself. "Yeah. He started being annoyed by the bakery and the customers. It was very unlike him. When we first met, he was so enthusiastic."

Given Tara's feelings about Henry, there seemed little point in concealing what they'd learned about Henry Nicholas's background. Maybe the key to his murder lay deep in his past? "Did he ever talk to you about an auto accident?"

"As a matter of fact, we did talk about one on the way here. It happened after he freaked out in the mountains on the road from San Ladron. There was an oncoming car..." Tara shuddered and let her voice trail off.

Marquetta's hand went to her heart. A worried look crossed her face as she gazed at Alex. Rick understood the reaction completely.

"We were almost in an accident on that road," Alex said. "Marquetta saved us."

"Sweetie, I nearly killed us because I let myself get distracted."

"You're both safe," Rick said. "That's the important part. Was Henry driving?"

"No. Actually, he'd asked me to drive over the mountain. We came around a tight curve. There was an oncoming car. It drifted wide on the turn, and Henry started screaming. He almost scared me off the road. I pulled over and demanded to know what had happened. He told me he'd been in an auto accident years before and still had flashbacks."

"Did he tell you anything more?"

"He only said he was in the car with friends. Otherwise, he wouldn't talk about it."

"Henry was the driver. He received a DUI for it. Nobody died in the accident, but there were injuries. I don't know how serious they were."

Tara's eyes moistened as she shook her head. She covered her mouth with her hand and sniffled. Looking at Kathryn, she muttered, "We really picked the winners, didn't we?"

The two women hugged again. It made Rick wish he didn't have more questions, but he did. No matter how difficult that might be. When Kathryn and Tara pulled apart, Tara looked at Rick.

"You know what? There was something else. When I went to the room to see Henry, he was talking crazy. He told me he was tired of letting others push him around. I thought he was referring to me dumping him and forcing him to leave the B&B. It just really ticked me off, and I tore into him. That made him even madder, and he said it was time to start settling old scores. I got scared and walked out on him."

"Did he say anything more specific?"

"No. But I got the impression that whatever he was talking about was somehow linked to the big plans he'd been making."

"And he'd never given you any indication of what those big plans were?"

"I'm really sorry, but no. He kept telling me he couldn't talk about it. All he ever said was we'd soon be living the good life."

Which would make sense if the plans involved stealing and selling artifacts on the black market. In Rick's experience, he'd never heard of a thief who expected their plan to fail. Obviously, Henry hadn't known he was being cut out of the scheme he'd helped start. Rick knew more than he'd known an hour ago. Maybe even enough to close in on the killer's motive. Otherwise, there might be no leads left.

49

RICK

ORDINARILY, THIS LATE IN THE day, sunlight would be streaming through the kitchen windows. But the fog was returning again and Rick felt darkness closing in. As though she could read Rick's mind, Marquetta flipped the wall switch. The room flooded with light from the recessed LEDs overhead. The brightness seemed to force the emotional darkness to recede. He wished this murder case could be solved so easily. At least he might now have a lead. "Tara, how old was Henry?"

"Twenty-eight. Why?"

"I'm working on a theory." Rick pulled out his phone and dialed Adam. He gave him a short recap, then said, "It's possible this whole thing is somehow tied to the accident ten years ago. Can you ask Walsh who was actually driving?"

"According to the report, it was Henry Nicholas."

"Adam, what if Henry wasn't really driving? Wasn't he a minor at the time of the accident? Depending on the timing, it could be he was covering up for whoever was behind the wheel."

"I'll find out who owned the vehicle. I'll also check with Walsh. Are you on your way back?"

"I just have one or two more questions before I leave here." Rick disconnected and regarded Tara. "I'm sorry. I know this is a lot to take in."

"It's okay. You have a job to do, and I really would like to see whoever killed Henry pay for it. I had no intention of going back to him, but I also don't think he deserved to die so young. He might not have been a great man, but he wasn't evil, either. You said you have another question?"

"Yes. Did Henry's change in behavior happen after you two decided to come here?"

"Absolutely. He didn't start his complaining until about a week before the trip. At the time, I was worried he might be getting cold feet, so I avoided making a big deal of it. But the reality is I think I knew then that things weren't going to work out in the long run."

"Thank you both. I appreciate your candid responses. Now, try not to let Alex pepper you with too many questions." He nudged his daughter with his elbow and winked. "I know she can be a little over-the-top."

Kathryn's gaze momentarily darted towards Alex, then she wrinkled her nose and said, "She's okay in my book."

"Mine, too," Tara added.

"Do you have time for some dinner?" Marquetta asked.

"I wish. I have to get back. Adam's got two of our suspects in custody and we're looking for the third. I'll call you later."

"Okay. I understand. By the way, I talked to Devon and his back was still acting up. He says he'll be here tomorrow, but I'm getting worried about him, Rick."

"If his back problem doesn't clear up soon, we'll have to find someone else to finish. Now, I have to run."

Rick kissed Alex and Marquetta goodbye and then made his exit. On the way, he kept wishing that Adam had all three of the conspirators in custody, not two. While circling the roundabout at Front and Main, he looked further down Front Street. He was only a half block from the Inn. Both Adam and Deputy Kama were tied up with Walsh and Pallett. If Max Rado was in his room, he could ask him to return to the police station and they could nail down the case against Pallett.

Instead of continuing up Main Street to the police station, Rick walked toward the Inn. Not wanting to deal with Ray and his attitude, he ducked into the back parking lot and went directly to Room 104.

After knocking, he considered putting aside his personal feelings about Ray. There was a chance—not a very good one, of course—that Ray would be cooperative and help him out without a lot of drama. Who was he kidding? He'd wasted time coming here and might as well get back to the station.

He left the same way he'd come in, taking the walkway out the back entrance. He'd just turned and was about to duck into the parking lot when he nearly collided with a man wearing a plaid flannel shirt and jeans. The man had a baseball cap pulled down low and was hunched forward, which made it impossible to see his face. He uttered a gruff, "Sorry," then stepped to the side. Rick recognized the voice immediately.

"Wait. You're Max Rado. Aren't you?"

"Who's asking?" Rado growled. A second later, he looked up and grimaced. "Oh, you. The consultant."

The hairs on the back of Rick's neck stood up. He'd been in tense situations as a reporter and recognized the voice of desperation. Coming here alone had definitely been a mistake. "That's right. With the Seaside Cove Police. You mind answering a few questions, Mr. Rado?"

"Can't right now. I'm in the middle of something." He sidestepped Rick and pushed ahead, pulling a key from his pocket as he walked.

Rick marched after him. He tried to keep a note of authority in his voice as he spoke, even though he knew his next words were based on a hunch and a bluff. "Are you trying to leave town? I can have an officer here in about three minutes. And they'll block the one road out of town. You can't get away."

Rado spun around. He approached slowly, a menacing swagger in his walk. "What do you want?"

"To know about you and Henry Nicholas."

"Nothing to know, Mr. Consultant. We just met here over coffee." Rado jerked his thumb in the general direction of the lobby, then turned around and started back to his room. He jammed the key in the lock and twisted the doorknob.

Rick's phone pinged with a message. He recognized the tone. It was Adam, but he couldn't take his attention off of Rado. "You're lying, Max. You've known each other since high school."

Rado muttered something under his breath as he removed the key and let the door slip closed. "Whatever. We knew each other, sure. Doesn't mean we were friends. Henry was the one who always wanted to tag along. A big pain, that's all he was."

"I believe he was more than that. How about this instead? He was the one who saved your butt from going to jail for a DUI? Am I right?"

"Don't know what you're talking about."

"Oh, come on, Max. We've uncovered too much of the truth for you to get away with that kind of crap."

Rado's jaw tightened. He straightened up, anger clearly painted on his face. "What are you saying?"

What the devil was he doing? Was he calling Rado a killer? If so, this was definitely not a place he should be alone. It was better to go easy and let Adam take over in an official capacity. He had the badge and the gun. "What I'm saying is, I'd like to know about you and Henry Nicholas. I'd also like to know why the four of you pretended to be strangers."

"Because we knew how it would look. Small town. Suspicious minds. Wagging tongues. You live here. You ought to know what I'm talking about."

Perfect logic if you were up to no good, thought Rick. "And Henry?"

"Me and Henry weren't friends. We drifted apart after high school. He went and did his little bakery thing while I worked at building an import business. We didn't have the same interests."

"Really? From what I've heard, you did when it came to the *San Mañuel*. You, Kiernan Walsh, Victor Pallett."

Rado's jaw tightened, then his demeanor changed again. "Look, I don't know what you heard, but you probably didn't get the whole story,"

"Okay. Why don't you tell me the whole story?" Rick put the last two words in air quotes, then waited.

"All right. Sure. Henry found out what was going on and he wanted in. He didn't have the connections to pull off the kind of business deals we were working on."

"By we, you mean you, Walsh, and Pallett."

"That's right. Me and Victor have been friends for a long time. We grew up together. And Kiernan, he's done work for me before, so I know he's reliable. But Henry? He always wanted what he couldn't have."

One thing Rick knew for certain—Max Rado was a true chameleon. He must have realized coming across as a jerk had only made things worse, and now he'd decided to pivot and use the nice-guy routine. Kind of like a game of good cop/bad cop all rolled into one player. Rick's phone pinged again with a reminder that he hadn't checked the message.

Rado took a menacing step toward Rick, but his tone was cool and calculated. "Maybe you should get that."

Glancing down, Rick noticed that Rado's hands were curled into fists. He had Rado on the edge. Who knew what might happen if he pushed further? But he needed help. And time. Somehow, he had to buy a chunk of it.

"Maybe I should." Rick took a step backwards and pulled out his phone and checked the message.

—*Pallett just confessed to being an accessory. We have to find Rado.*

"Anything important?" Rado asked.

Rick shook his head and tried to sound casual. "It's a friend making plans for tonight. Guy will keep texting me every two minutes if he doesn't hear from me. I'll send him a quick text."

"Suit yourself." Rado backed away and pulled out his key again.

Rick tapped the reply icon. With only a few seconds to shoot off a message, he wrote, *SCI Help.* He could only hope Adam understood the hasty acronym and could get here before this got out of hand.

Rado had just taken a step into the room when Rick called out, "What did you have that he wanted? Plans to make a fortune off the *San Mañuel?*"

Keeping his hand on the doorknob, Rado stepped back into the walkway. He glared at Rick for a moment, then switched to a resigned tone. "Yeah. But it didn't work out. That archaeologist wants to keep all the stuff her team brings up. I know what she'll do. She'll sell it herself."

Rick didn't take the bait, but used the momentary silence to pocket his phone. Getting into a theoretical discussion of ethics about what would happen to the artifacts after they'd been catalogued and examined was not where he wanted this conversation to go. It was a rabbit hole with no good ending. "I understand your frustration. You thought you had a solid plan for everyone to make some money, and Flynn turned you down. But wasn't Henry the one who brought the deal to you?"

Rado pulled in a slow breath, then let it out between his teeth. "You've been talking to Kiernan."

The clock was ticking. Adam should be on his way. But he hadn't replied. What was going on? There was only one thing Rick could do. He had to keep the conversation going. "You're right. I have been talking to him. From what he's told us, Henry brought the information about the *San Mañuel* to him, and then he came to you."

Rado waved off the comment. "The *San Mañuel*'s been on my radar for a long time. In my business, you have to stay on top of what's going on. You think I wouldn't know about something this big?"

"He didn't mention that part. So you're saying Walsh is trying to make you look bad?"

"Could be. He's done work for me, but we're not tight or anything. It's also possible he's just shooting off his mouth about something he knows nothing about. That would be classic Kiernan."

There was one way to find out if that was true. A pop quiz. He needed some irrefutable fact. "So Kiernan's got the story wrong? You've been working on a deal for the *San Mañuel* for a while?"

"Long time. Yeah."

Behind Rado's cool exterior, Rick could see the anger and desperation churning. Where in the world was Adam? Help should have been here by now. At least a minute ago. Rick desperately replayed the events of those seconds when he'd sent the message for help. What could have gone wrong?

"I'm impressed," Rick lied. "How long have you been planning this operation?"

"Almost three years. I've been monitoring the situation ever since the discovery. It was time to make a move."

Like a lightbulb flashing on in the middle of the night, the reason help hadn't arrived became crystal clear. Rick had been in such a hurry that he'd pocketed the phone before he made sure the message was sent. He was alone. And he had to keep cool, no matter what.

"Wow. Three years. That's a lot of planning."

"I just had to work on it off and on. But yeah. It was a huge amount of work."

And a lie. The *San Mañuel's* exact location had only been discovered a little over a year ago.

50

RICK

RADO PUSHED OPEN THE DOOR to his room and ducked inside. Rick moved into the doorway, intending to block the other man's exit. Surely Adam would be looking for him. All he had to do was stand here and delay Rado's departure.

But as Rado crossed the room to where a gray duffle bag sat on the bed, a small, pink baker's box on top of the dresser caught Rick's attention. The hairs on the back of his neck rose again, and Rick stepped into the room.

Rado hoisted his bag with his left hand, then strode toward Rick until they were standing so close he could smell the man's breath. Sweet. Sugary. A hint of cinnamon. Mary O'Donnell's words came rushing back—*he does have a wee bit of an afternoon sweet tooth.*

"I'm leaving this Podunk town. See you later, Mr. Consultant," Rado growled.

"I don't think so." Rick's voice sounded confident, but his insides churned with a blend of rage and fear as he reached down to flip open the box.

Rado's right hand flew up to shove Rick aside. Rick countered with a sideways thrust. The sound of bone hitting wood filled the room, and Rado squealed in pain. The duffle landed with a thud on the carpet, and Rado doubled over. He cradled his wrist in the crook of his left arm, groaning as he slumped down onto the edge of the bed. Slowly, he tried to raise his other hand, as if signaling surrender. He wheezed, "Okay, okay. That's my bad wrist, man."

Keeping Rado in his sight, Rick opened the box. Inside, there were two cupcakes. They'd been decorated with hearts. In the center of one, there was an engagement ring made of gold and silver icing.

"This was the box Henry brought with him."

Still cradling his right hand in his left arm, Rado stared at the box. Slowly, his shoulders began to shake. He looked down at the floor and muttered, "Stupid Henry."

"Why'd you kill him?"

"What kind of fool do you think I am? I got nothing else to say to you."

Though the man was still defiant, Rick had little doubt he would eventually talk. He pointed at the cupcake with the decorative ring on top. "I'll bet when we cut open that cupcake, we'll find an engagement ring. It was the ring Henry was going to give to Tara."

Max turned his attention to the box. His mouth opened and he shook his head. He still cradled the hand that had hit the dresser. The impact had been hard, but not so much that it would cause this kind of pain...unless he had a preexisting injury. Rick wanted to smack himself on the forehead. He knew exactly how that injury had happened. "You were the one injured in the auto accident ten years ago. Weren't you?"

"Yes." Rado grunted a couple of times, then drew a ragged breath and moaned, "It's over. I've screwed up my entire life." He coughed out a breath. "Twice."

Rick moved closer to the door, partially to keep it propped open and partially to provide a quick escape should Rado turn violent. "You were the one driving the car, weren't you?"

Rado looked up at the ceiling. His eyes glistened with tears. "Yeah. Henry was in the back seat. It was the first time he ever got drunk, and he wasn't doing good. I convinced Victor and Kiernan to move him into the driver's seat and swear he was driving. Henry went along with it later because he wanted to be one of us."

"He was under age, unlike the rest of you. Right?"

Rado hung his head and nodded.

"And after the accident?"

"We all stayed really tight until the trials were over, but after that, things broke apart. Me and Victor remained friends, but Henry went his own way."

"And Walsh? Did he stay friends with Henry?"

"Kiernan never felt right about the whole accident thing. He drifted away afterwards. I think he stayed friends with Henry because he felt guilty, but he kept in touch with me. We were never the same, though."

So Walsh had been telling the truth. And that meant Rado had not only blamed Henry Nicholas for an accident that wasn't his fault, but had also tried to steal his get-rich plan. He laid the scenario out for Rado, who stared at the floor until Rick finished.

"Like I said, I've screwed up my life twice now."

From the corner of his eye, Rick caught a movement. He shot a glance in that direction and held up his hand to stop Adam from entering. All he needed was a couple of minutes. "You won't be able to blame anyone else this time, Mr. Rado. You're out of options."

"I know. I think I have known since I pushed Henry and he fell into the dresser. I was always a risk taker. One of those guys with guts who'd roll the dice no matter what the odds. I've just taken too many hits in a row." He grimaced and raised his wrist with his other hand. "No pun intended."

"Walsh said you lost a lot of money the last time you worked together. How much did you lose?"

Rado let out a sigh. "Everything. That was the moment when I realized I hadn't been smart about the risks I'd been taking. Too many stupid choices."

"Starting with the auto accident?"

"Should've taken my punishment right then and there. Would've saved me all this." He stared at the dresser. It was an exact duplicate of the one in Henry Nicholas's room. "Henry'd probably still be alive, too." He paused, then added, "I didn't mean to kill him. We got into an argument and he came at me. I pushed him and he tripped." Rado barked out a disgusted laugh. "Over his own feet. Guy was a klutz."

"What did you do when he fell?"

"I called Victor. He's chill under all kinds of pressure. I figured he'd know what to do. He told me to get out of the room before I left DNA evidence."

If the call had gone to anyone else, Rick imagined the advice would have been to call 9-1-1, but with Victor Pallett, the choice to leave the chaos made perfect sense. Rado would have plenty of time for self recriminations. Maybe eventually he'd realize how he could have done things better, but for now, Rick was going to take the confession as a win. He breathed in a sigh of relief as he gestured for Adam to enter.

After Adam had advised Rado of his rights and put him in the back of his vehicle, Rick asked, "How'd you know to find me here? I tried to send you a text, but I must have missed the send button."

Adam cut his eyes back toward the Inn. "Ray." He chuckled. "Apparently, your little conversation with Mr. Rado upset a couple of his guests. They called the office, demanding that he deal with the argument going on in the courtyard. He called me to complain. I put two and two together and realized it had to be you."

"Two and two? What do you mean?"

"The munchkin called me right after you left the B&B. She said you'd just left, but she wanted to be the one to tell me what she'd done. After she'd unburdened her guilt, I told her it was no problem. All Francine did was be herself. And Alex, well, she's only a kid. Francine should have known better. I'll have a talk with her. Anyway, when you didn't show up within ten minutes, I figured you'd stopped somewhere. And when Ray's call came in, I knew it had to be here."

"Huh. Imagine that. Ray Villari actually helped me out for a change."

"Send him a Christmas card." Adam clapped Rick on the back. "Good job, by the way. And thanks for your help. Now, go home. Kama and I will be turning these clowns over to the sheriff. After we get rid of these three, it's all up to the system."

While watching Adam pull out of the parking lot, Rick decided to talk to Ray and thank him. He found Ray at his desk in the office, peering at the computer monitor.

Rick cleared his throat, then said, "I wanted to say thanks for calling Adam."

Without looking away from the screen, Ray grunted, "Just doing my civic duty."

So much for a Christmas card. Rick grimaced and started to back away. "Okay then. See you around, Ray."

Rick had taken only a few steps when Ray called out. "Hey. Was that guy really the killer?"

"Yes. He confessed, and I suspect the coroner may yet come up with some DNA evidence to seal the deal."

Ray snickered and nodded to himself. "Good job. Glad you got him." With that, he turned around and went back into his office.

All the way home, Rick thought about his brief interaction with Ray. The compliment hadn't been much, but it was the nicest thing Ray had ever said to him. Who knows? Maybe there was hope for at least a cordial relationship yet. Or not.

Upon walking through the front door of the B&B, Rick breathed in the aroma of sautéed onions, tomatoes cooking, and freshly baked bread. He hadn't been very hungry on the walk home, but he suddenly realized he was famished.

He also heard voices. Women laughing. Talking. Alex's voice, somewhere in the middle of it. It sounded like contained chaos. And it was all coming from the dining area. He poked his head around the corner and looked into the room. Four of the tables for four had been pushed together and were covered by a white tablecloth. Marquetta and Alex sat next to each other. Next to them was Traci Peterson. Marquetta's mother sat at one end and lined up on the other side were Anita Jones, Kathryn Larkin, and Tara Nicholas.

"This looks like quite the party," Rick said.

Alex turned around in her chair, then rushed over. He scooped her up in his arms, and this time he didn't even feel like making a joke about how she was growing. He kissed her forehead.

"I love you, kiddo."

"I love you, too, Daddy. Did you get the bad guy?"

"Max Rado did it. The case is officially closed. My part of it, anyway."

Marquetta poured Rick a glass of wine and brought it to him. She kissed him, and said, "You're free to get married then?"

"Mrs. Soon-to-be Atwood, I most certainly am."

"Then you're welcome to join us." She handed him the glass. "But you have some catching up to do."

Rick raised his glass in a toast. "In that case, let's drink to smooth sailing from here through the wedding!"

51

ALEX

Hey Journal,

Today's the wedding! Daddy and Marquetta get married and I can officially start calling her Mom. I kinda accidentally on purpose snuck it in yesterday and she said she really liked the way it sounded! I'm so over-the-moon. I can't believe this day is finally here!

And even the weather seems like it's happy because it's gonna be perfect, too. Lots of sun. (Our fog went away early this morning!) A nice breeze. (Not super gusty like it has been.) And best of all, no murders!

You know what, Journal? Something awesome happened last night. We had the rehearsal dinner at the Crooked Mast, and when Cecelia was seating us, she asked Marquetta what she was doing for music. When Marquetta told her we were using a boombox, Cecelia volunteered to play. Even Marquetta didn't know Cecelia played violin, guitar, and keyboards. And then, after that, Mr. Grayson said he would cook for Marquetta this morning. What's super amazing is that she took him up on the offer! That's like twice this month she's let somebody else in her kitchen! And one of those times was cooking with guests. I'm like...wow.

All the guests who were here last week are gone. I guess Anita, Kathryn, and Tara are becoming friends. They had a long time to get to know each other 'cause Anita drove them back to LA. It sounds like they're all gonna stay in touch. They even said they might come back for a reunion! Yay! We like repeats!

Gotta go! It's time for the wedding!

Xoxo

Alex

A hand gently touches my shoulder. My breath catches and everything around me gets all blurry. Traci squeezes my shoulder and pulls me a little closer. I lean into her. I don't usually like frilly dresses, but the one I'm wearing is the most beautiful thing I've ever worn. It's a pale purple...Traci called it violet. Mine doesn't have sleeves, and it's got a ribbon at the waist. Traci's dress is the same color as mine, but it's a different style. She says it's the adult version. I don't care. The dress I'm wearing makes me feel pretty. And light. And free. And beyond happy.

My dad is wearing a tux. When I saw him, he told me he had it in New York and never got rid of it. He's super handsome. And standing here in the gazebo next to Traci, seeing him and Chief Cunningham across from us, I think my heart is gonna burst. When we arrived in Seaside Cove a year and a half ago, I never thought I'd feel this way again.

Cecelia's been playing *Somewhere Over the Rainbow*, but when she finishes, she gets a signal from Mr. Gray and starts playing the here comes the bride song. And when Marquetta steps out from the French doors, even Grandma Madeline puts her hand to her heart and starts to cry.

Watching Marquetta...my future mom...walking slowly along the path to the gazebo, I think she's the most beautiful bride I've ever seen. She's holding onto Mr. Gray's good arm. Marquetta told me last night she chose him to give her away because after her dad and Captain Jack died, Mr Gray was the closest thing she had to a father. Her lacy top is simple, but elegant. All the fluffy, tulle layers in the skirt are rustling in the breeze. It almost looks like she's walking on air.

I swipe at my cheek. When I look up at Traci, she's got tears coming down her cheeks, too. She's known Marquetta all her life, and now she gets to stand next to her on the biggest day of her life. In a way, I'm jealous of Traci. I wish I could've known Marquetta all my life. But when I think about it, I'll be with her every single day from now on, and Traci only gets to see her a few times a week. I guess maybe I am the lucky one.

Traci's candles are all around us. The scent is super faint, but having them flickering in the breeze, and with the ocean in the distance, the gazebo is like something magical—like part of a fairytale. Even the music is awesome! Cecelia is super talented and is way better than that boring string quartet Grandma Madeline wanted.

The B&B's full this week, and most of the guests are here watching. We gave them all invitations yesterday and told them all they had to do was bring themselves, but I didn't really expect so many to skip sightseeing for a wedding. Even Lydia's here with her husband. They showed up early this morning, and between the two of them, they finished all the B&B work a couple hours ago and then helped set up for the wedding.

Marquetta and Mr. Gray are at the base of the stairs. Chief Cunningham goes over to help Marquetta 'cause Mr. Gray's kinda wobbly with what he calls his 'broken wing.' Typical for Mr. Gray, he shakes off the chief's arm and gets up the stairs on his own. Marquetta waits for him, then lets him walk her the last few steps to meet my dad.

Everything gets blurrier. It's hard to see what's going on. Then Traci's pulling me closer to her again. I guess I've been blubbering, but through my tears I can see Marquetta smiling at me. Then she holds out her hand and I rush to her.

I feel her arm around me, pulling me closer and squeezing me tight as she says the words, "I do."

52

ALEX

Hey Journal,

We got an email from Tara after the wedding. She wanted to wish my dad and Marquetta the best. She's back in her shop and says she's getting together with Kathryn and Anita on Friday night. We're gonna do a video call. These new locks Kathryn put in are super nice—they never stick like the old ones did sometimes. The three of them are talking about coming back here sans men. When I asked my dad what that meant, he told me I'd figure it out soon enough.

After the wedding ceremony, Chief Cunningham told my dad Dr. Turner matched some DNA on Mr. Nicholas's body with Max Rado's. Between that and finding Tara's engagement ring in the cupcake, he's totally going to trial. It even sounds like Mr. McNasty is gonna get charged for being an accessory. I think it's awesome after what he did here. That was all I heard before my dad caught me listening. Oh well, I've already got plenty for my next Cove Talkers Newsletter story.

It's been a super long day. Even though we had help to prepare for the wedding, it was a lot of work. I never realized how much trouble it is to get married! But even with all the hard work, it was an awesome day. When I marry Robbie Sachetti, I want my wedding to be just like Mom and Dad's.

OMG, Journal. I have a mom again. A real one who loves me. Pinch me! Seriously! This is like so awesome. Marquetta is my mom! I wish I could've seen better during the ceremony, but Mr. Van Horn videoed the whole thing. I'm gonna watch it like ten times when he sends me a copy.

The biggest surprise for Mom and Dad (so awesome I can say that!) came after the wedding. That's when we told them about Operation Honeymoon. Lydia and Matteo and Mr. Grayson helped me organize everything. LOL, they didn't have a clue that they were going away. It's only a couple days, but Mr. Grayson's gonna do the cooking. The O'Donnells will supply breads and muffins from Crusty Buns. And me, Lydia, and Matteo will run the B&B. Isn't that awesome? Because I'm staying here while they go away, it makes me feel like I'm making a contribution to the present, too.

You know what? I'm happy to be left behind. Not only will I be contributing, but Mom and Dad will have some time alone. They both deserve to be happy. Even more than that, with them getting to be alone, I'm hoping Operation Baby Brother is going full speed ahead!

Xoxo

Alex